Nov 24/2011 (2)

THE LUCK OF THE HORSEMAN

THE LUCK OF THE HORSEMAN

Bill Gallaher

TouchWood
Editions

TouchWood Editions
www.touchwoodeditions.com

Library and Archives Canada Cataloguing in Publication
Gallaher, Bill
    The luck of the horseman / Bill Gallaher.

Print format. ISBN 978-1-926741-10-9
Electronic monograph in PDF format. ISBN 978-1-926741-62-8
Electronic monograph in HTML format. ISBN 978-1-926741-63-5

    I. Title.

PS8563.A424L83 2010   C813'.6   C2010-903679-4

Editor: Marlyn Horsdal
Proofreader: Sarah Weber
Cover image: Glenbow Archives, NA-862-5

We gratefully acknowledge the financial support for our publishing activities
from the Government of Canada through the Canada Book Fund, Canada
Council for the Arts, and the province of British Columbia through the
British Columbia Arts Council and the Book Publishing Tax Credit.

Mixed Sources
Cert no. SW-COC-001271
© 1996 FSC

The interior pages of this book have been printed on 100% post-consumer
recycled paper, processed chlorine free, and printed with vegetable-based inks.

1 2 3 4 5 13 12 11 10

PRINTED IN CANADA

This one is for Dan and Les and Brent and Judy.
Good friends always.

CONTENTS

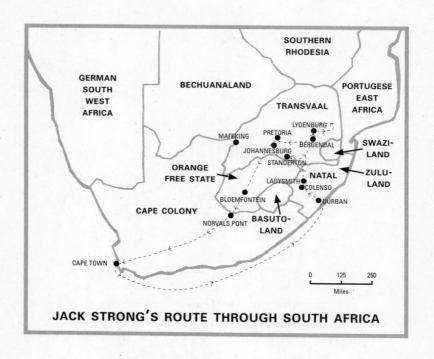

JACK STRONG'S ROUTE THROUGH SOUTH AFRICA

SOUTHERN
RHODESIA

GERMAN
SOUTH
WEST
AFRICA

BECHUANALAND

PORTUGESE
EAST
AFRICA

TRANSVAAL

LYDENBURG
MAFEKING
PRETORIA
BERGENDAL
SWAZI-
LAND
JOHANNESBURG
STANDERTON
ORANGE
FREE STATE
LADYSMITH
NATAL
ZULU-
LAND
COLENSO
BLOEMFONTEIN

CAPE COLONY
DURBAN
NORVALS PONT
BASUTO-
LAND

CAPE TOWN

0   125   250

Miles

Background

WHEN CALEB CAINE LEFT his home and an abusive, alcoholic father behind, he changed his name to Jack Strong, after his dime-novel hero, "Wild Jack Strong." Events led to his involvement in the Saskatchewan Rebellion of 1885, chronicled in the first volume of this trilogy, *The Frog Lake Massacre*, after which he went home to Victoria. Volume Two opens 10 years later, with Jack's return to the prairies.

ONE

Reunion

TRAGEDY STANDS JUST OFF-STAGE in everyone's lives. For the lucky ones, it never makes an entrance; for me, it burst on and stole the show. Afterward, it had required only a toddler's step to go from desperate meditations to the whisky that dulled my mind as it honed my feelings of guilt and self-pity. I'd been drunk for two months, ever since I arrived in Calgary, but I'd had enough of being inside myself; it was time to crawl out of the hole I'd dug before it got so deep that I couldn't. Being idle had only made matters worse, so I decided to head down to Fort Macleod to see Sam Steele. More than 10 years had passed since I rode with him on the trail of Big Bear and even if he couldn't use my help in the hunt for the Blood Indian wanted for murder, there was no harm in getting reacquainted. And I'd be surprised if Steele didn't know every ranch owner in southern Alberta and wouldn't provide me with a letter of introduction. I needed the kind of hard work that can heal an ailing mind, and there was no denying it.

I outfitted myself with everything from a bedroll to boots and warm clothes for the winter, as well as a lariat and a lever-action Winchester rifle with shells and a scabbard. Then I went to the livery stable and bought a nicely disposed cow pony called Sam, which was short for Samantha, for Sam was a mare. I paid a paltry sum for her—in 1896 more people were using bicycles to get around town because they were less finicky and didn't have to be fed—and shopped around until I found a used saddle that didn't require breaking in and would go easy on both horse and rider. Then I bought saddle-bags, filled them with grub and when I was ready, tucked my cash into my moneybelt and pointed Sam south.

Sam was plain and brown, and I'd seen prettier horses but she had a fine temperament and was smart as a whip. She loved it when I spoke softly to her. Her ears would prick up as if she were hanging on every word because a true friend was speaking them. Some horses can take you outside yourself, not necessarily to let you forget your problems entirely but to not remember them for a while, and Sam was that kind of horse. And like me, she had been penned up too long and was eager to be moving. I let her set the pace, sat back and enjoyed the scenery.

It felt good to be breathing fresh air instead of saloon smoke, and it helped me ignore the strong thirst for a drink that nagged at me during the first couple of days. October can be a fine month on the prairies; the mornings were crisp and frosty while the afternoons were above freezing with a warming sun. I saw plenty of cattle, gathered in small bunches here and there as they usually do, but spotted very little wildlife, even though the prairie was teeming with it. Granted, there was evidence everywhere, in tracks and droppings, but I saw nothing but gophers and a lone coyote skulking over the horizon. The only sounds I heard were an occasional bird call, creaking leather and horse hoofs meeting prairie dirt.

It was a hundred miles to Fort Macleod and when I reached the Oldman River, I could plainly see the North West Mounted Police post on the south bank. The water level was low because of the dry weather, so I left the trail leading across a bridge into town, forded the river and climbed the far bank to the post, a large but orderly collection of whitewashed buildings.

I went directly to the administration offices and asked a young constable if I could see Superintendent Steele. He informed me that the superintendent was unavailable and inquired about my business. I told him my name, my reason for being there and that Steele would know me because I had ridden with him during the 1885 rebellion. His eyebrows rose at that bit of information and he went off to see if it would impress his boss. He returned a few moments later.

"Superintendent Steele will see you, sir."

The rise in his level of respect was quite apparent. He ushered me into the office where Steele sat behind a large oak desk.

"Wild Jack Strong!" he thundered, his eyes absorbing me at a glance. "I wondered if you had dropped off the face of the Earth!"

He came around the desk and shook my hand, even more imposing than ever. He had put on a bit of weight over the past decade but he wasn't fat, just burlier. There wasn't the slightest suggestion of softness about him, so the extra pounds may have come from the drink that I could smell on his breath. When the rebellion ended, he had taken an extended leave in Winnipeg before returning to the mountains to police the railway construction camps. His work there earned him an invitation to the driving of the last spike at Craigellachie and put him on the first train from the east to reach the west coast. From there, he went to Battleford to clean up the post, which had lapsed into chaos after the rebellion. He promptly rid it of people unwilling to work toward improving relations with the Cree but a personality clash with his superiors got him sent to Fort Macleod with a reduction in command. Later, he went to British Columbia where he quelled a potential Indian uprising and built the post now known as Fort Steele. He returned to Macleod and married Marie Harwood, the daughter of a country gentleman, and subsequently became the commandant of the district. Whether he was or not, Steele had always looked like a man in command of something important and today was no exception.

He indicated a plain wooden chair for me to sit on and returned behind his desk. His chair groaned as he settled into it.

"Did you ever get back to the coast? That's where you're from, isn't it?"

MEMORIES WASHED over me, cold as a north wind. It was my mother I had gone to see. I had written her letters from the prairies but received no answers. Had she given up on me? That definitely wasn't characteristic of her and to my mind there were only two answers: my drunken father had gotten to the mail first or—and this was what worried me most—she was ill and unable to write.

Victoria had grown immensely during my two-year absence, particularly the James Bay area, and I barely recognized the house in which I'd spent the first 15 years of my life. It had been repaired and repainted, and there was no laundry hanging to dry in the yard. Was that a positive sign? Had my father turned over a new leaf and found steady work so that my mother didn't have to wash other people's dirty clothes? It was probably too much to hope for. Whatever the case, it had changed enough that I thought I ought to knock on the door instead of walking in. I was surprised when a matronly, middle-aged woman answered, wiping her hands on her apron.

"I'm looking for Mrs. Caine," I said.

"Oh, dear." Her hand flew to her mouth. "I'm afraid she doesn't live here anymore. She's passed on."

I sucked in air and nearly choked on it. I knew what "passed on" meant as well as anybody but asked inanely, "Do you mean she's moved somewhere else?"

"No! As I understand it, the poor woman had had about all she could take from her husband and drowned herself just off the point." She motioned behind her.

"What? When?" My voice sounded as if it were coming from some faraway place.

"Last February. We bought the house from her husband for a pittance. A shameless man he was."

By then she could see the effect the news was having on me. "I'm afraid I've . . ."

I cut her off. "That's all right, ma'am. Thank you."

I turned swiftly and hurried off the porch and out the gate before I embarrassed myself. I walked, head down, shoulders hunched, the few short blocks to Beacon Hill Park, scarcely noticing them, and found a secluded spot among the trees. I believed that my father had killed my mother, perhaps not by holding a gun to her head, but by robbing her of every reason she might have had for living. In the course of time I would learn that in the early hours of a rainy, February morning someone saw her walk into the icy sea off Laurel Point. By the time an alarm was raised and a boat launched to search for her, she was floating face down, drifting on the ebb tide toward the strait, along with the rubbish cast into the harbour.

I tried not to cry, tried to hold everything inside, but feelings of guilt breeched the dam and tears came anyway. Why hadn't I come home sooner? And why hadn't I written more often? Even if my father had been intercepting the letters, he might have missed one of them. She must have thought I had been killed or had deserted her, just as her husband had, in every way but his presence. Images of my drunken father filled me with a murderous rage. I wanted retribution. I would find my father and make him pay, and I knew where to begin looking for him.

I went to the rundown saloons first and when I didn't see him, asked the bartenders if they knew or had heard of Cal Caine and where he might be found. Some knew him well, others merely recognized the name, yet no one knew of his whereabouts. They hadn't seen him for a few days but didn't think he had left town. A few suggested trying the saloons in Esquimalt.

It was nearing midnight when the cab clattered over the Point Ellice Bridge and along the Esquimalt road. It had begun to rain. I felt depressed and frustrated. The murder in my heart that had precipitated the search had dissipated somewhat; nevertheless, I still wanted to find my father. I had no idea what I would say or do when I did but I wouldn't be able to rest until I confronted him.

On the outskirts of the village, we stopped at a sleazy saloon-cum-hotel called the Anchor Inn. I paid the driver and stood there for a few moments in the light drizzle. Amber splashes of light from houses and gas lamps dotted the main thoroughfare; otherwise it was draped in midnight black. Noise from the bar spilled out onto the street. As the cab turned and rattled toward Victoria, I wished for a moment that I had gone with it. But it was too late. I opened the door and went in.

The place was crammed with dock workers and sailors hell-bent on forgetting their occupations for a while, as tough-looking a lot as I'd ever seen. The air was thick with smoke, the stink of unwashed bodies and a piss trough somewhere in the back. I wove a path to the bar, ignoring the hard stares directed my way: there was no mistaking me for one of their own. At the bar I caught the busy keeper's attention.

"What can I get you?" he asked.

"Nothing. I'm looking for Cal Caine. Do you know him?"

"I know him. Who's asking for him?"

"I'm his son."

The man's eyes saw me for the first time. "You damned well are." He seemed to toss a decision around in his mind for a moment, then said, "He's in the snug. Second one on the left." He nodded his head toward the rear where two three-quarter doors led to private rooms partitioned off from the main part of the saloon.

"Is anyone with him?"

"Only Vicky, but she won't do you no harm." The barkeep winked. "You might want to knock before you go in."

"Sure thing. Thank you."

I snaked among the tables, through the babble-laden smoke and din. I could feel my heart pulsing in my ears. I hesitated for only a moment at the door, then pulled it open without knocking.

Vicky was a straggly, over-used tart who didn't seem to mind the hand on her breast or the leer on its owner's face. Surprised, my father jerked his hand away. Vicky straightened her blouse.

"What the hell . . . !" A scowl crossed my father's face, followed by astonishment when he recognized me. "Caleb! What the hell are you doin' here! Where you been?" He peered up at me but his eyes lacked focus. He was drunk and slurred his words, and made no effort to stand. "Your mother . . . she deserted me, goddamn her hide, and so did you! You let me down, Caleb." There was as much whine in his voice as belligerence.

I couldn't believe that this pathetic excuse for a man was the same person who had once filled me with fear, whose mere presence could make me tremble. For the first time I suddenly felt more powerful than my father, who sensed it and appeared to shrink in size. God, how I wanted to punish him, punch him, grab him by the throat and squeeze the life out of him. No one would have missed him and the world would have been a much improved place for it. But I couldn't; it wasn't in me, and besides, my help wasn't needed. My father was already well down the path of self-destruction. I leaned on the table with both hands and stared hard at the grizzled face, the vein-streaked eyes. Vicky sat there, transfixed. I craved words that would define what I felt, biting words, devastating words, but all that came to rest on my tongue was that my father was a blight on the human race. Yet I didn't say it. I didn't need to because I saw that knowledge reflected deep in his eyes. I left him with his wretched whore and miserable life, and stomped through the saloon toward the front door, uncaring of the faces staring at me. A drunk lurched to his feet, wearing a silly grin and said, "Hey, you're Cal Caine's boy. Lemme buy you a . . ."

I never let him finish. "The name's Jack Strong," I said. I put my hand on his chest and shoved him back in his chair, the force of it nearly sending him arse-over-head. I stormed past and out of the saloon, prepared to take the anger left in me out on anyone foolish enough to follow. No one did.

It was raining heavily but I was damned if I would stay even remotely close to my father. I didn't bother trying to find a cab and began walking back to Victoria. Late though it was, a few wagons bedecked with lanterns splashed by as I hastened along the dark road. The driver of one, travelling in the same direction, stopped and asked if I wanted a lift. I never so much as glanced at him, just shook my head and kept walking.

I didn't want to spend money on a hotel room or have to talk to a clerk to get one, so I found a dry spot beneath the Point Ellice Bridge and curled up there for the remainder of the night. The rain dripped off both sides of the span like beaded curtains, offering a feeling of sanctuary. But I never slept a wink and the time dragged by as though it was afraid to pass. Everything I never said to my father I said tenfold in my mind and I was brilliantly articulate, until I realized that I would eventually have to let those thoughts go or they would cripple me forever. My father, at the very least, had given me life and then showed me how not to live it, and that fundamental truth could be my salvation. When the dawn finally broke and I could see the cloudy sky reflected off the water, I felt moderately better, even though I hadn't slept.

A month or so later, in Vancouver, I read in the newspaper that my father's bloody and beaten body had been found in the alley behind the Anchor Inn, lying amongst some garbage. The police had no clues as to who the murderer or murderers might be and I would have bet anything that they weren't expending a great deal of energy to find out.

I did not think that I had a single tear left for my father but I was mistaken. They came unbidden: uninvited guests who did not know when to leave.

IN ADDITION to being swamped with work, Steele was not the kind of man who would want to hear my life story or reminisce, so to answer his question, I simply said, "Yes, sir. Things didn't quite work out the way I hoped, so I decided to come out here. Been up in Calgary for a while."

"Our good fortune," he remarked. "What brings you down this way?"

"I needed a change and I was hoping you might be able to use me on the hunt for the Blood Indian."

"Like old times."

"Yes, sir. Like old times."

There were several newspapers on Steele's desk and even though they were upside down, I could easily read the headlines: "Murderer Still at Large," "Indian Eludes Pursuers, Riding Away on a Policeman's Horse—Not Caught Yet!"

I had read about it in Calgary. A Blood Indian by the name of Black Feather had allegedly murdered another Blood named Antelope's Backbone and then shot and wounded the farming instructor on the reserve. The Bloods were part of the Blackfoot Confederacy which also included the Peigans; their reserve was between the St. Mary's and Belly rivers. The word was that Black Feather had gone crazy and was thirsting for more blood. Being on the run, he'd likely be riding hard and would have to change horses often, and a Blood was more adept at stealing horses than most Indians. He might also decide to slaughter a heifer if he was hungry, so ranchers and farmers in the area were on edge about that, too, let alone the safety of their families. But what had really piqued my interest was the fact that Sam Steele was in charge of the investigation.

A couple of days later, the news around Calgary was about a shootout with Black Feather down by the Belly River. Again, though, he managed to escape, this time on a NWMP horse that he had stolen, and was leading the entire police force and half the Blood nation on a fruitless chase. Politicians in

Ottawa were demanding to know why it was taking so long to catch the culprit, which seemed to me a question that only someone who had never been out west would ask. They didn't know how vast this part of the country was, how rapidly a man could vanish in it.

Steele spoke, commanding my eyes again, and offered some details of the case that were not in the papers. Apparently, Antelope's Backbone, the murdered man, had been missing for a week or more before searchers discovered his body in a shed on the Blood Reserve. When the coroner conducted his preliminary examination at the scene, he noted that the body was lying on its side with its head resting on a folded jacket. There was dried blood around the nose and mouth, more on the clothes and hands, even on the penis, though the man was wearing coveralls. But there were no exterior wounds to suggest a cause of death. They took the body to the Big Bend detachment where a police surgeon was to perform an autopsy. Before it began, however, word came from the Blood people that Black Feather had confessed to the killing.

Antelope's Backbone had been in the cowshed having intercourse with Little Rabbit Woman, the wife of Black Feather, who sneaked up on the lovers and aimed his rifle through the chink between the logs. Antelope's Backbone looked up when he heard the cocking of the weapon and Black Feather shot him in the eye. It was Little Rabbit Woman who closed the victim's eyelids, concealing the wound, tucked the man's penis into his pants and placed the jacket beneath his head.

Black Feather had also confessed to shooting the reserve's farm instructor, but no one was yet saying why.

Steele sighed. "I was beginning to believe that the Bloods were settling down. Their children are attending school and learning English, they have productive gardens and cattle herds, and most of them have traded in their buckskins for our style of clothes. But just when you think you're making headway in civilizing these people, something like this happens.

"I can always use a good man but the fact is we don't know where Black Feather is going to show up next. Choose a point on the compass and your guess would be no worse or better than mine, or anyone else's for that matter. If you've got the time to wait until we gain more intelligence, we might be able to send you in the right direction. Meanwhile, the last barrack on your right as you go out the front door should have some empty beds in it. You can help yourself to one but you'll need your own bedroll. The man at the livery stable will tend to your horse and I'll ensure that the kitchen staff know you're entitled to eat in the mess. I'll send for you if I need you." As an afterthought, he added, "Kind of you to think of us, Strong. Thank you."

You could never accuse Steele of wasting time with idle chit-chat, so I took my leave. I sensed that the operative words in his instructions were "as you go out the front door."

But the man had a lot on his mind and the extent of his frustration was evident the very next day when he had Black Feather's entire family arrested and brought into the guardhouse for aiding and abetting the fugitive. He did not need warrants for these arrests, as Indians were wards of the government and such formalities were not required. By the time he finished, there were 26 of them, mostly women and children, the youngest only a few weeks old. Personally, I have never found any infant threatening, but when Steele's authority was tested he had only one answer and that was "Steele's Law." This meant that you did whatever was necessary to accomplish your goal, even if it didn't mesh precisely with the Queen's law. But then, communications were slow and if you had to wait for approval for everything, it might come too late. And "late" was not a word in Steele's vocabulary.

He summoned me to his office early on my second morning at the post. He had a job for me. It wasn't much but with many of his men out on patrol, he was shorthanded and hoped I would help. Rumour had it that Black Feather might be heading west for the mountains and in case he slipped through, Steele was sending two men from the small detachment at Pincher Creek over to Fort Steele, in British Columbia, to prepare them for the possibility of the fugitive's arrival. The men required provisions and pack horses for the journey, and my job was to deliver them.

Well, he was right. It wasn't much but it was better than sitting around twiddling my thumbs. They loaded four horses and Sam and I set out immediately for Pincher Creek, some 30 miles to the southwest.

The last thing Steele said to me was about Black Feather, in the event I ran into him; it was vintage Steele. "He's a natural soldier, Strong. A perfect example of what a man can do when he is put to the test. And he's never left the old ways behind. You will want to keep an eye out at all times."

TWO

Black Feather

IT WAS AN EASY ride to Pincher Creek, over wide open, rolling country, along a well-used track that crossed the southern end of the Peigan Reserve. I saw neither hide nor hair of anybody or anything, let alone Black Feather. The temperature was dropping rapidly and when I was a few miles from the detachment, it began to snow heavily, flakes as large as silver dollars that stuck to the ground and soon covered it. Badly rutted, the road was not difficult to follow and I pulled in to the Mountie post late in the afternoon, just as it stopped snowing.

Sergeant Bill Wilde was in charge and was rankled that Steele was assigning two constables elsewhere, leaving him with one. Nevertheless, he didn't forget that I had completed a voluntary assignment for the force and made sure both Sam and I were fed and quartered. I let him know that I was keen to join the hunt if something developed while I was there.

Well before dawn the following morning, the two men and the pack horses set out on the long ride to Fort Steele. Later, as I was preparing Sam for a leisurely ride back to Fort Macleod, the detachment had some visitors. Two cowboys rode in at a good clip, one a giant of a man on a huge horse. They had brought word from Steele that confirmed Black Feather was indeed heading into the mountains and would probably make his run somewhere in the hills south of Pincher Creek. The superintendent had ordered Wilde to mount a patrol with anyone willing to volunteer for the job and go after him.

The sergeant would have loved to have the two men that he had dispatched to British Columbia but he couldn't send a courier with orders for them to return; if Black Feather slipped through the net, the people farther west would still need warning. All that aside, he also had an order from a senior officer and would therefore fulfill it regardless of the difficulties.

"Well, Jack," he said to me, "if you still want in on the hunt, it looks as if you've got your chance."

Wilde left his last constable in charge of the detachment and he and I, along with the two cowboys, rode south. The sky had cleared some but it had snowed again during the night and more than a half a foot lay on the ground. It was cold, the temperature well below zero; the country had gone from fall to winter over the span of a day.

We rode in single file, with Wilde leading. Sam and I looked tiny compared to the Mountie, who was not only a big man, but rode an enormous black stallion, a magnificent animal that looked strong enough to gallop to the coast and back without stopping to rest. As for the sergeant, he towered above me and I stood six feet without my riding boots. His thick moustache made him seem every bit as severe as he was, and when he spoke, most men paid attention. A strict, law-and-order, spit-and-polish man, he was cut from the same cloth as Sam Steele and had come to the Mounties from the British army in 1882.

The cowboys' names were Leonard Davies and Jim Spencer. Leonard was thin and freckled, with a shock of red hair sticking out from beneath his hat. Jim was quite the opposite. While he matched Wilde for height, he was broader and heavier and none of it was flab. Wavy black hair, a black moustache shaped like an inverted chevron and dark eyes emphasized a handsome face well seasoned by the weather. Both men were cowhands at the Rocking M, a large spread north of Fort Macleod, but had left for the winter. Rather than head out for another round on the grub line—riding from ranch to ranch doing menial tasks in exchange for food—they reasoned that getting involved in the hunt would be much more interesting. They had appeared at the NWMP post about the same time as the latest information about Black Feather landed on Steele's desk.

By mid-afternoon, we were less than 20 miles south of the detachment when we came to a deep coulee cut by a creek narrow enough to straddle. Wilde signalled a stop. He pointed to hoofprints in the snow along the bank. They came from the east, around a bend in the meandering stream and disappeared to the west around another bend. We urged our horses down the slope, stopping short of the tracks, and Wilde dismounted to examine them. His assessment was immediate. "Two horses," he said. "Both unshod. It has to be Black Feather. He has a pack horse with him, and the last horses he stole were Indian ponies."

I nodded. "This creek is cut deep enough into the land to hide a mounted man and who would need to do that more than Black Feather?"

"No one that I can think of," Wilde replied dryly.

The tracks led us west for perhaps a mile, then climbed a high embankment and went over the edge. We halted and Wilde swung down from his horse.

"You boys wait here while I take a look. Make sure there are no surprises."

He climbed the bank to the rim, removed his hat and peered over. He remained motionless for a few moments, then slid from his perch and returned to the bottom, brushing the snow from his uniform. He got back on his horse.

"There's a farmhouse, maybe 150 yards away, and the front door seems to be open a crack. There's no smoke coming from the chimney and I couldn't see any movement. I think it's deserted, but that's exactly what Black Feather would want us to think if he's in there and planning an ambush. So, we will have to proceed with caution. I can see a haystack behind the house and several clumps of trees and bush beyond it, so this is the plan. Jim, you stay here and keep an eye on the front of the house while the rest of us head up the creek and into the cover of the trees." He looked at Leonard. "Once we're there, you make your way through the trees to a point where you can cover the far side of the house. If you come across Black Feather's horses hidden there, hustle back and let us know. Jack will stick with me and we'll use the haystack for cover. Now don't take any chances. If Black Feather's in there and makes a run for it, holler at him to halt. If he doesn't, you have my permission to shoot. Just don't shoot each other, if it's not too much to ask."

The three of us followed the creek, leaving Jim behind. I took my Winchester out of its scabbard and levered a cartridge into the breech. Leonard did the same. Two hundred yards farther on we dismounted and, leaving the animals ground tethered, clambered up the bank into the woods.

"This is better than I expected," Wilde said, as we stopped to assess the situation. "There are no windows in the rear of the house." To Leonard, he added, "Swing around to the other side but stay in the trees anyway. We'll wait till you're there before we move."

Leonard hurried off and once he was in position, Wilde drew his revolver and said, "Let's go."

We left the woods, hunched over, moving slowly in the fresh snow, which made a soft crunching sound as our boots compacted it. The absence of windows allowed us to bypass the haystack and go directly to the rear of the house. But as we stole by, we could see that someone had recently spread hay out on the ground for feed.

We crept along the creek side of the house as quietly as we could, but if Black Feather was inside, he would have had to be deaf or asleep not to hear us. Ducking beneath a window, we made our way around to the front where a single step took us onto a covered porch. We stood next to the door, pressed flat against the wall, listening. Then Wilde called out something in Blackfoot that I guessed was an order to Black Feather to come out. The house remained silent. Using the barrel of his gun, Wilde pushed the door wide open. The squeak was loud in the still air. Then he did the bravest or most foolish thing I'd seen in a long time. With his gun out in front of him, he walked upright through the door. I fleetingly debated following him but figured the best thing to do was to stay right where I was in the event Wilde took a bullet and Black Feather came running out. I half expected to hear gunfire and to have a dead Mountie on my hands, but the only sound was boots on a wood floor as Wilde moved through the house. In seconds, he came striding out. "It's empty," he said and motioned for Jim to come forward, then went to the side of the house and beckoned to Leonard.

"I'll go get the horses," I said. My legs were quaky from relief as I returned to the bottom of the coulee, led the three horses to the haystack and loosened some more feed for them. When I got around to the front of the house, Jim and Leonard had joined Wilde.

"I've been telling the boys that Black Feather's been here," Wilde said to me. "This place was broken into—he was probably looking for food—and some of the haystack was spread out for two horses. And it wasn't that long ago. You can see his tracks leading off to the south. He can't be too far ahead of us, so we'd best get moving."

I had been so focused on the house that I hadn't spotted them, but the tracks heading south explained why Wilde was bold enough to walk through the farmhouse door. He'd seen them and deduced correctly that Black Feather had gone. Perhaps his act wasn't as crazy as I thought, but some Mounties believe that the mere sight of their uniform is enough to make even the foulest of villains drop to his knees and beg for mercy.

We stayed at the farmhouse only long enough to let the horses eat, then picked up the trail, which was dead easy to follow across the undulating landscape. The air felt colder and the lowering clouds that darkened the sky looked laden with snow. A heavy snowfall would obliterate Black Feather's trail, so Wilde suggested increasing our pace a little. A mile or so farther we reaped the reward of our efforts. As we crested a hill above a tributary of the Waterton River, we spotted our quarry, 200 or perhaps 300 yards below. He was cooking food over a small fire.

He hadn't seen us. Yet instead of withdrawing and devising a plan of action, Wilde spurred his horse forward, down into the coulee, leaving the rest of us to follow. There was very little snow here, only patches; nevertheless, the footing was treacherous and slowed our progress. Black Feather couldn't miss seeing us and his voice echoed through the still air in a war song. Ignoring his pack horse, he leapt on a still-saddled paint and prodded it diagonally up the far side of the draw. It was plain that the horse was tired and working hard to get to the top.

Wilde stopped and yanked his rifle from its scabbard. He took aim and fired two shots, neither of which hit their mark. Perhaps he had hoped that it would frighten Black Feather into surrendering but it didn't. He crammed the rifle back into its scabbard and took off after the Indian. By the time we reached the bottom of the coulee, Black Feather had gained the rim with a good head start. Wilde's big black scaled the slope without difficulty and reached the top before Leonard and I were halfway there on our smaller mounts. Jim's horse, as big as Wilde's, was carrying a heavier load and kept pace with ours. Once we were out of the valley we could see where Black Feather was headed. Not far to the west were low, densely forested foothills which, with night approaching, would provide a perfect place to evade his pursuers.

The three of us set off at a gallop, trying to catch up to the Mountie, but our horses were no match for the black and neither was Black Feather's. Wilde was closing the distance between them rapidly and was near enough that he had his pistol out. He was calling to Black Feather to halt. *You bloody fool*, I thought, *are you trying to get yourself killed?* But I think he figured that the fugitive would yield to his authority and he could capture him alive. Instead, the Indian swivelled in the saddle, raised his weapon and, without taking aim, let off a shot toward Wilde.

The bullet hit the policeman and drove him back in the saddle. He hung on for a moment, then plummeted to the ground. The black pulled up. Black Feather turned his pony around, sped the few yards to the fallen Mountie and fired another bullet into him. Then he deftly swung down from his horse, vaulted onto the black and was thundering toward the forested hills before any of the rest of us could get off a shot. I shouted at Jim to keep on Black Feather's trail. Leonard and I reined up where Wilde lay inert in the snow. We both jumped down to see if we could help him but he was past anything we could do. He looked at me but his eyes were focused on something beyond, perhaps the path he was about to travel. Blood gurgled from the side of his mouth and he died as I lifted his head in my hands. I felt life drain from his body—it was the strangest sensation I had ever experienced.

"Shit!" I said, a hot anger rising to a boil within me. I

wanted to get on Sam immediately and resume the chase but we couldn't leave Wilde's corpse there to be chewed on by animals. We loaded him on Black Feather's horse and Leonard, who was familiar with the area, said that he would retrieve the pack horse Black Feather had left in the coulee and head for a ranch house that he knew of, six or seven miles to the east. He wished me luck and I tore off after Jim and Black Feather, both of whom had dropped from sight beyond a rise a quarter mile ahead.

I had barely gathered speed when I heard a gunshot. Coming over the rise and into a broad valley, I saw Jim part way down the slope, dismounted, with his rifle out and Black Feather melting into the distance, well out of range.

I came abreast of Jim as he was remounting. His face was stoical, but he was angry too. It was there in his eyes. "Is Wilde gonna make it?"

I shook my head. "He died. Leonard is taking the body to a ranch nearby. It's just the two of us now. Do you want to turn back?"

"Some other time maybe but not today."

Together we loped down to the valley bottom, across an icy stream and up the far side. We were closing in on the timbered hills, which were cut by sparsely wooded valleys. Beyond were the mountains. Soon the terrain became more rugged and forced us to slow our pace. Black Feather's trail followed a narrow valley into prime ambush territory, so we stopped to plan our next move.

"This don't look good at all," Jim said.

"Maybe we ought to split up," I suggested. "You could climb to the ridge on the left and ride along the tree line while I stay in the valley. I think one of us should stick to the trail, in case it veers off to the right into the timber."

If it did, I would fire two gunshots five seconds apart and wait until Jim joined me. The higher ground would afford a better view of the lay of the land and he might even spot Black Feather.

Jim wove his way to the ridge and I headed into the valley. It was crowded with a variety of boulders, scrub trees and deadfall, but Black Feather had laid out the path of least resistance for me. It was eerie going up that valley, alone, in the gloom of approaching dusk, and I don't think my eyes stopped moving, searching everywhere, for any sign of movement or anything that might suggest a trap. I saw nothing. Even so, I was nervous. It was one thing to hunt an animal; it was yet another to hunt a human being. Not one of the deer I'd hunted had ever laid a trap for me. So I moved slowly and kept my Winchester across the saddle, ready for use at a moment's notice. Occasionally I caught glimpses of Jim on the ridge, not far ahead, which allayed my fears somewhat. If anything moved, he would surely see it.

The valley widened and I saw Jim, perhaps a hundred yards ahead, coming down the slope to join me. All of a sudden, he stopped and lifted his rifle. At the same time, my eye caught a movement on a bluff ahead and to my right. It was Black Feather, on foot at the tree line, with his rifle aimed at Jim. The black stallion must have been somewhere in the woods behind him. Grabbing my Winchester, I dismounted and pulled Sam into the protection of a small thicket. Black Feather was about 300 yards from my position—a long shot even for a marksman—and I doubted that he could hit me, but I didn't want Sam to catch a wayward bullet. I fired off two rapid shots and wondered why he wasn't responding and why Jim wasn't shooting either; he was close enough for a good shot. But Black Feather stood there defiantly for a moment or two, then turned, entered the forest and was gone. I swung onto Sam and in a few moments joined Jim, who was cursing his Lee-Metford carbine. It had jammed on him in the frigid air and he wasn't able to get a shot off.

We urged our horses up the slope and into the trees that had swallowed Black Feather, hoping there might be an open meadow a short distance beyond, but there was nothing save the primeval forest and the descending darkness.

THREE

Big Jim

IT WAS TIME TO call it a day. It would be impossible to track Black Feather through the thick timber at night and the horses needed a rest so we reckoned we might as well bed down and look for the trail at first light. I didn't think Black Feather would be travelling much farther either, which meant we wouldn't lose too much ground. We returned to the valley floor and found a poplar grove for cover and firewood. Nearby there was a small, stream-fed pond and I broke through the surface ice so that the horses could drink. The warmth of a fire would be welcome and I figured the trees hid us well enough that we would not be easy targets.

The bitterly cold air turned our breath into white puffs of condensation as we gathered wood and got the fire going. There was plenty of deadfall around, so we stacked enough to keep the fire blazing all night, thankful that there was no wind to make it colder. The sky was heavy with stars that were beginning to fade in the east with the rise of a brilliant full moon. We boiled water for tea in our tin cups and chewed on some jerky for supper. I put small chunks of it in my mouth and worked it around a bit, so that my saliva softened it. It was less tough and more flavourful that way. We had had a long day in the saddle and both Jim and I were tired but we were too tense to sleep, or I was anyway. His demeanour left the impression that nothing much bothered him.

Jim Spencer was in that class of human beings who are easygoing and therefore easy to like. He had grown up in Wellington, a coal-mining town on Vancouver Island, where his father worked in the mines and, like me, had left home at an early age. In fact, we were kindred spirits in more than that, as I discovered after asking him about the scar that paralleled his right eyebrow. It was the legacy of a father much handier with his fists than his tongue. Jim had tried to defend his mother one night from those awful weapons and had his forehead split open for his effort. His father wasn't the town drunk, though, and ultimately deserted them. To put food on the table, Jim left school early and took a job in the mines but a year or so later, his mother died of pneumonia. With nothing to keep him mining coal—a job he had hated with a passion—he had drifted into the Interior and found work at a ranch, washing dishes and doing other menial chores. He discovered there that he loved horses.

The owners willingly taught him to ride and rope, and eventually hired him on as a cowhand. Everyone called him "Big" Jim because another cowboy named Jim worked on the ranch. About three years later, restlessness and a desire to see more of the country had drawn him to Alberta. He got a job at the Rocking M and then rode on the grub line over the winter months in exchange for food and a bunk. He didn't much like that, as there wasn't an owner or foreman around who didn't eye him suspiciously because of his size, afraid that he might eat them out of house and home. When the fall roundup ended at the Rocking M and there was no offer of steady work, he had ridden to Fort Macleod to see if his services might be needed on the hunt for Black Feather.

"That is one crazy Indian we're followin'," he said. "Did you see him on the ridge provokin' us?"

"Yeah. But I don't think he's so crazy. He's doing what he thinks he's supposed to."

He looked at me sceptically. "You might want to explain that."

"When Black Feather killed Antelope's Backbone, he knew that if he was caught by white men he'd be swinging from the end of a rope . . ."

Jim interrupted. "But the law might have let him off. After all, wasn't his wife lettin' Antelope's Backbone poke her? That's a good case for manslaughter if there ever was one."

"Sure, but Steele told me that Black Feather had never bothered to learn the white man's ways. That means he wouldn't know anything about our laws except that if you kill someone, you get strung up for it. I'll bet it's as simple as that to him. And a true warrior never dies on the gallows. He dies in battle or by some other means of his own choosing. Not only that, if white men decide his fate he'll be put in a box and buried underground and that can be a terrifying thought to some Indians. How could their spirit journey to the Sand

Hills if it's trapped underground for eternity? The Indian way is to leave the body in a special place above ground where the spirit is free."

"But what about Wilde? Why didn't Black Feather keep on ridin' after he fired the first shot. Why did he turn around? It looked to me as if he wanted to make sure Wilde was dead. Seems pretty bloodthirsty, if you ask me."

"My guess is that when he killed Antelope's Backbone, Black Feather believed he was a dead man anyway and had nothing more to lose. In other words, if he's going to the Sand Hills regardless, he'd prefer to arrive like a warrior rather than an old woman. He also needs someone important to announce his name before he gets there, someone he's killed. In the old days, he would've gone out and found an enemy Indian chief to kill, but nowadays any important person will probably do, even a white official. That's likely the reason why he tried to kill the farm instructor, and why he made sure Wilde was dead. Now, when it comes time for him to enter the Sand Hills, his name will be known there as a great warrior, because someone important will have spoken it. Too bad it had to be Wilde."

"You seem to know some about Indians. What's your story, Jack?"

"My story? In some ways, it's not much different from yours, I suppose." I told him about my father, and he nodded knowingly, as if all fathers liked to beat their sons. I told him about my old friends Bill Cameron and Big Bear, the massacre at Frog Lake, being a captive of the Indians and how I met Sam Steele. I touched the bullet scar on my cheek. "Got this at Loon Lake while we were on Big Bear's trail."

"Jesus." Jim was clearly impressed. "Everyone was talkin' about that mess at the time. But you were actually there!"

"Before it all happened I spent more than an evening or two with Big Bear in his lodge, listening to his stories and hearing about his people's ways. He was one decent human being who got the short end of the stick. He was Cree but they're not that much different from the Bloods."

"So where have you been hidin' for the past 10 years?"

"Out on the coast, working at a lumber mill in Vancouver."

"You look like a man who's seen a lot more than the inside of a mill."

I presumed he was referring to the dark half-moons under my eyes. I grunted. "I'm bushed, Jim. I think I'll turn in."

I walked out beyond the circle of light cast by the fire, relieved myself, then got into my bedroll. I did not elaborate because what had happened out on the coast was not a topic for discussion. I had tried before and could not make my voice rise above the screams in my head, the hands that reached out for me in my dreams and the guilt corroding my soul. Well, only a fool believes he has complete control over his life and denies how much chance figures into it: the luck of the draw. You think you choose life but in reality, it chooses you.

I HAD met her on the steamer from Victoria to Vancouver, after the confrontation with my father. The weather was glorious as we steamed past the myriad small islands dotting the straits. A brisk wind was growing some teeth and the ship rose and fell heavily over the waves combing out of the north-west. I was standing at the rail when the door leading to the staterooms flew open and a girl came out with a young boy, his face an odd shade of green. I had seen them on the dock before boarding the ship, standing with her mother and another younger brother, and instantly recognized her, though I'd only seen her once before. I had been chained to a stump in Gastown, being punished for public drunkenness, when she and her family had passed me on their way home from church. I could not forget that lovely face nor the fact that her father was the manager of Hastings Mill and had all but thrown me out of his office when I had gone there looking for work.

The girl and boy came to the rail, not far from me. Before I knew what I was doing, I had sidled over.

"Hello," I said. I was confident that my appearance had changed enough that she wouldn't recognize me; nevertheless, something in her expression suggested that she had seen me before but couldn't quite place where. She was probably around 18 years old and wore a light blue dress with white lace at the cuffs and neck. Her long, sandy hair was combed straight back and tied at the nape of her neck with a blue bow that matched perfectly the colour of her eyes. And they were not ordinary eyes. They could stop the smallest of thoughts from crossing a man's mind and tie his tongue in knots. A dusting of freckles covered the bridge of her perfect nose and there was a healthy blush to her cheeks. Her skin looked so soft that it was all I could do to resist reaching out and gently laying my hand on it; I was sure it would have been like caressing the finest silk. I stood more than an arm's length from her and yet the heat rose in me so intensely that I might have been on the parched prairies in high summer. The girl left me breathless.

There was an air of shyness about her but I couldn't tell if it was her natural demeanour or for my benefit. Yet even though she was reserved talking to a stranger, she was not aloof. We made small talk. She explained that she had been in Victoria for a holiday with her mother and two younger brothers, the youngest of whom stood with her, less concerned about the stranger beside him than about emptying the contents of his stomach over the rail.

"I wish I could have stayed," she added. "There are so many shops and things to do. Vancouver is such a bore, even before it burned to the ground."

"My name's Jack Strong," I said.

I searched her eyes to see if she recognized the name from the dime westerns but if so, she didn't show it. And before she could tell me her name her little brother, who had been turning even greener, suddenly began retching. Whatever it was he'd had for breakfast splattered against the rail, some of it onto his sister's dress.

"Oh, dear!" she cried, pulling a handkerchief from her sleeve. She dabbed at the spots on her dress before tending to her charge. Then she cleaned the residue from the corners of his mouth. "Are you feeling better, Willy?" she asked, and the youngster nodded.

"I want to go in now," he whined, grasping her arm.

She glared at him as if little brothers were the bane of her existence, which they may very well have been, then turned and said, "You must excuse me."

In a trice, the two of them had gone through the door leading to the cabins, the boy tugging her impatiently.

I lingered in the vicinity, hoping she'd come out alone

but she didn't. I wandered around the ship, as other passengers were doing, enjoying the fine weather, and much later saw her and her family heading to the first-class lounge for lunch. She glanced my way and must have said something to her mother who turned her head briefly to look. I repaired to the second-class lounge and gnawed on a leathery meat listed as roast beef, with potatoes and carrots boiled dry, and passed the time by trying to guess the girl's name. I decided that it must be Rebecca.

After I finished eating I went back out on deck and encountered the family returning to their stateroom. The girl brought up the rear, herding the children, who seemed to be her responsibility. I gave her and the family a nod and a tug on my hat. The mother kept her eyes averted, as if I didn't exist. When the rest had gone inside, the girl hurried over to me and shoved something wrapped in a napkin into my hands. When our fingers touched I felt more than the package pass between us. Something akin to an electric current ran clear to my shoulder and spread across my chest. I knew that she had felt it too when I saw her eyes flicker wide.

"For you," she said, and spun on her heels as if to rejoin her family before she was missed. She had nearly reached the door when she stopped in her tracks, half-turned toward me and called, "Charity!"

Charity? Why would she say that? I knew the napkin contained food but I didn't need food and I certainly didn't need her charity. Pride filled me and I considered throwing the package into the sea, but it suddenly dawned on me that she was telling me her name. It was one name that hadn't crossed my mind but, yes, it was perfect, as was the slice of apple pie she had given me, which tasted all the better for coming from her hands. She had rightly assumed that such delicacies weren't available to second-class passengers and had given me a gift.

That was the last I saw of her until we disembarked in Vancouver, by which time I was all but consumed by a powerful need to see her again. And, with any luck at all, on a much more intimate basis.

IN THE morning I felt in better spirits than I had for a while. The lack of alcohol was restoring the self-confidence it had stolen. Jim and I saddled our mounts, ascended the slope and found Black Feather's trail. A horse as large as the black couldn't pass through those woods without leaving noticeable clues in its wake. Before long, we reached the spot where the fugitive had spent the night. There was no evidence of a fire or any animal entrails to suggest that he might have captured even a small rodent to eat.

"He must be cold and hungry," Jim said.

"No doubt. But he'll be more used to it than we'd be."

Carrying on, we came out of the forest into a thinly treed valley paralleling the one we'd camped in. There was much more snow here and Black Feather's tracks were clear as they turned from the mountains and bore east, seemingly back toward the place where this whole episode had begun.

We increased our pace, leaving the wooded hills behind and following the trail, which ran like an indelible line through the snow. By mid-morning, a brisk wind rushed out of the mountains and pushed us along as the tracks led through gentle valleys and over low buttes. The wind grew in strength and blew the snow in great clouds that obscured the horizon and eventually, Black Feather's tracks. I didn't think it mattered.

"I bet he's heading back to the reserve, for some reason or other. Maybe for food."

"What if he's turned north or south?" Jim asked. "We'll never know it in this weather."

"Then he's fooled us good. But I don't think so. More than likely there's something at the reserve he needs."

"With any luck at all, he's goin' there to give himself up. Anyway, if we've lost him, we're headin' in the right direction for Fort Macleod."

The sun might have been warming in calm air, but the wind had pulled the rug out from under the temperature and sent it tumbling. I had never been so cold in my life, despite the heavy coat and gloves that I wore. Jim felt the cold too and we tied our bandanas over our heads and under our chins so that our ears wouldn't freeze and put on an extra pair of thick woollen socks. My toes remained numb.

We forded the Waterton River, which was icing over and shallow, and some time later the Belly River, which formed the western border of the Blood Reserve. Along the way, we came upon a place where the black horse had pawed through the snow for something to eat and later on, droppings, which were still soft on the inside. We weren't far behind our quarry.

Darkness fell and the wind died. A bright moon reflecting off the snow lit the land and Black Feather's tracks were soon visible again. We kept on moving, chewing jerky to sustain ourselves and stopping only long enough to let the horses paw out some grass, take the stiffness out of our legs and restore some feeling in our toes with a little foot stomping. Sam was handling the arduous trek pretty well, all things considered. Her head was drooping a little and she was showing signs of fatigue, but there was still some spark left in her. We plodded on, growing wearier by the minute.

"We must be gettin' close to the Blood camp," Jim said.

"Then we might as well ride on in and see what's happening. I wonder if they'll help him. The way he's been shooting people, they might be more scared of him than anything else and if so, they might be tempted to capture him and hand him over to Steele. But you never know, especially if they're his kin."

We heard shouting and a cacophony of barking dogs before we reached the camp so we surged forward at a gallop and came to a cabin, its windows and open doorway bright with lamplight. In front, three men were struggling with a fourth, trying to restrain him. As we got closer, the fourth man was clearly recognizable as Black Feather. When he saw us, with rifles drawn, the fight drained out of him like water through gravel.

We hauled him inside the cabin where he collapsed onto the dirt floor, his face gaunt and his clothes filthy. He was exhausted, but then he'd been on the run for a few weeks now and without food for probably two days. We picked him up, stripped off his gun belt and put him on a chair. He spat at one of his Indian captors and said something in Blood.

The reply was incomprehensible but I believe one of the words was "Steele."

The man Black Feather had spat at spoke some English. He said that his name was Crow Foot and that Black Feather was his brother. Black Feather had accused him of betrayal but Crow Foot told him that he had had no choice, that he was only obeying Mr. Steele's orders and that it was better this way.

North Axe, one of the three Bloods who had captured Black Feather, set off for a small Mountie detachment several miles north to fetch the police. While the others kept an eye on Black Feather, I went out and tended to the horses, putting them in a stable that was little more than a sod roof on three walls, the open side away from the prevailing wind. I spread out a bunch of hay and returned to the cabin.

The five of us, Jim and me, Crow Foot, Black Feather and another Blood named White Man, filled the small cabin. Of the Indians, only Crow Foot spoke English so most of the conversation was in Blood and I was too tired to bother asking him to translate everything. But I did learn some things. It seemed Black Feather had been hiding in the trees a few hundred yards from the cabin for more than an hour before he finally decided to approach his brother's door. Crow Foot was more or less expecting him, and when the dogs began barking in the middle of the night, he and the others went out and grabbed the fugitive before he had a chance to change his mind and run. That was when we had turned up.

I asked why he had captured his brother instead of helping him escape. He replied, "Mr. Steele told me that if my brother came here and I let him escape, I would be punished for it. Not only that, I was afraid for Little Rabbit Woman. I figured he might want to kill her for makin' him lose face. He had a lot of crazy ideas in his head."

Beyond obtaining that bit of information from Crow Foot, I could only sit there and let the Blood language, in all its complexity, wash over me. It belonged to the same linguistic family as Cree and while some of it sounded familiar, I hadn't used that language for more than 10 years and had lost much of what I knew. The result was that Jim and I were odd men out and could not understand most of the conversation.

A fire was blazing in the stove and the heat was both welcome and stifling after two days out in the frigid weather. Generally, these cabins were notorious for cooking your top half and freezing your bottom but since my bottom half already felt frozen, it was all relative. Anyway, I was grateful to be off Sam and glad that the hunt was over with nobody else hurt or killed. Once Black Feather was in the law's hands, Jim and I could return to Fort Macleod.

Black Feather was restless at first but eventually settled down, his arms pulled inside his blanket coat which, without his gun belt, hung on him like a tent. An hour passed and everyone grew quiet, but no one, other than Black Feather, was interested in sleeping. I didn't think it would take more than an hour for North Axe to get to the detachment, which meant that it would be another hour or so before he arrived with the police.

Black Feather looked to be asleep. His chin was resting on his chest and his breathing sounded like a soft snore. His long, coal-black hair framed a face that was stern even in repose. I had been staring at him for half a minute or more when I noticed a rivulet of liquid trickling down his buckskin leggings onto the hard earthen floor. *By God*, I thought, *he's*

pissed himself! Suddenly, Crow Foot jumped to his feet, start-
ling everybody. He had noticed it too, only he knew that it
wasn't urine. It was blood. Black Feather opened his eyes at
the commotion but they lacked focus. I jumped up too and
with Crow Foot's help yanked his brother from the chair and
tore the blanket coat off. An awl fell to the floor. Black
Feather had it hidden in his coat and had somehow managed
to reach it, push his sleeve up and pierce a vein in his arm
with none of us noticing anything. He was slowly bleeding to
death.

"Get me a rag, brother, or something I can use as a tour-
niquet," I said to Crow Foot, who fetched a piece of rawhide.
I tied it around Black Feather's arm, above the puncture and
staunched the flow of blood. I didn't know if we were in time,
though; a lot of blood had leaked down his clothes and onto
the floor. He was weak, so Jim lifted him bodily, carried him
over to the bed and laid him out. The wound in his arm
looked terrible and he had done it without making a sound
or changing his facial expression. He lay there passively, as if
he were willing himself to die.

Just before sunrise, North Axe came back with a policeman, a young, energetic constable eager to take charge. By
then Black Feather was awake and apparently going to live to
see the hangman. We led him outside where Crow Foot had
hitched up a wagon. He was compliant and passive, his fate
now out of his own hands and in someone else's. We had to
help him on board, as if he were an invalid. Then, with the
constable as an escort, Crow Foot steered the wagon toward
the detachment and jail.

FOUR

Cowboy

JIM AND I RODE north in early spring, after wintering at Fort Macleod and giving evidence at Black Feather's trial. He was found guilty, not for killing Antelope's Backbone, which the court deemed manslaughter, but for the cold-blooded murder of Sergeant Wilde. We did not attend the hanging.

As witnesses, Jim and I had been put up at the post, which saved us having to pay for bed and board. Before we left, Sam Steele, as he had done after the hunt for Big Bear, tried to persuade me to join the North West Mounted Police. It was tempting, more than it had been the first time, because I felt rudderless and surmised that the structured life of a policeman might bring some direction to mine. But I ultimately decided against it. My sense of the job was that it entailed mostly menial work, punctuated by very brief periods of intense excitement. Cowboy work could be menial too, but

there wasn't always someone barking orders at you. When I
asked, though, Steele did not hesitate to provide me with a
letter of introduction to Marcus Clarke, the owner of the
Rocking M, saying, in effect, that while I was short on ranching experience, I could ride and was long on hard work and
responsibility.

Jim was also a means of introduction, as Clarke had told
him to come back in the spring if he wanted to. "You won't
find a fairer, more generous man than Marcus," Jim said.
"I've heard that he could paper his walls with the IOUs he has
from cowboys down on their luck."

Jim and I had become fast friends over the winter. Though
he was big and tough, and only someone suicidal would want
to cross him, there was a side to him that was almost paradox-
ical, the side I admired most. He could sing like an angel, his
tenor voice soaring to the high notes and diving to the low
notes, pitch-perfect. He would break into song with little
prompting and needed none at all if he'd had a drink or two.
He loved the popular tunes of the day and sang them as if he
meant every word.

The sky was split by a chinook arch as we rode and the
land was a patchwork of brown and white, the buffeting warm
wind quickly melting the little snow that remained. There
wasn't much activity at the ranch and Marcus Clarke himself
greeted us.

Clarke was tall, thin and slightly stooped, and the wire-
rim glasses that he wore lent him the bearing of a professor
rather than a rancher. He looked to be in his 60s and he
reminded me of Steele in the way that he was completely in
charge, although he had a twinkle in his eyes that the Mountie

lacked. He handed us over to his foreman, Don Johansen, saying of me, "This fella rode with Sam Steele, Don. Maybe we could use his help come roundup time."

Tough and sinewy, Johansen had a handlebar moustache you could use to throw a rope over and lynch a man. His eyes flickered down and up as he took full measure of me and his response was swift and affirmative. The actual preparations for the roundup would begin in a month or so, he said, and I'd be one of his wranglers. In the meantime there were plenty of odd jobs around the ranch to keep me busy, and some of the boys would be more than happy to share their wealth of knowledge with me. The contract was a handshake.

It was a joy to watch Jim work with horses. He was in full control all the time and the animals knew it. In one instance, Johansen had two mean broncs that none of the other cowboys would touch because their standard, more gentle techniques were useless. Jim took the first one, a large, beautiful bay with fire in its eyes, and rendered it unable to buck by snubbing its nose to a pole in the middle of the corral. Then he threw on a saddle and cinched it tight. Ignoring the stirrup, he grabbed the horn and vaulted onto the animal. Another cowboy released the rope and it became a contest between wild beast and man. The word was that Jim never lost. He gripped the animal with those powerful legs of his and he was there till the horse either gave in or dropped dead from exhaustion. I'd seen smoother riders, for Jim could be quite jerky in the saddle at times, but there was no unseating him. The horse flew around the corral in a frenzy of bucking, futilely trying to rid itself of the hateful burden it carried. Then Jim yelled for the corral gate to be opened.

Instinctively, the bay headed for the open space and tore out onto the prairie, disappearing at a full gallop over a low ridge in the distance. I was all set to ride after them, worried that Jim might not be able to hang on, but none of the cowboys were bothered by it. A dour-looking ranch hand standing next to me said, "Keep your eyes on that ridge." Sure enough, a few minutes later, horse and rider reappeared, the animal at a controlled trot, Jim sitting tall in the saddle. He rode into the corral, dismounted and handed the reins to another man.

"Let's see if the other one's got any more to show than this one," he said.

If broken horses had some way of communicating with unbroken ones about riders, I've little doubt that they would have recommended either surrendering or running in the opposite direction at Jim's approach.

One of the old-timers said that he figured Jim was the most courageous men he'd ever met. But in my opinion what Jim had wasn't courage. Courage was something most of us can find if events demand it, even when we are scared to death. Jim hardly had to muster up anything; he was mostly fearless. I had seen the same quality in Sam Steele. He and Jim were not like the rest of us ordinary mortals, who experience fear in varying degrees. They would have a hard time even describing it unless they asked someone or looked it up in the dictionary. The aplomb and grace with which they faced danger made you enjoy being in their presence, made you feel that all was right with the world and, if it wasn't, then it was probably manageable.

My old friend Bill Cameron, from Frog Lake, taught me to ride but it was Jim Spencer who taught me about horses.

To him, they were as individual as human beings; he could assess their unique character traits straight off and use them to his advantage. He knew horses inside out, *understood* them as if he and they were part of each other, which I swore they sometimes were. What he didn't know about them could be printed in block letters on a child's thumbnail.

He also taught me how to use a lasso. I practised daily until I could snake the loop onto the neck of a horse from 50 feet, with Sam at a full gallop.

He showed me the most widely used breaking-in technique. He'd snub the horse to a post in the centre of the corral and allow it to run in a circle. When it settled down, he would approach it slowly, talking softly. Once he had gained the animal's confidence, he would begin stroking it, on the withers, chest, belly and rump, getting the animal accustomed to his touch and, just as important, showing that he meant it no harm. Then he'd take as much time as he needed to get it used to a bridle, and after that he'd call it a day. In the morning he'd rub the animal with a burlap sack or a rain slicker to get it used to the feel of something foreign on its back. The next step took two men. Jim would get me to hold the reins while he threw a saddle on the horse. Then he'd climb on and use his great strength to pull its head high, so that it was hard for it to buck, and let it trot around the corral. He'd never let the horse forget who was boss. If it bucked, he quirted it; if it didn't he'd stroke its neck, speaking gently all the while. When he felt it would accept a rider, Jim would nod his head and I would open the corral gates to let the animal run. Most bronc busters had a rider follow them out, but Jim wouldn't have it. "I wouldn't take the horse beyond that gate if I didn't think I could ride it back."

I never saw a horse throw Jim, which was strange because of the disjointed way he rode. Yet the saddle was like a magnet, holding him on. What he did was not teachable; you could either do it or you couldn't and Jim was one of those men who could.

The horses had an easier time shedding me, at least in the beginning, and my first ride wasn't so much a ride as it was a determined bid to stay in the saddle as the horse whirled and crow-hopped across the corral. I landed on my backside more than a few times and during those first days my rump was sore and my neck stiff. Jim was uncritical. "You're willin' to give it a try, Jack. You can't ask a man for more than that."

Jim's other passion was cattle, though he held a less charitable view of them. "They're about a teat short of an udder when it comes to brains," he said, "but you can't beat 'em when they're on the cookstove."

He explained the mechanics of a cattle drive to me. Depending on the size of the herd, the animals were usually kept about six or seven abreast. Experienced cowboys rode "point" at the front of the herd and it was their job to keep it moving in the right direction, 10 to 15 miles a day, so the animals wouldn't lose too much weight. Other cowboys acted as "swingmen" on each side of the herd and they were responsible for keeping it in line. Still others rode at the end in the "drag" position. They made sure that the rearmost animals kept pace with the rest and that there were no stragglers.

"And there are always stragglers, Jack. You can bet your chaps and saddle on it."

Drag was not a sought-after position on the drive, especially if the trail was dry and dusty. "But that's where you begin to learn how to trail cattle," he added. The lowest position on a drive or a roundup, though, was the wrangler, the man who tended to the other cowboys' horses, which was where I was starting.

"No one likes ridin' night herd either. There's always somethin' that can spook those flighty creatures into a stampede, even the night man if he isn't careful. Best thing to do is sing to them. It isn't that they like music—it lets them know where you are and that you're not a wolf or some such thing. Even so, some of my best performances have been on the night watch."

You could smell the earth now, on the breeze spilling out of the mountains that formed a ragged profile in the west. Full spring had come to southern Alberta as it does to few places in the world. The weather was balmy, wildflowers bloomed everywhere and the grass turned to the very definition of green. The ranch throbbed with excitement and the cowboys were eager to go to work.

FIVE

A Get-Rich-Quick Scheme

THE ROCKING M BECAME a much busier place as the men prepared for the roundup, mainly getting their gear in order and readying the horses they would need. Most had their favourites; because the roundup was a couple of months of long days and hard riding, each man required from 7 to 10 horses. As wrangler, my job was to look after the horses, (called a remuda) during the day while another man tended them at night. I did my job well and the men respected that. Most of them called me Wild Jack because they had read the books.

The Rocking M wagon set out in mid-May. By "wagon" I don't mean a single wagon; I mean the entire outfit, which included a chuckwagon and two wagons carrying a mess tent, sleeping tents and bedrolls, together with other personal items belonging to the cowboys. Men representing other ranches, and therefore other brands, rode with us as well. They were called "reps." (The Rocking M had reps in neighbouring drives.) There were no fences, so the semi-feral cattle wandered far afield during the winter months and brands invariably intermingled. The reps, who brought their own horses and wagons, would take charge of any of their own cattle. Naturally, there were new calves to contend with, but they rarely strayed from their mothers so it was usually obvious who they belonged to.

At night, we kept the remuda far enough from the camp that the noise wouldn't bother the animals and every morning, about five, the night wrangler brought them to the camp and into a temporary corral I made by stringing rope between the wagons. By then the cowboys would have had breakfast and would catch whatever horse they wanted for the day, saddle up and fan out in different directions ahead of the wagon, searching the coulees, thickets and hills for cows. By mid-morning they would usually have enough to drive to the camp which, along with the remuda, would have moved to a predetermined spot perhaps 10 miles farther on, depending on the terrain. Then they would head out for more and be finished that part of their job by mid-afternoon. The cattle were separated by brands, and calves were temporarily taken from their mothers and branded. The next day the routine would be repeated. When the collection of cattle grew large enough, say around 2,000, the reps and some Rocking M cowboys, who had come out specifically for the task, would drive their respective herds to their home ranges for summer grazing. Then the entire process would begin again until an area of several hundred square miles had been covered.

It was hard, bone-wearying work in the heat and the dust, and occasionally rain and mud, for everyone involved. As for me, when I wasn't tending the horses, I was gathering and chopping wood for the fire and performing any other task the roundup boss required to keep the camp running smoothly. By the time eight in the evening rolled around and the night wrangler took the horses off my hands, I was ready for my bedroll.

The days ran into one another. It was mostly a solitary time, except at meals when there was great camaraderie among the men. Breakfast and lunch were hurried but supper was more leisurely, a time for sharing stories of the day's ride. The cook would work his magic with his cast-iron pots and pans, rustling up steak and beans, some sourdough bread and maybe a few dried-fruit pies. We capped it with strong, hot coffee and sat around the chuckwagon, some men leaning against the wheels, others squatting or sprawled out on the prairie grass, and every now and then someone would ask Jim for a song. He'd wrap those dulcet tones of his around a sentimental favourite and send more than a few cowboys off to their bedroll in a fit of melancholia.

Few of them ever talked of marriage—you couldn't lead this kind of life and have a wife at the same time—but there was nothing quite like a love song about a beautiful woman to get a man thinking about what he might be missing. Once, after Jim had rendered a fine version of "I'll Take You Home Again, Kathleen," one of the older cowboys ruefully remarked, "Home is what we don't have. Other than my saddle and bedroll, everything I own is in a box under my bunk at the ranch."

"We've got a roof over our heads—most of the time anyway—and enough grub to fill our bellies," someone else said. "What more does a man need?"

Another chimed in, "How about a good poke on a regular basis? And a tent or a bunkhouse ain't real homes. They both belong to somebody else."

Then, from a cowboy fully committed to the occupation, "A woman can complicate your life in more ways than I care to think of. Better to pay for a poke every once in a while than for the rest of your life."

There was laughter and a few nods of agreement, and on it went. But I wondered if any of them had even the vaguest notion what it was like to really *want* to share your life with a woman.

UPON MY return from Victoria to Vancouver, I stayed with my old friend Joe Fortes, who was rebuilding his house; it had been destroyed in the great fire of 1886 that reduced the town to ashes. We agreed that some hard work would provide the best means of coping with what I had learned in Victoria and Joe offered me a room and food in exchange for help with his house. There was a lean-to on the property that served as his temporary home, but it was too small to accommodate both of us, so we made a tent from a tarp in the new building and I put my bedroll on the floor. Joe got a pencil and a small board and wrote on it "Jack's Place," and nailed it to the unfinished wall. The accommodations, though modest, would save money because I wouldn't have to stay at a hotel. More important, it was a way of repaying Joe for all the help he'd once given me.

I was pleased to be busy and to put to use the carpentry skills I'd learned at Frog Lake and Fort Pitt, and no one appreciated this more than Joe. We finished framing the walls and began putting on the roof. The weather remained warm and sunny and it felt satisfying to be working outdoors, burnished by the sun.

When the house was completed, I needed to find a paying job. Luckily, with Vancouver rising from the ashes of the fire there was plenty of work around, but I figured Hastings Mill was the best place to apply because of the excellent pay. But first I'd have to get past Alexander McRae, Charity's father, who was still the manager. Would McRae recognize me from my stint on the stump and the previous interview? Joe and I talked about it and concluded that it was best to be forthright and speak to McRae man to man, openly and honestly. It wasn't something that I was keen to do but any other course of action was cowardly. Besides, I had matured enough that I wasn't about to pussyfoot around and, as Joe pointed out, "You don't need to be beholden to any man after what you been through."

I reasoned the best thing to do was establish my presence in town first, and the easiest way to do that was to let the newspaper know about my involvement in the Frog Lake massacre and the hunt for Big Bear. Joe, always willing to help out, stopped by the newspaper office to tell them about his recently arrived guest. The reporters had run out of fire stories and had milked the arrival of the first train from Montreal for all it was worth so they were eager for some fresh news. One came over to the house to interview me and the story made the second page, a full column, headed "Hero of Massacre Returns Home."

I was no hero, but thought it a damned fine title that might open a door or two.

I waited a few days before going out to the mill and spent much of the evening before thinking of what I should say. In the morning I was pleased at how calm I felt. It had to be because I had faced worse things than Alexander McRae since I'd last seen him.

A recent downpour had soaked the boardwalk on the way to the mill and made the planks slippery. Overhead, the sky was a deep blue where it showed through the clouds. A smell of salt air, seaweed and lumber tinged the air. The inlet waters were dark and rippled and looked oily. Near the mill's general store, empty barrels stood along the edge of the boardwalk, and behind the store, a tugboat sat on the ways, its bottom being scraped and repaired. The ferry to Port Moody was tied to the dock as were two lumber ships. A few others were anchored well offshore.

The mill hadn't changed much since I was last there, except the office building had received a fresh coat of white-wash. I walked in. McRae's door was closed and the same clerk was sitting behind the same desk, guarding the entrance with the same air of superiority.

"I would like to see Mr. McRae."

"Do you have an appointment?" The clerk seemed to expand in size and looked prepared to throw himself bodily in front his boss's door to prevent my entry if I hadn't.

"No, but tell him Jack Strong is here to see him."

In McRae's office, I thanked him for seeing me. His face showed hints of a smile. "If the story in the newspaper is true, then I decided it was only fair to give you a hearing."

"It's mostly true, sir. You know how the papers tend to exaggerate."

"Nevertheless, you should be commended. Are you looking for work?"

"Mainly, sir, but I've also come to apologize. What I did two years ago was stupid and inexcusable. Too much whisky when I should have known better. I've learned a lot since then, believe me."

I hoped a contrite, mature approach would appeal to McRae and it did, for some of the rigidity he had displayed upon my entrance dissipated.

"I'm sure you have," he said. "Stupidity always comes easy to the young." He paused, thinking. "All right, Strong, apology accepted. I'm going to give you a chance. You've earned it."

"Thank you, sir."

I moved into the mill's bunkhouse and went to work on the dock, loading huge timbers on ships bound for far-off ports. I was dog-tired by day's end but not so tired that I couldn't think about Charity and ways to get closer to her. When I heard that she attended weekly square dance sessions that were open to anyone, I wasted not a second joining.

Unfortunately, the sessions were led with a tight rein by Mrs. McRae, so the only time I could get close to Charity was during a change of partners. Yet each time we met it was as if an electrical charge had been set off between us. In the promenade position, when we stood hip to hip, our left hands joined in front of my waist, our right hands joined in front of hers, she squeezed so hard I almost winced. Yet she could have broken every one of my fingers and I would not have minded.

I had mixed feelings about those evenings: they brought me closer to Charity, but it was never close enough. There was always the unassailable rampart of her mother set between us and I felt thwarted. I wanted more than anything for us to have some time on our own, and though I feared it might never be possible, an opportunity finally presented itself.

During a huge outdoor anniversary party thrown by the mill, I was able to steal a few moments alone with Charity. I approached her during a pig-chasing contest that she was watching.

"Hello," I said.

"Hello!"

She almost sang it. She had her hair tied in a bun for the races, a style that made a lot of women look severe, but not Charity. Her perfect face did not need framing. Even the light bead of sweat on her upper lip and the dark patches spreading from her armpits did nothing to detract from her beauty. Indeed, several exquisite fantasies flashed through my mind about other means of provoking a similar physiological reaction. We arranged to meet behind the food tent when the crowd gathered to hear her mother perform an aria and her father give his annual speech.

"I won't be able to stay long," she warned.

That she would consent to a clandestine meeting for even a few moments made me want to shout it out to the world.

The afternoon dragged by until at last there was an announcement that everyone should gather at the stage. When I saw Charity duck behind the food tent, I made my way there as casually as possible with my heart in my mouth. She giggled as I joined her. We sat side by side on the ground, leaning against the tent, facing the water, she with her legs straight out and her hands clasped on her thighs, me with my legs drawn up and my arms resting on my knees. Our shoulders touched ever so lightly and I didn't want to move a hair for fear of disturbing the connection. Charity was still, too, for the same reason, I hoped. We were quiet for what seemed like an eternity but couldn't have been more than a few seconds.

I found my voice first. "I'm glad you came."

"I couldn't not come." She was a little breathless, perhaps from the boldness of her actions.

Without thinking, I reached for her hand. She anticipated it and met mine halfway. I grasped it and squeezed tightly, kneading her knuckles with my thumb. She squeezed back and there was more pleasure in that simple act than I thought possible. She laid her head on my shoulder and I pressed my cheek against the top of it, breathing in the scent of her hair.

"I need to see you again," I said. "Not like we have been. More like this, with no one else around. And I can't wait for another holiday." In fact, I was willing to smash protocol to smithereens to see more of her.

Charity was silent for a long time before she said, "It can't be like this. It will only lead to trouble. We should start on the right foot. I think the first thing to do is to have you invited over for tea."

I half-laughed; it was a preposterous notion. "Your father would never allow it!"

"But I think my mother would."

"Your mother doesn't like me."

"Oh, no! That's just Mother. She's much more under-standing of these things than Father. He only *thinks* he's the head of the household and I think that between Mother and me, we could change his mind." She gave my hand a squeeze, let go and stood up. Brushing off the back of her dress, she added, "I have to go, Jack, before I'm missed. Please trust me."

I watched her as she ran off to join her family. I wanted to believe that she would accomplish her goal, but I wasn't optimistic.

I should have had more faith. Three years later, Charity and I were married.

WHENEVER THE opportunity arose for Jim and me to talk, we usually turned to the future, as the past wasn't something either of us cared to dwell on. He knew when I cut our con-versation short during the hunt for Black Feather that there were things I did not wish to talk about. And, much as he loved the camaraderie and the wide open spaces, he confessed that he was feeling more and more like putting down some roots, finding a woman and raising a family, maybe even having a small ranch of his own.

My heart lurched at the mention of a wife and family, envious that a man was able to even think of it. But all I said was, "Women are as scarce as fir trees out here. And buying a ranch on a cowboy's wage isn't something you hear about every day. Unless you're expecting an inheritance."

"No such luck. Been savin' a little, though. Maybe one day."

The more I'd come to know Jim, the more I liked him. He was a comfortable man to be with, rock solid, reliable and straight as a lamp post. Right or wrong, you always knew where he stood and if something needed to be done, he would do it without complaining or asking why someone else wasn't doing it. I felt certain that he'd make a great business partner, so I told him that I had some savings too, that I had dreamed of owning a ranch for a long time and maybe we could help each other by pooling our money. We could start small and with a little luck and a lot of work, turn it into something bigger. If he found a wife, then we'd build a fine house off on its own for the two of them.

"I'm not sure I could scrape up half for even a small property," he said doubtfully.

"You put in what you've got and when we start turning a profit you can pay me till you own half."

We discussed finances and agreed that we would need jobs in Calgary over the winter. We would stay out of the bars and not gamble. Barring any unforeseen expenses, we might be able to garner the necessary cash by next year.

"That's okay by me if it's okay by you."

We shook hands on it, but as things turned out, more favourable circumstances arose.

As the summer rolled on and men came and left, talk around the camp at night often turned to the recent gold strikes on the Klondike creeks. Some men speculated on the life of luxury they would live if they ever struck it rich, while others couldn't imagine doing anything other than what they were already doing. Two men said they were going to outfit themselves and head north as soon as their contracts ended in the fall. It was an exciting adventure to contemplate and got my blood pumping, although I remembered an old prospector once saying, while he reminisced about the Cariboo gold rush, that more men went flat broke than ever struck it rich. He had also said that most of the big money had been made from mining the miners, not from mining gold, and I wondered what Jim and I could sell that the miners would need. We didn't have to search very hard to find the answer.

Some of the ranchers spoke of shipping cattle north, that there was huge money in it, but the logistics were daunting. A Calgary rancher-cum-meat packer named Pat Burns, however, had already tried it with modest success and was planning to ship even more. I said to Jim, "This is what we've been waiting for. When work is done in the fall, I think we ought to go to Calgary and have a chat with Mr. Burns."

Jim perked right up. "But what we really need to make it pay is some cattle of our own. Do we have enough to buy a small herd and pay the rail and steamship costs to get them there? It won't be cheap."

"I think I know a way around that. Why don't we talk to Marcus Clarke? I'll bet he'd consign a few head to us."

Jim agreed and we worked out a deal to present to Burns. Autumn took longer than usual to show itself but when it did, we hurried to Calgary.

Burns was big, tough and smart, with an indomitable spirit unfettered by an inability to read or write, and one of the friendliest men I've ever met. He owned several ranches, and his meat-packing plant in Calgary sent beef to various places along the railway line. He was never afraid to take big risks, and shipping cattle to the Klondike was his latest one. He had tried driving a small herd across the Chilkoot Pass, but it proved far too challenging for the cattle and most of them died. Those that made it arrived as sides of beef and none too fresh at that. Nevertheless, he still made money and knew he could make even more if he could only get a herd closer to Dawson before having to slaughter and dress the animals.

When Jim and I met with Burns, he spoke of another route, west of the Chilkoot, called the Chilkat or "Grease Trail" because the Indians there traded in eulachon oil. It was longer but much flatter and bypassed most of the serious rapids on the Yukon River, ending at Fort Selkirk, a settlement that was only 135 miles upriver from Dawson. An 1897 guide to the Yukon-Klondike mines said that though the route was well timbered, there were large stretches of open grass for livestock. We could only speculate on the truth of that but it also said that a toll had to be paid at the trailhead, and that kind of negative information usually tends to be accurate. It didn't say how much the toll was but we suspected it wouldn't be much of a bargain.

"I'd be surprised if we got away with anything less than a dollar a head," Burns said.

He wanted to ship 180 head by this alternative route but it would be a tough haul and so far, he had only two men willing to take on the challenge. "Now you have four," Jim said, and I threw in, "But only if we can add some cattle of our own to the herd, plus we want five cents a pound for helping deliver yours. We'll provide two more experienced cowboys and pay their wages too."

"Too large a herd could be unmanageable and more costly to ship to Alaska," Burns said. "How many head are you thinking of adding?"

"Twenty," I said.

Burns nodded. "That shouldn't be a problem. They your own?"

"They will be," I replied. "And I can guarantee that they'll be the best stock, tough and hardy, and capable of handling rugged terrain."

"What about the extra men?"

I was quite sure that we could get the two men from the roundup who said they were going north, since we would be offering them free passage to the gold fields. I told him about the cowboys, two smart swingmen from the Rocking M, and his response was, "Well, if they were good enough for Don Johansen, they're good enough for me."

Burns had no reservations about Jim and me. He had heard our names in connection with the Black Feather affair and also knew that I had ridden with Steele during the rebellion. We drew up a contract and signed it, Burns with some squiggly lines that were his signature. Then Jim and I returned to the Rocking M in the first snowfall of the season to talk to Marcus Clarke.

The rancher was clearly excited about our adventure and more than willing to let us have 20 of his best steers on consignment. His single condition was that we pay him twice the going rate for beef on the hoof in Calgary, regardless of whether we got them to the Klondike or not. That was fine with us; we figured we'd get 10 times that. Unlike Burns, Marcus didn't want any papers signed when a handshake would do. "The way I see it," he said, "I'm only risking some animals. You boys'll be risking your necks."

Back in Calgary, we found the two Rocking M men who had indicated they were changing careers at a cheap hotel that was a haunt for wintering cowboys. Dick Grant and Percy Hall had come from small towns in Ontario, harbouring dreams of being cowboys. Grant was about my age, tall and slender, with muscles like ropes, while Hall was a few years younger, of medium height, with a rounder face, long side-burns and what was commonly called a "killer" moustache, one that drooped around his mouth in the fashion of western lawmen. He had chocolate-coloured eyes that gave you his full attention when you spoke. They had heard of Burns's proposed expedition and initially weren't much interested in it, but they were now discovering that outfitting themselves and getting north was an expensive undertaking. To that end, they had found work washing dishes at different restaurants, which didn't pay much, but kept them out of the bars. They weren't exactly overjoyed with our offer but they accepted it and said they would be there when we needed them.

Our plan was falling nicely into place. We had the cows and we had the men and we hadn't had to put out a cent of our own money. We were set.

Burns sent a message to come meet the other two men who would be making the trek with us. Bill Henry was a short, confident man in his late 40s, his dark hair flecked with grey, his face creased and leathery from years exposed to the elements. He was a taciturn, triangular-jawed man who had been around cattle and horses most of his life. Andy Anderson, the second man, was a cowboy from Wyoming who had come north on a cattle drive and decided to stay. He was in his 30s and, like Dick Grant, thin and wiry. When he laughed, which he did frequently, it was staccato, like bullets from a Gatling gun.

Marcus gave us what work he could and the winter and spring passed slowly. Toward the end of May, Dick and Percy came down to the Rocking M to help Jim and me drive our 20 head of cattle to Calgary. Marcus wished us well and we told him the next time he saw us we'd be wealthier men.

He laughed. "That's the spirit!"

As Burns was supplying the horses, I sold Sam to the livery stable from which I'd bought her. I hated to part with the old girl, because she'd been an exceptional horse and an even better companion, but she wasn't built for the terrain awaiting us. Besides, she had lived her life on the prairies and in the foothills, and deserved to spend her remaining years there. I trusted the owner to ensure that she went to someone who would treat her well.

By early June, we had purchased all our camping gear and provisions for the trail and loaded 200 head of cattle, 22 pack horses, five saddle horses and one milk cow onto a train and were steaming through the mountains to Vancouver. Three days later, we were sailing northward on a ship crowded with animals and would-be miners.

SIX

The Grease Trail

THE SHIP'S CREW WINCHED a long ramp onto a pebbly, slightly sloped beach in the Chilkat River estuary, just south of the tiny mission community of Haines, and we unloaded our supplies and animals. We had been six days at sea and were glad to be on solid ground and active once again. Even more important, the animals had been so crowded on board the ship that they had not been able to lie down for a proper sleep. We drove them to a broad, grassy area between the beach and the forest where they could eat and rest for the long haul to Fort Selkirk. The ship's whistle blew in salute as she gathered steam, her Plimsoll line riding high now that she had shed most of her heavy cargo.

It was a pretty spot, with the colours of the sunset reflecting off the flat surface of the water. Flanking the inlet were dark, tree-covered mountains, one of them pyramid-shaped, and to the north was the wide swath cut by the Chilkat River. We pitched camp, boiled some rice and coffee, and afterward determined the order of our watches for the night. Then we sat around talking longer than perhaps we should have; I expect it was because we were excited. When we awoke the next day the easy part of our journey would be over and the hard part would begin.

In the morning, the weather remained fair as we trailed the herd along the wide beach, past the mudflats of the estuary, into the broad valley of the Chilkat. Snow-capped mountains soared behind the smaller, forest-draped hills lining the valley. A warm, late June sun streamed down on us and the insects were already ferocious. A solitary house sat near the shoreline and a woman with a child waved as we passed by.

Among cattle, as among humans, there are leaders and followers, and they soon sort themselves out. (The dominant ones are always more aggressive, slightly larger and first to the best feed.) To use this verifiable truth to our advantage, we split the herd into three sections, placing a half dozen of the best leaders in the first section and two dozen willing followers in the second. The remainder of the animals, compelled to obey their herd instincts, brought up the rear.

About a half mile into the valley, we came to a large tent at the side of the trail. Standing in front were two men, both with revolvers in shoulder holsters and one with a rifle cradled in the crook of his right arm. In his mid-40s, he was tall and weather-beaten, and his long blond hair flowed from beneath a broad-brimmed black Stetson. His sideburns and moustache were neatly trimmed and his moose-skin moccasins reached his knees. He raised his left hand, palm out, signalling us to stop. I was leading with the pack horses and reined up.

"Morning," he said in an even-toned voice. "I'd bet my last dollar that you're heading for Dawson."

"Yup," I agreed. "With any luck at all."

He grinned affably. "Well, friend, you're gonna need a lot more than luck. In fact, if you want to use this trail to get there you'll need exactly $2.50 for every cow you've got behind you, plus 50¢ a horse and 20¢ a man."

The charges seemed so preposterous I nearly laughed. Just then Bill Henry joined us and I filled him in. His eyebrows rose and he exclaimed, "Jesus! The last we heard it was a buck a head."

"You got old news, my friend," the man said, still smiling. "It's now $2.50."

"And what gives you the right to more than double it?" I asked, unable to stop the indignation from creeping into my voice.

He swung the rifle up. "This."

"Whoa!" I said. "Point that thing somewhere else, mister, for God's sake. Why don't you tell us what's going on here? We're reasonable men."

His name was Jack Dalton and he'd been transporting goods through the area for years. He had almost single-handedly blazed the trail between the estuary and the Yukon Divide, which amounted to the first half of our overland journey. Only about 40 or 50 miles of it was in Alaska and the rest was in Canada, but the only way around it was to take the Chilkoot Pass instead.

"That kind of work ought not to go unrewarded," he said. "And I don't intend to let it. There's a maze of valleys up there that'll eat a man whole if he don't know where he's going. You'll feel better about it if you think of it this way— the toll charge ain't a whole hell of a lot considering how much that beef of yours'll sell for in Dawson."

I couldn't argue with that, provided we got most of them to Dawson, nor could I argue with the rifle still pointing at us. Neither could Bill. We paid. Dalton filled us in on what to expect along the trail and marked places that our map didn't show. Although I thought that we were being bilked, I liked the man. He had no shortage of charm and I soon began to think our money was well spent. We also learned that a handful of men with a herd of 150 cattle from Oregon and another of similar size out of Washington had preceded us by one and two weeks respectively. Other parties, without cattle, had gone through before them when snow still lay on the ground, most notably one with two women and another of 36 men. All had pulled sleds.

"Those first herds through will have made the trail as plain as day, so you may not need my markers," Dalton said. "Unless they got lost, of course, but I don't see that as my problem."

We may have given Dalton the money grudgingly, but it proved to be the wise thing to do. Farther along the trail we heard that he was not a man to fool with. Had we not paid his toll, he might not have shot us but he certainly would have made our lives miserable. Some herders had tried to ignore him the year before and he kept them off the main trail for nearly 200 miles. In places where it ran open on one side of the river, he forced them by gunpoint to the opposite, tougher side. By the time they reached Fort Selkirk, most of their cattle had died on the rugged terrain.

We left Dalton behind and covered 12 miles more effortlessly than we had anticipated, following the river, which we crossed once at a shallow ford. According to Dalton, it would be like that for another 50 miles, until we left the river valleys and began climbing to the Chilkat Pass. But for now, the animals needed rest, so we found an adequate grazing spot that the previous herds hadn't eaten and trampled, and camped for the night. The easy passage, the spectacular scenery of the valley and the blue sky made a man feel good to be alive and optimistic about the journey ahead.

After three uneventful days, we forded the Chilkat for the last time and turned west, into the broad and beautiful valley of the Klehini River. The mountain peaks gleamed white with snow and a vast glacier loomed high to the south. The level of the river was low compared to the Chilkat and its rocky shores tormented the animals' feet, as did the occasional talus slope we had to traverse. The lead cattle bellowed and balked at the unstable footing but once we got them on it, the rest followed without a problem. Occasionally, the poor condition of the trail forced us into the forest which, along the river, consisted mostly of poplar, alder and willow. At a place called Pleasant Camp we passed from Alaska into British Columbia. Several mounted policemen were constructing log buildings, which would become the Customs post and living quarters. Meanwhile, they camped in tents. Some cows grazed nearby, food for the winter.

Ten miles farther on, the trail left the river and began to climb northward to the Chilkat Pass. We'd barely noticed any ascent at all over the miles we'd covered from the trailhead, but now the land began to rise rather steeply through forested hills, with wide spaces between the trees but very little undergrowth and no grass for the animals to feed on. We gained considerable altitude as the trail climbed and dipped repeatedly over the 15 miles to the pass's summit. It took us a few days to reach that point, by which time we had ascended well above the tree line. The weather slowly deteriorated so that being closer to the heavens felt more like a descent into hell. The wind gathered strength and rain fell in sheets, with wicked thunder and lightning. There was no place to hide as jagged bolts of lightning struck the ground around us. The herd was spooked by it but we kept the lead animals under control and avoided a stampede.

When the storm had passed and the sky cleared, we could take in our surroundings. To the west rose a barren, snow-streaked, saw-toothed range and to the east was a ridge of lower, rounded mountains, with snow-capped peaks beyond. The pass itself was wide open country, a prairie-like expanse stretching off into the distance with plenty of grass, willow bushes and sparse stands of scrub spruce. Purple fireweed bloomed prolifically as did a variety of other colourful flowers. Now that the rain had stopped and the clouds had lifted, it was much cooler and the temperature fell to near freezing at night. It felt as if we were near the top of the world.

We camped beside a small lake and shot several ptarmigan, which were everywhere and completely unafraid of us. Dick Grant, who was as skilful a cook as he was a cowboy, whipped up some ptarmigan stew, complete with gravy and dumplings. It beat our meat staples of bacon, salt pork and beef jerky hands down, and was even better than the trout and grayling we'd been catching since we left the coast.

There was good feed for the cattle, too, and plenty of water, as there had been the entire way so far and, according to Dalton, should be all the way to Fort Selkirk. This was important because well-fed and watered cattle are much easier to handle than hungry, thirsty ones. They sleep better at night, and tend not to get cranky, although some are born that way. Best of all, they retain their weight, which meant money in our pockets.

The days were long—almost 24 hours of daylight—and because we could see where we were going, long stopovers were unnecessary. When there was good feed around and the cattle needed rest we stopped briefly and got some sleep ourselves, then moved on, regardless of the time of day. We scheduled night herding—for want of a better term—so that no one spent more than two hours on watch. Nevertheless, it was always the worst part of the day for me because I had too much time to think.

OUR WEDDING was held at the McRae residence at 10:00 A.M. on a fine April morning. The house was crammed with guests and Joe Fortes stood proudly as my best man. Charity all but floated into the room, on her father's arm, a veiled angel in white. After we exchanged vows, I lifted the veil to kiss her and my knees turned watery. She was beautiful beyond any telling and I knew I lived a charmed life.

A carriage pulled by four white horses carried us to the dock where we boarded a steamer to Victoria. The McRaes had booked and paid for a suite in the capital's finest hotel, the Driard and when the bellhop had left and we were alone at last, we stood there for a moment, apart, unable to quite believe it. Then we were in each other's arms.

I wanted to undress her but the complexities of her apparel were beyond the dexterity of my fumbling hands. She gently pushed them aside, kissed my cheek and went first to our luggage and took out a nightgown, then went into the washroom to change. My imagination ran wild, so I busied myself by adjusting the lamps in the bedroom and living room until the light was just right. When she came out, dressed in her floor-length nightgown, I thought I was dreaming. I took her in my arms and felt her exquisite softness beneath the thin material. We kissed, long and deeply. When I brought my hand around to cup her breast, she moaned and said, "Oh, Jack, I love you so. We've waited so long."

"Much too long," I croaked. I could barely speak, so consumed was I with love for her. I had never known true passion before that moment. I lifted the gown over her head and let it fall to the floor. I kissed her mouth and her perfectly formed breasts, knelt and kissed her belly and the mound above her thighs. Then I stood and led her to the bed. The feelings coursing through me were beyond anything I'd ever imagined, a combination of love and lust so intense I was near combusting.

We experimented and explored each other's bodies until we knew every crease and tiny mole. We made love until we were sore and our mouths were chafed red from kissing. Even then we could not seem to get enough of each other.

The following year, our first child was born, a sweet baby girl who was the spitting image of Charity. We named her

Rebecca and she captured my heart so quickly that any dis-
appointment I might have had about her gender was
overshadowed by the fact that we had brought into the world
another human being as beautiful and bright as its mother.
Yet it had been a difficult birth for both mother and
daughter, and the doctor advised that any future pregnancy,
if it occurred too soon, might be life-threatening.

Charity was nearly inconsolable. She wanted at least a
half-dozen children, as quickly as possible, for she had
enough love for that many, and more. Motherhood comes
naturally to most women, but for Charity it was a state of
grace.

McRae spoke often of my future and said he was grooming
me for bigger things. He moved me around at the mill so that
I knew and understood its various aspects and, when the clerk
left, insisted that I take the position. "This is where you can
begin to learn the business end of running a mill, Jack," he
said. "Admittedly, some of the work is boring, and some of it
is complex, but there's nothing you can't handle. Learn it
and pay heed to what I'm doing and one day you'll be able to
manage an operation like this yourself."

I listened only because Charity was part of it. My dreams
were not of managing sawmills. They were of a ranch somewhere, perhaps in the foothills of Alberta, and my enthusiasm
for it infected Charity. Every payday we put aside money for
a down payment but the problem lay in telling her parents,
who saw us on a path of their own design.

More than once I had dropped hints to McRae of Charity's
and my intention to buy some land and start a small ranch,
but he was the kind of man who, if he didn't want to believe

something, never heard it. "Yes, of course," he'd say and then carry on thinking that no one would be so foolish as to renounce a well-paying, prestigious career for the vagaries of ranching.

Charity worried about her father and how he would react when he was forced to face the truth. "He will be so disappointed."

"I know. But he left home himself as a young man and came west during the Cariboo gold rush so he must have had dreams, too. I'm sure he'll understand ours."

"Yes, he did have dreams. But he didn't take someone's daughter and grandchild along with him."

I couldn't argue with that; however, we had to live our own lives.

We continued saving money. We would have had plenty for our purposes if we sold the house, a wedding present from the McRaes, but I didn't believe it was ours to sell.

"The deed is in our name," Charity pointed out.

"But we didn't buy it. Your father did."

"It was a gift, Jack." She was puzzled by my contrariness. "There were no strings attached, for Heaven's sake!"

"Of course there were and they were meant to tie us here. Your father likes to control people, my love. You, of all people, ought to know that. Have you forgotten what life was like as a teenager?"

She sighed. "No. But Father has always had the best intentions."

"Your father's a fine man, Charity, but he doesn't understand that not everybody wants what he wants."

This complication affected only us, of course. For the

McRaes, these were the best of times. Their daughter was happy and they had a grandchild whom they absolutely adored. They doted on her, and Becky was a child worth doting on. She had the same sandy hair as her mother and the same span of freckles across her nose. She was precocious, too, and grasped things faster than most children her age. Her ability to use relatively sophisticated words and phrases at an early age was astonishing, but Eleanor McRae said that Charity had done the same thing. And like her mother, Becky always saw the bright side of life and was curious about everything, right down to the tiniest bug in the garden. A small tidal pool at the beach could keep her absorbed for hours and she would protest loudly if she considered that we were taking her home too soon.

TWENTY MILES beyond the summit, the trail descended into another broad valley, a few miles wide in places, flanked by spectacular mountains and brooding cliffs where it narrowed. The Tatshenshini River had cut this valley and it was supposedly prime moose and bear country, although we saw neither animal. They could hear us coming for miles and made themselves scarce. We saw plenty of eagles, though, huge birds with six- to seven-foot wing spans, soaring too high in the heavens to feel threatened by us.

The timber wolves weren't bothered much either. We soon had to be extremely vigilant when we stopped to rest and began putting a pair of men on watch at a time. They were cunning devils, those wolves, much smarter than coyotes, and seemed to know when one of us might be able to get a clear shot at them. We did our best to discourage them with a bullet in their direction but even so, they killed one of our cows that got separated from the herd in a driving rainstorm. It was a typical wolf kill. One had, in a single slash with its razor-sharp teeth, severed the animal's hamstrings, disabling it, while another tore open its jugular. They hadn't yet ripped into the flesh when Jim happened upon them. Though he had only a hurried shot with his rifle, he dropped one of the pack while the rest ran off. The dead wolf looked big enough to carry off a bull. Jim skinned it and we butchered the cow for fresh meat for ourselves. We hated losing her—it was a matter of pride—but Jim and I heaved a small sigh of relief that there were still 20 cattle with Rocking M brands. The dead cow was one of Burns's animals.

There were several muskegs along this stretch of the river, home to mosquitoes whose thirst for blood was insatiable; they were far worse than on the high plateau where the frequent winds made them manageable. For the most part, the trail circumvented the muskegs by entering the forest where the bugs weren't quite as bad. That is, they stopped a hair short of driving the animals completely mad. But it was dangerous, for the wolves had not forgotten the taste of blood and stalked us mercilessly.

Some three weeks after leaving the coast, we passed into the Yukon Territory and reached Dalton's post, a rambling log structure 120 miles from his toll tent. Since Pleasant Camp we'd averaged only about 6 miles a day, but the cattle were healthy and hefty, which bode well for us in Dawson, and the trip to date had been easier than we had expected. Sometimes it's hard to find good men to ride with but I was fortunate. My companions were among the best.

Ike Martin, a grey-haired, amiable man, ran the post and was delighted by our appearance. He was an employee of Dalton's, who mostly tended the store while his boss was on the coast collecting money from would-be trail-users. The store had been there long before the area became part of the route to Dawson, created to trade with the Indians whose village was a mile or so down the Tatshenshini River. Dalton brought in extra supplies to cater to the gold-rush trade, but nothing was cheap. We supplemented our stock of flour with a 50-pound bag that cost a whopping $25. However, if all went well we'd soon be on the other side of such skewed transactions and that provided some consolation.

We rested for a day at the post, enjoying the sun that beat down on us, and then set off again, downriver, past the barking dogs of the Indian village, and climbed to a ridge that rose 800 feet to another vast plateau. Behind us and below we could see the post and the village and the Tatshenshini which had flowed north to this point but now curved in a broad arc and began a southward journey to join the Alsek River and the sea. We could see it twisting for miles down the valley. The Coast Mountains rose to the southeast and to the southwest were the giant peaks of the St. Elias Range. To the northwest, the direction in which we were headed, smoke from a forest fire obscured the horizon.

After viewing this panorama, Jim commented, "Sorta makes a man feel puny, don't it?"

"Or bigger than he ought to," I said.

It rained again, hard and slanting and we were miserable and cold by the time we reached the Dezadeash River. We spotted a cabin in the trees but found it locked and deserted except for a snarling dog. We presumed it was there to deter visitors while its owner was out panning. Twenty miles farther on, the valley narrowed between steep cliffs draped in clouds and it was here that we saw the first hard evidence of the forest fire we'd spied from a distance and which the heavy rain had apparently extinguished. The canyon was an eerie graveyard of charred trees, devoid of life. The damp, burnt-out smell along this stretch made the animals nervous. The ground was rocky and treacherous, broken-leg territory, and we had to ease our way through it, when the herd instinctively wanted to run.

Like the Tatshenshini, the Dezadeash River curved to the west before it also dipped south to join the Alsek. Near the high point of its arc, we saw another cabin, this one sitting on the bluff above the river, with sweeping views in all directions. An affable, loquacious French Canadian named Paul Champagne lived there, along with two partners who were down on the river working their claim. We accepted an invitation to stay for dinner but insisted on providing the meat, as the beef we had wouldn't last. When the partners returned, Dick Grant, who had become our de facto cook, fried some beef liver and steaks, and Champagne made johnny cakes and custard for dessert, which proved a nice change from our customary wild berries and milk. It was a sumptuous feast for being served in the middle of nowhere.

In answer to our query, Champagne said that he had been to Fort Selkirk and knew the route we'd be taking, not well, but enough to describe it and offer a flavour of what it was like. This information was welcome, as Dalton's detailed knowledge had extended only as far as the Dezadeash River.

Champagne told us that 10 miles north of the cabin, we would cross the Yukon Divide, which separated the rivers flowing to the Pacific Ocean from those flowing to the Arctic. From there to the fort was a vast plateau of rolling, spruce-choked hills, cut by muskeg-filled valleys that seemed to go off in every direction.

"Some of dose muskegs can swallow a man and 'is 'orse 'ole if 'e isn't careful," he said. "And dey are as monotonous as dey are dangerous. Da same t'ing day after day. By da time you reach da fort you'll be 'appy to 'ave it be'ind you."

Having already come 150 miles, we were halfway to Fort Selkirk. Granted, we'd still have more than 100 miles to go from there to Dawson but we would complete that part of the journey by raft. We'd face new challenges then but we didn't know just how welcome the change would be, for Champagne was right: it was indeed tiresome country.

We plodded across its sameness, day after day, its capricious weather dogging us like a millstone, following the trail left by our predecessors. The muskegs were exasperating and one steer strayed into quicksand and couldn't be extracted despite a Herculean effort on everyone's part. It wouldn't budge and only sank deeper. Like the loss of the cow to the wolves, it wasn't a defeat we suffered gladly, the value of the animal being secondary to the principle of the matter. Once again, though, it was a Burns cow and Bill put it out of its misery with a bullet to the head. Its death was made even worse because we couldn't butcher it for food.

Then we came to a spot where the herd that preceded us had run into trouble. The trail was badly churned up, and the tracks veered off to the east on better ground but we suspected that they'd lost a cow or two before realizing that the muskeg was impassable.

Bill trotted over to me. "I wonder if what they found over yonder was any better than this? Or maybe the whole damn lot of them were sucked into a bottomless bloody mud hole."

Like the rest of us, Bill had had his fill of muskegs. "I suppose it wouldn't hurt to check it out," I said. "See how far east they had to go before they turned north again. If it's too far, maybe we can find a better passage to the west. I'll get a fire going and have some tea ready when you get back."

Bill and Andy rode off. I built a small fire, filled the kettle from a creek, threw some tea leaves in and set it on the fire to boil. By the time it was ready, they had returned. "It isn't too bad that way," Bill said. "Still quite boggy but it's passable."

"It probably wouldn't hurt to see if it's any better the other way," I said. "You boys have some tea and Jim and I will take a look. If the ground will hold him and his horse, it'll hold anything."

I whistled to Jim and we set off together. It had begun to rain so we pulled our slickers out of our saddlebags and donned them. The rain and low clouds added to the dreariness of the landscape.

We rode into a broad side valley that looked inviting for the first 10 minutes until we encountered another muskeg. It was small, only about 50 yards across, but the steep slopes on either side of it made it impossible to go around. Beyond, another valley cut off enticingly to the north.

"That might be a better route if we can get through this," I said.

I eased my horse forward into the muskeg and we sank

only halfway to the animal's knees. He was tentative but the footing appeared to be fine and I urged him on. All of sudden, the solid ground beneath the soft top gave way. When the horse's front legs began sinking, he panicked and launched himself forward, as if it were a stream he could leap across but all he did was take us farther into the muskeg. He lunged again and twisted in his attempt to escape and instead of staying with him I placed both hands on his neck and pushed myself off. By this time my legs were in the muck and felt as if they had anvils tied to them. I fell on my side with a splat.

The horse was struggling wildly to free itself but was only sinking deeper. I could see the terror in its eyes. I got a mouth full of muskeg and began choking and thrashing about myself. The mud added a hundredweight to my body and began pulling me down. I tried to swim but my legs were useless, and sinking my arms into the muck only made it worse. I tried to shout but all that came out was a choking sound. Thoughts of Charity and Becky flashed through my mind. In the next instant a strange calmness enveloped me. Then I felt something hit my face and heard Jim yell, "Grab the rope, Jack!"

I reached for it with every ounce of strength that I had, felt its roughness as I wrapped it around my right arm and wrist, grabbed it with my left hand and held on tight. Jim had the rope turned around his saddle horn a couple of times and his horse was backing up to free me from the sucking quicksand. I was afraid my arms were going to be pulled from their sockets but in a moment or two I was being dragged along the surface and then onto solid ground, spitting out mud as I went.

I lay on my side gasping, then saw Jim above me. "You all right, partner?" he asked. He looked as if he didn't know if he should be concerned or laugh his head off.

When I caught my breath, I said, "I think I might make it, thanks. I owe you one. I wouldn't have got out of there on my own."

Jim helped me to my feet. My knees were shaky, my shoulder joints ached and my arm was sore where I'd had the rope wrapped around it. At the edge of the muskeg there was a pool of water and I staggered to it, rinsed my mouth out, washed the mud from my hands and face and let the rain take care of the rest. I returned to where my horse and I had entered the bog but it was as if he had never existed. He had completely vanished, saddle and all, without a trace, although my hat sat partly submerged, its crown jutting from the surface, a monument to misfortune. I shuddered at what would have happened had Jim not been there. I climbed behind my friend and we doubled back to the others.

They were sitting by the fire enjoying a cup of tea. Bill took in my muddy clothes and grinned. "It's just a guess, mind, but it looks to me like we're heading east for a while."

We stripped one pack horse of its load and redistributed it amongst the others and I rode bareback over the final 50 miles to Fort Selkirk. The place had been our goal for so long it had taken on almost mythical proportions, but on the fifth day of September we saw smoke curling skyward from the settlement and finally arrived, sweat-soaked and bone-weary.

The community sat below the confluence of the Pelly and Yukon rivers. Besides the local population and transients, there were more than 200 soldiers of the Yukon Field Force, posted there to assist the police in keeping the peace and to prevent the thousands of Americans streaming into the country from taking it over. Not far downstream there was an Indian village of identical log houses, all in a row on the bluff above the water. We hired a half-dozen men from the village at 50¢ a day each to help us build the rafts for the final stage of our journey, slaughter the animals and accompany us to Dawson.

Most of the trees around Fort Selkirk had already been converted into rafts, which forced us upstream some distance to where the forest was thick and the trees straight as masts. Over the next two weeks, we built three rafts, each 75 feet long and 36 feet wide, with long oars at each end for steering. They were awkward vessels to handle at first, but generally seaworthy and, once we got used to their contrariness, quite manageable. We floated them down to where the cattle were and spent the next week slaughtering and dressing the animals and loading the carcasses on the rafts, working long hours until we were dizzy from exhaustion. We sold the horses to the Field Force for a tidy sum and at dawn the following day, shoved off into the broad Yukon River as it curved northward.

SEVEN

A Place Where the Insane Gather

I STEERED THE LEAD raft out into midstream with the large oar mounted on the stern. Fully loaded, the vessel was less cumbersome to handle than I expected. Nevertheless, poles lay at each side of the raft should we need them to push ourselves off gravel bars. I was accompanied by Jim and two Indians, neither of whom spoke English. We communicated by hand gestures, facial expressions, grunts and words, unintelligible, but usually understood. They'd been on the river many times and knew what to look for, so they spent much of their watch at the bow. Behind us, Bill Henry and Andy Anderson and two Indians manned the second raft, while on the third were Dick Grant and Percy Hall, also with two Indians.

We skirted a small island opposite the fort and saw the charred remains of a Hudson's Bay trading post—the original Fort Selkirk—that had been attacked and burned to the ground by Indians in 1852. Beyond, a black wall of columnar rock on our starboard side soared 450 feet above us as we drifted slowly past at about four or five knots. The columns, impressive at first, went on for nearly 20 miles and began to feel more like prison walls. I was glad to see the end of them. Now, mountains sloped steeply into the river, reminiscent of the inlets we had passed on our sea voyage to Haines. And grey clouds clinging to the hillsides made it about as inviting as the land between the Yukon Divide and Fort Selkirk.

We drifted on. The river was filled with small islands, and selecting the best channel between some of them was often pure guesswork. Now and then we'd see a tattered flag where some thoughtful souls had marked the way. There was so much silt in the water that we could hear it scraping along the logs of the raft and the bowmen had to be on their toes in order to avoid grounding. Good fortune was on our side for there had been about two days of heavy rain prior to our taking to the river and this had raised the water level substantially. I would not want to speculate on how difficult it would have been to get those vessels off a gravel bar in the middle of the river without completely unloading them first. It also might have meant losing some of our payload and that would have been catastrophic, especially with success so near at hand.

We built cooking fires on board for lunch and only stopped at night before it got dark. Here the Indians were well worth their pay. They knew the food that the land had to offer and gathered wild onions and mushrooms that we fried with our steaks, and there were always blueberries for dessert.

Other than the soft, raspy whispering of the silt beneath us, the wilderness was utterly silent as we floated through it.

Only twice was it disrupted. The first time was when a grizzly bear feeding on berries near the river was frightened by the sudden appearance of our rafts. It bolted up a short slope with amazing power and agility for such a large animal. Jim fetched his rifle but by the time he got it to his shoulder to fire, the bear had found safety in the forest.

"Damn it," he cursed. "That was one helluva fine rug that ran off into the bush."

Surprisingly, it was the first grizzly we'd seen after being warned that they might eat most of our stock before we got halfway to the river. But like almost everything else we'd heard third- or fourth-hand about the trail, it had proven to be unreliable information.

The second sound that disturbed the deep silence was the throb of a paddlewheeler's engine as the vessel steamed around a curve in the river. As she drew near we could see passengers lining the deck and even from 75 yards Sam Steele was recognizable; his scarlet tunic and commanding bearing suggested that he was no less than the ship's captain as she churned by, giving us a wide berth, on her way upriver. I waved my floppy-brimmed hat at him and he, along with others at the rail, waved in reply, but I didn't know if he recognized me from that distance. His wave, like the others, was probably a polite response to ours.

According to newspapers a few months earlier, Steele had been transferred to the Klondike to exercise some form of control over the miners flooding into the area. But he was apparently leaving, which seemed to me to be a short posting. I wondered why. Maybe there was a family emergency. Or maybe it was the war that had recently broken out in South

Africa. It would be like Steele to want to jump headlong into the fray.

We bobbed a bit in the vessel's wash, then she disappeared around another bend and left us in silence again, with a thin veil of smoke that settled like fog on the river. The encounter had been all too brief, but it was as if civilization had sent one of her best representatives to prove her existence and boost our spirits.

The mountain walls that had been hemming us in eventually slipped behind us, and the land became flatter and marshy. Now and then we passed crude cabins built alongside small creeks emptying into the Yukon. We saw no signs of their occupants who were probably panning for gold in the feeder creeks. A large river, unnamed on our map, joined the Yukon from our left and was so choked with milk-coloured silt that it turned the main stream grey. There was a labyrinth of islands here, the passages between them clogged with enormous snags. Branches and roots from gigantic trees reached out for us like the skeletal arms and fingers of some horrific monster, but it was the ones we couldn't see, underwater, that were the most hazardous as they grabbed at the rafts and threatened to bind us permanently. It was an eerie world, even for an adult's imagination, and went on for miles. We pulled in at Stewart Island for the night, thankful to be past the labyrinth and temporarily off the river.

We drifted on for two more days until we rounded a great bluff and there lay Dawson City, stretched out along the right bank for more than a mile. We were lucky to find room to moor amid the steamers and other craft tied along the shoreline.

We had done it. The long journey was over and Jim and I hadn't lost a single animal and spoilage was negligible. He was grinning like the Cheshire Cat and pounded my shoulder so hard I reckoned for a moment that I might have to seek medical attention.

We'd barely got our rafts secured before the buyers, who had seen us coming, descended on us. Bill made things easy for himself by selling Pat Burns's cattle in a single lot to the Mounties for 75¢ a pound. Jim and I sold ours in smaller lots at $1.00 a pound, plus we got 50¢ a pound for the hides, which averaged about 80 pounds each. Bill also paid us a nickel a pound for our work in getting Burns's cattle there, which didn't hurt him a bit. And since the surrounding hills were stripped bare of anything that resembled a tree, we sold the rafts for an exorbitant sum and split the money between the six of us and the Indians for their help building them. In total, Bill collected more than $60,000 after expenses. How much he himself got out of that was not a topic he was willing to discuss. Jim and I made a total of $11,000 from our cattle and what Bill paid us; nearly $1,000 went toward expenses, which included paying the Indians a little extra, and $100 bonuses to Dick and Percy. We earmarked another $1,600 for Marcus Clarke, a figure based on doubling the $40 which he would have received for selling his cattle on the hoof in Calgary, then added another $400 because we might not have been holding all that cash in our hands were it not for him. In the end, Jim and I had $8,000 to split, enough profit to turn many a miner in Dawson green with envy.

With the responsibilities and difficulties of the drive behind us, the six of us felt worn to a nub. Yet the speed with which we converted our stock into cash enlivened us significantly. We sought out a bath house first, then a restaurant, then a saloon.

Dawson was a subarctic oasis in a great desert of mountains and muskegs, working hard to put itself on the map faster than any city in history. Only a year before, it had been nothing more than an unnamed collection of tents and a few buildings. Now it rivalled most western Canadian cities in size and offered pretty much the same amenities. Luxurious hotels abounded, as did fancy restaurants. It had an opera house and other places of entertainment such as saloons, dance halls, vaudeville theatres, motion-picture theatres and whorehouses. It even had telegraph and telephone service. People of high society lived and worked alongside the lower classes. Doctors and lawyers rubbed shoulders with murderers and thieves, and sometimes they were one and the same. Everybody knew everybody else's business, and secrets were as closely guarded as the headlines in the daily newspapers. You could buy anything you wanted if you had the money; if not, your chances of survival were scant. It was a crazy place, filled with crazy people, because if you wanted to be there you had to be somewhat crazy to begin with.

There were about 15,000 people in Dawson and twice that many on the creeks in the surrounding area. Human beings filled every valley and gulch with their bodies, their tents and any equipment deemed necessary to extract gold from a shovelful of gravel. The hills were shorn of their trees and the streams had metamorphosed into flumes, although some men swore they could have washed the gravel with their sweat. For a few, their hard work bore fruit, as all of the main creeks to the southeast of Dawson—Bonanza, Eldorado, Hunker, Sulphur and Dominion—were gold-bearing. But the surface gold was gone and the miners were now sinking shafts inch by inch through permanently frozen ground to bedrock, which in most cases was 25 feet or more below the topsoil, hoping to find the motherlode. Few people were more optimistic than miners.

Jim and I had bought mining licences in Vancouver on the off-chance that we might want to try our luck but it was not for us; our minds were on different things. Dick and Percy, on the other hand, had signed onto the drive for only one reason and as soon as they had rested and outfitted themselves, they went off into the hills to muck for gold. Bill and Andy prepared to depart on the next steamer south. They intended to drive another herd of cattle to Dawson the following year, a smaller one, which they would buy outright and try to bring in alive. They knew that the profit would be enormous and it would be all theirs.

Jim said to me, "We need to get out of this place as soon as possible, partner. Every day we spend here costs us about an acre of land down south."

I agreed. The money we had was barely enough to buy two feet of frontage on an empty lot in Dawson but it was plenty for our purposes. Before we left, we put the money in belts around our waist.

"How does it feel?" Jim asked.

"Like a ranch holding up my pants," I grinned. "And I hardly know it's there."

We joined Bill and Andy on the steamer and escaped the lunatic asylum that was the Klondike. We had not dipped a single pan and left without a single regret. We stood on deck, held our mining licences out into the breeze, let them go and watched them waft gently down to the water, like autumn leaves, where the current carried them toward Dawson.

EIGHT

Ghost from a Distant War

MARCUS CLARKE HAD NEVER entertained any doubts that we would return successfully and, indeed, said that he would not have given us his prime beef if he had. We had made him a very happy man. "You boys just got me a new stable built, and then some" he said. "This calls for a celebration." He went to a sideboard and retrieved a bottle of whisky. "I've been saving this for exactly this occasion." He poured three generous tots and raised his in salute. "Here's to you boys, and here's to those wonderful rectangular things with a leg on each corner."

The 20th century rolled in with a display of fireworks and drunken revellers in the snow-swept streets of Calgary. Jim and I spent it quietly, joining a few friends for drinks at the Alberta Hotel. Among them was Pat Burns who was eager to have us lead another drive to Dawson come summer. We flatly declined. We were through working for other people. We would only work for ourselves from now on.

"Don't let me disillusion you, boys," Burns said, "but unless you're born rich, you're always working for someone else. And the marketplace can be the cruellest master of them all. If you don't mind some advice, the only way to be success-ful is to always do what you have to do. But maybe I don't need to explain that to you."

He didn't. And it was good advice coming from a man who never let an opportunity pass without doing exactly what he had to do to take advantage of it. We let him know our plans because few people knew the land market better than he did. He said he'd be glad to keep an eye out for us, adding genially, "Although I don't know if I need you boys as competition."

We made enquiries at several estate agents' offices to see if there were any small ranches available that matched our pocketbook. There was one near Medicine Hat and another closer to Edmonton, areas that didn't interest us, but most agents were positive that something would come along if we were patient. Well, I had plenty of patience and didn't mind a brief holiday. The drive to Dawson had been tough and demanding, and a little rest and relaxation was overdue. We took rooms at an inexpensive hotel and lay low but it wasn't long before we grew bored. Spring would be on us before we knew it and so far nothing had developed. Then I picked up the local newspaper, as I did every morning.

On the front page was a list of the men killed in action in South Africa where the war between the British and Boers had been under way for several months. A small Canadian contingent had already gone to assist the British but most people assumed the war would be of short duration and our soldiers would be home soon. That wasn't how it turned out, however, and now the newspaper contained a list of the Canadian fallen. The majority were young men, single and barely in their 20s, and one was a family man who had left a wife and children behind. The names were in alphabetical order and as I read down them, toward the end, my heart stuttered when I came across the name of William Ironside Scott.

IT WAS a Friday night in May and Victoria, where Charity, Becky and I had gone for a holiday, was busier than we'd ever known it to be, with revellers, both locals and out-of-towners, set to celebrate Queen Victoria's 77th birthday. The Driard Hotel was bursting at the seams with guests but we had pre-booked our suite and went directly to it after checking in. With a long day behind us and another ahead, we wanted to get Becky into bed as soon as possible. While Charity soothed her with a bedtime story, I waited in the living room, in front of the window overlooking the city.

Across the harbour, I could see that the new legislative buildings, replacing the old Birdcages, were nearing completion. The street lamps had come on and the town was still busy with carriage and foot traffic, people strolling along the sidewalks enjoying the warm evening air. A trolley went by, clanging its bell. I was thinking of how bad things often gave rise to good things and vice versa, when Charity appeared. She was a perfect example of what I was thinking about. If my father hadn't been a drunk and beaten me, I would not have left home when I did and would probably never have met her. In that regard, my father's life hadn't been a complete waste. Now I couldn't imagine my life without her.

She came to my side and I slipped my arm around her shoulders.

I said, "That didn't take long."

"I think it's called sheer exhaustion." She rested her head on my shoulder.

I turned and took her in my arms and kissed her long and softly, then held her face between my hands. I was still excited by her beauty. I kissed her forehead and the tip of her nose.

"Do you have any idea how much I love you?" I asked.

"Yes. I can feel it in the gentleness of your hands and the tenderness of your voice. It's there as surely as my love for you."

We undressed each other in front of the window, feeling decadent and exhibitionist, though we were on the hotel's top floor and there were no other tall buildings in the vicinity. She whispered in my ear, "I don't want you to use a condom tonight, Jack."

I was concerned. "Have you forgotten the doctor's warning? How dangerous it might be if you get pregnant again?"

"But that was five years ago and I've never felt better! I don't want Becky to be our only child. I want to her to have brothers and sisters."

We discussed it for a while but she was adamant. After all, the doctor had really only said not to have more children too soon. There was nothing to worry about, she insisted, so in the end I acquiesced. We went to bed and made love; not the frenetic, passionate love-making of old but gentler and more deeply realized. And when I spilled my seed inside her it felt the most natural and right thing to do.

Later, we had wine sent to the room and sat on the bed and toasted each other. Charity glowed with happiness. We decided that after our return to Vancouver we would tell her parents of our plans to investigate properties in Alberta.

Charity sighed. "I can't say I'm looking forward to telling them. They will be so hurt."

"Well, it isn't as if they haven't been given all kinds of clues even if they do seem to ignore them."

We finished the wine and in sheer contentment fell asleep in each other's arms.

A pamphlet in our suite outlined the activities planned for the weekend, which would take place over four days, Saturday to Tuesday. We divided Saturday and Sunday between the beach and a train ride through the farmland on the Saanich Peninsula. On Monday we went to the boat races on the Gorge waterway but it was Tuesday's celebrations that I had most wanted to see. They included a large military parade with much pomp and circumstance sure to impress everyone and, best of all, a mock battle, scheduled for Esquimalt. It would be the grand finale of the festivities and was touted to be spectacular.

Breakfasting at the hotel that morning, Charity was afraid that the gunfire and exploding cannons would alarm Becky, who was not in her usual good mood. "I think she might be developing a fever, Jack, so why don't you go on your own? Becky and I will enjoy some quiet time in our rooms."

"Come with me to see the parade, at least. Becky will love it and it might even cheer her up. There should be plenty of cabs around when it's over to bring you back here. Maybe we could take the streetcar over." I reached for Becky's hand. "Would you like to go for a streetcar ride, honey?"

Though there were trolleys in Vancouver, Becky had never been on one and it piqued her curiosity. Her eyes brightened and she nodded her head. "Yes!"

Charity said, "All right then. Just a streetcar ride and we'll come home."

Extra cars had been brought out from the barn to handle the crowds, but even so, we were lucky to get seats. Charity sat next to the window with Becky on her lap while I held Becky's hand. After the next three stops the aisle was jammed with passengers clinging to straps dangling from the ceiling, while others filled the platforms at the front and rear of the car. The heat was suffocating every time the streetcar stopped, even with all the windows wide open, but if Becky was bothered by it she didn't let on. If anything, I thought she looked more energetic. As the car swayed along the line, the excitement was tangible and the hot, summer-like air flowing through the car crackled with loud chatter. Seated in front of us was another family with a pretty, freckle-faced, red-haired girl about Becky's age, who peeked shyly over her mother's shoulders. Becky, who wasn't at all shy, said, "Hi!" which caused the girl to retreat.

Weight restrictions on the Point Ellice Bridge required the trolley to stop momentarily, to allow the one preceding to cross on its own. As it reached the far side, ours crept onto the bridge along with a one-horse carriage and a bicyclist. Dozens of people were crossing on foot. Beneath the bridge, several boaters were enjoying the holiday and warm weather on the water, and they waved. Suddenly, there was a loud cracking sound and the streetcar dropped. It continued forward for a second or two, then there was an even louder noise as the span it was on began to collapse. The world shifted onto a different plane; everything appeared to be in slow motion. The streetcar tilted to the right and there were shouts of alarm. We were seated on the left side of the car and I yelled to Charity, "Hang on!" when there was really nothing to hang on to except the seat in front of us. I saw her grab it with her left hand, while her right arm still encircled Becky. I let go of Becky's hand and threw my left arm around Charity's shoulders, grabbing Becky's tiny arm with my right hand. They both fell against me and Becky cried, "Oh, Papa!" We tumbled out of our seat on top of other people.

The car turned completely on its side and plunged toward the water. I heard Charity's voice but didn't know what she said for it was lost amid the screams of terror from the other passengers. Yet above it all, I could hear the bridge timbers splintering and popping like fireworks. Then, with a horrific jolt and splash, and the sound of shattering glass, we hit the water. I tried to hold on to my loved ones but the impact tore them from my arms. Water flooded into the open windows and the trolley sank into the cold, murky depths of the channel. I could see nothing, but all around me was chaos as I felt the kicking, struggling bodies of other passengers. I reached out, hoping that I might catch hold of Charity or Becky, but got instead a trousered male leg that gave no resistance. I let it go. I fought to hold my breath, a single thought flashing through my mind: that my life and the lives of those I loved surely could not end here. Then something thudded against my head and I blacked out.

I regained consciousness face down, retching and coughing water. I believed I was still in the streetcar and panicked, thrashing frantically, trying to grab something to keep me from being dragged down even farther.

"Whoa, whoa!" a male voice said. "Take it easy, son. You're safe now."

Two pairs of hands gently turned me over and I sensed the hard earth below me and saw blue sky and a bright sun above. There didn't seem to be any warmth in it, for I started to shiver uncontrollably. Two men knelt beside me and one, an elderly, silver-haired man with a kind face, threw a blanket across my chest and torso. Slowly, I became aware of my surroundings. I lay stretched out on what might have been someone's front lawn, near the water's edge and what was left of the bridge. I could see other survivors in my immediate vicinity but none that I recognized. Close by was the limp body of the shy little red-haired girl. Fear ripped through my heart like a bullet. I tried to sit up but could not. My head ached badly and I had a violent urge to vomit.

"My wife! My daughter! Where are they?"

"Easy, son," the kindly old man said again. "You've had a nasty blow to the head and you need to stay lying down. We're going to get you to the hospital right now, but tell me your name and the names of your wife and child, and we'll try to find out if they're among the survivors. Many of them were taken to the far shore, so don't despair."

Yet besides the vicious headache, despair was precisely what gripped me and I barely got our names out before I fell

into another black hole, the light above me receding to a fine
point before it was gone altogether.

When I awoke the next day in the hospital I was informed
that Charity and Becky had not survived. I had lost the most
loving, lovely wife and beautiful daughter that a man could
ever hope for and it was all my fault. Why had I encouraged
Becky to come on the streetcar ride? If I hadn't, she and
Charity would have returned to the hotel and would be alive
now. And why hadn't I died with them?

Charity's parents came to help with the arrangements to
take the bodies home to Vancouver. The three of us were in
a dense fog most of the time. The Methodist Church on
Princess Street was jammed with mourners for the funeral
service and the two coffins sitting by the altar were closed.
There was a sea of flowers, mostly roses, and I found the
smell sickening. Roses would forever remind me of funerals
and this one in particular.

The procession to the cemetery seemed miles long and
the clip-clop of horses' hoofs and the grinding of the
hearses' steel-rimmed wheels on the macadam surface grated
on my soul. Townsfolk lined Westminster Road to pay their
respects and even the streetcars did not run. But difficult as
the procession was, it didn't compare to the final act of
lowering the coffins into their graves. How does a man do
that and retain his sanity? Perhaps he never really does; I
didn't know. All I knew, and knew with stark certainty, was
that the blossoming trees and colourful flowers in the cemetery, the spectacular blue mountains forming a backdrop,
and the sun beaming down from a cloudless sky on the crowd
of mourners was not the real world. For me, that was a dark,

cold place, unfit for habitation; a place where funeral dirges played in the heart forever.

When I thought I could handle it, I returned to Victoria because I had someone to thank. I had learned that a young man named William Ironside Scott, who was also on the streetcar when the bridge collapsed, had pulled me out of the water. Not only had Scott rescued me, he had gone into the water three more times to rescue others and was the biggest hero of the tragedy.

Scott was personable, lithe and muscular, and well known around Victoria, even before the accident. An oarsman of the first order, he was the junior single sculls champion for the Dominion of Canada. He was also the stroke oar of the International Champions of America, yet he wore it all with great modesty. He offered his condolences and said he was relieved that the newspaper hadn't known of our meeting, for a reporter would have pestered us no end. That he had been able to help was only because he had been in the right place at the right time.

"Even so, Bill, I owe you my life."

"You owe me nothing, Jack. You would have done the same thing," Scott said with conviction.

Perhaps I would have. I did not know. And despite Scott's claim, it was a debt that would always remain on the ledger.

THE NEWS of Scott's death both stunned and upset me. I read it again and still could scarcely believe it. The image of Scott—that of a vibrant young man with a powerful zest for living—had remained with me over the years. I couldn't imagine him dead but he had lost his life in a battle at some obscure place called Paardeberg Drift. I suddenly felt shallow and contemptible. While I was sitting around Calgary twiddling my thumbs in relative luxury, he had made the ultimate sacrifice for Queen and Empire.

Beneath that article was another, about a slaughter at another place, Spion Kop. British soldiers had climbed to a hilltop in a dense mist, thinking that they had taken the high ground, and hastily dug a long trench. That they could get down only a foot and a half into the hard, rocky ground proved fatal. When the mist lifted in the morning, they discovered to their horror that there were three hills surrounding them, all higher and all occupied by Boers. They were sitting ducks and by the time the firing stopped, the dead lay three deep in the long trench which had become a mass grave. Nearly 400 men died, as many went missing or were captured and 1,500 were wounded. Boer losses were minimal in comparison.

The final article involved Lord Strathcona, the man who had driven the last spike on Canada's national railway. He had made a "munificent offer" to provide funds to create a voluntary force of 500 men and 500 horses to join the fight in South Africa. It would be called "Lord Strathcona's Horse," and its commander would be Sam Steele. Steele had actually been in Halifax preparing to depart for South Africa with the Canadian Mounted Rifles when he received word of his new command. The force was to consist entirely of westerners who were excellent horsemen and sharpshooters, and they were to have the best mounts available. He had hopped on the train immediately and was on his way to Calgary.

That Steele would be in command made my decision easier, although I would have joined anyway. I owed that much to the man who had saved my life. A third reason was provided later by Marcus Clarke who agreed that it was my duty to go. I owed it also to the country I lived in, which allowed me to conduct my life in any way I saw fit as long as I didn't violate too many laws.

Jim was not happy when I told him. "Christ, partner, that's insane! You want to go off and get yourself killed just when we can make somethin' of our lives? It's not even our war. It's halfway around the bloody world, for God's sake! Besides, if we don't find some land soon we may be priced right out of the market."

"I have to do this, Jim. I'll explain some other time. But why can't you get the land for us? I trust your judgment and you have my word that you'll hear no complaints from me."

It clearly wasn't the way he had seen events unfolding but he sensed that it was futile to argue. He sighed. "All right, I'll get the land. You make sure you come back in one piece."

Three days later Steele arrived and recruiting began in earnest. I was first in a line of more than a hundred men. When the hall doors opened, I saw Steele himself among the officers seated behind a long table, preparing to enlist people. I walked over to him and he smiled. "Ah, Strong. You've returned from the Yukon, I see."

So he had recognized me after all. Somehow it didn't surprise me.

He arose and, reaching across the table, shook my hand. He was more imposing than ever as he motioned me to sit down on the hardback chair opposite him.

"Did you manage to make it to Dawson with your load of beef?"

"Yes, sir."

"A very profitable enterprise, I should think."

"Well worth the trouble, sir."

"I'm sure. You've invested it wisely, no doubt?"

"My plan is to buy a ranch as soon as I can find something suitable. Actually, I've formed a partnership with Jim Spencer."

"Ah, Spencer. A good man. Will we see him today?"

"Not likely, sir. He's staying behind to buy the property before there's nothing left that we can afford."

Steele noddded. "Well then," he said, shifting some papers on the table, the small talk over with. "Shall we get down to the business of why you are here?"

"Yes, sir. I was hoping you could use me in South Africa."

"Indeed we can. Dare I ask what prompted your decision?"

"A number of things. Mostly the death of a friend at Paardeberg Drift."

"I see." He paused, reflecting on my comment. "You wouldn't want to let something like that cloud your mind, Strong. You'll need to keep your wits about you over there."

"I understand, sir."

Satisfied, Steele presented the paperwork and briefly explained my obligations, and I signed a one-year contract of service as a private soldier in Lord Strathcona's Horse. Steele swore me in and said that the Horse would be much the better for my presence and that if I kept my nose to the grindstone there would be a promotion before we left the country. Then he gave me my first assignment: joining several other volunteers on a train bound for Fort Macleod. We were to meet with Dr. Duncan McEachern, a veterinary surgeon responsible for purchasing the force's mounts, and be his wranglers.

Outside the hall I was surprised to see Jim's large shape at the rear of the line. Partly annoyed and partly pleased, I went over to him. "There's no property for sale in there, Jim. I checked."

"I'm not here to buy property," he deadpanned. "I'm here to protect my interests. Nothin' more."

NINE

The Horse

DR. DUNCAN McEACHERN WAS a capable man who knew horses inside out, literally, but wasn't much of a rider. With a handful of us as wranglers, he spent the next two weeks visiting every ranch between Fort Macleod and Calgary, buying healthy, sturdy horses that were broken and trained. McEachern was prepared to pay anywhere from $80 to $120 for one. Unfortunately, the Canadian Mounted Rifles had preceded us through the area and bought most of the top animals, which forced him to import 41 from Montana. We also had to take many unbroken ones as well.

We seemed always to be in the saddle during those bitterly cold days, riding from ranch to ranch and driving the newly acquired animals to convenient loading points on the Fort Macleod–Calgary rail line. From Calgary, they went in strings of 90 to 100 to Lansdowne Park in Ottawa where the regiment had been assembled for basic training. I accompanied the third string and got to camp at the end of February.

Home, for both men and horses over the next two and a half weeks, was six identical buildings facing the Lansdowne Park race track. They had been built to hold livestock during exhibitions and there was a distinct barn smell about them that we did not find objectionable. Against each long side wall were hastily constructed, straw-lined double bunks that slept two men lower and two men upper. Down the middle of each building were three wood-burning stoves that barely took the chill from the air.

Jim was already there, training the animals that I had helped gather. He was not happy; he disliked the regimen of army life and having to wear a uniform. "You get separated from these horses, partner," he groused, "and this place is no fun at all."

I can't say that I liked it much either. Ottawa was an endless round of parades, mounted drill, rifle practice, stable duty and having to listen to men we considered less intelligent than ourselves barking orders at us. But a means of escape for Jim, me and a handful of other volunteers was the time we spent breaking and training horses. The work came with some nice side benefits, particularly for Jim who would soon be humming a different tune about being in Ottawa.

We acquired a sort of celebrity status in town, and civilians, especially young women, would gather around the corral to watch us. Because of his ability, Jim always took the big, mean broncs and people loved to watch him ride. He gained many fans in the crowd, mostly girls, who whistled and loudly cheered him on. Some of them, grateful not only for the entertainment, appreciated the sacrifice the soldiers were making for the country and let it be known that they would be available for supper. That's how Jim met Maggie.

Margaret Benson, or Maggie, as she preferred, had hair as raven-black as Jim's and was merely pretty until you spoke to her and sensed the beauty that radiated from within. She was open and honest, and not at all reticent around the opposite sex. She was in her early 20s and came from a large family with nine siblings, eight of them brothers, so she knew how to take care of herself around men. A blind man could see that she was attracted to Jim almost immediately.

I accompanied Jim and Maggie on their first date, escorting Maggie's friend, Beth, a nondescript young woman who, like me, was only along for the ride. They led us down-town to the Clair de Lune, an expensive and busy restaurant where the waiter brought us platters of roast beef smothered with gravy and vegetables, from which we helped ourselves, and a large carafe of French red wine. The wine oiled Jim's vocal chords and after dinner he broke into "After the Ball," singing it directly to Maggie. The restaurant came to a stand-still as Jim's fine tenor soared through the smoky air. When he was done, everyone in the place broke into spontaneous applause.

Maggie had tears in her eyes, as did Beth, not because it was a sad song, though it was, but because it was so beautifully rendered. Even I had shivers along my spine. I think Maggie fell in love with Jim at that moment and I'd bet a month's pay that Beth did too. As Jim was singing you could see in Maggie's eyes what was in her heart. She was completely smitten. And if the way Jim looked at her and spoke to her was any indication, it was clear that he was as well. I was happy for my friend but I admit to no small degree of envy.

The restaurant returned to normal again and chatter filled the air, probably much of it to do with Jim's performance. Indeed, a few people even stopped by our table as they left to pay Jim compliments. One man said, "You should be on the stage instead of in that army uniform."

After he had gone, Maggie said, "He's right, Jim. Why aren't you?"

"I suppose because there isn't a stage in the country that's as comfortable as a horse. I'd rather sing for a herd of cows than an auditorium full of people any day."

"But they would love you. Probably by the thousands!"

Jim was silent for a moment, perhaps thinking about what he would say or debating with himself whether or not he should say what he was thinking. Finally, he spoke. "Maybe thousands would love me. But it's the handful that might not that bothers me." His eyes dropped and I think even he was surprised by his candidness. Women and wine can do that, though. They may not always bring out the best in a man or even the worst but it's pretty well guaranteed that they'll bring out something honest. And it occurred to me that his unwillingness to perform professionally was the only area in which Jim's immense courage failed him.

Jim met Maggie only four days before we shipped out and he spent all of his free time with her. He was never a demonstrative person, nor was he overly talkative, but he became animated when he spoke of Maggie, and he spoke of her often. As we prepared to leave Ottawa it was plain that he would rather have stayed behind but he had committed himself and wasn't the type to bemoan it. Instead, he was eager to go and get the war over with so that he could come home and begin where he had left off with his wonderful discovery.

"Seems like you might have found the girl you want to put down roots with," I said.

He was noncommittal. "Time will tell. It's a long way from here to South Africa and back."

But beneath that placid exterior I sensed he was anxious about losing her.

Meanwhile, we were fitted with uniforms. They were made distinctive from the regiments preceding us by high riding boots and Stetson hats, much like those worn by the North West Mounted Police. As well, they issued us mess kits, Lee-Enfield rifles, Colt revolvers, lassos, compasses, California stock saddles for the horses and a generous supply of tobacco, which I gave to Jim, never having acquired the habit myself. We drilled and drilled some more, with and without the horses, but anything done horseless the men considered a colossal waste of time. Few of them understood that it had little to do with horses and more to do with learning to obey orders, the hardest thing of all for men who had spent most of their lives as cowboys.

Steele briefed us on the state of the war. He stood in front of a large map of South Africa, showing the British colonies of Cape Colony and Natal, and the Boer colonies of the Orange Free State and the Transvaal. "Not only have the Boers stripped British citizens of their civil rights in Boer territories here and here," he said, slapping the map with a pointer, "and treated them abysmally, they have violated the rules of war by murdering wounded soldiers and massacring innocent civilians. These are a brutish people by any measure. They laid siege to the British towns of Ladysmith in Natal, and Kimberly and Mafeking in the Colony, here, here and here." He again slapped the map in what we could only guess were the appropriate places. "Kimberly has been relieved and so has Ladysmith after four unsuccessful attempts, but, Mafeking has not. God only knows what beastly things the poor citizens will suffer there if relief is not forthcoming. It may be our task to provide that relief but we must be prepared for anything."

He went on stoking us, then dismissed us with this declaration, "In Africa we will be pitted against an evil foe whose atrocities are unparalleled since Attila the Hun. They must be struck down!"

We removed our hats and waved them, cheering. What man would not want to strike a blow against such evil?

Three weeks after our arrival in Ottawa the regiment, divided into A, B and C squadrons, was marched from Lansdowne Park to the train station amid the cheers of thousands of well-wishers. Some of the men were lucky to board the train with all their clothes on, as the crowds, mainly young women, tore at them for souvenirs. Many lost their hats, and nearly everyone lost a button. Some were patted in places they never expected. I missed the furor, as I was busy loading the horses, but many soldiers later referred to the incident as their first experience with hand-to-hand combat. None said it complainingly, mind you.

Maggie refused to come out for the departure and said goodbye to Jim the evening before, in tears, Jim told me afterward. It wasn't something she wished to celebrate. To see him on a train that would ultimately carry him off to a war from which he might not return was more than she could bear.

In Montreal, even larger crowds greeted us as we detrained and marched through town, led by a brass band. In excess of 30,000 people saw us off at Bonaventure Station. It puffed a man up, made him think that he was something more than an ordinary soldier.

The train ploughed through deep snow into the Maritime provinces and made it to the docks in Halifax on March 15. McEachern thought that the local stables might be harbouring glanders, a highly infectious and fatal disease among horses, and had us load them directly onto the ship. A day and half later, thousands of Haligonians gave us a tumultuous send-off, and the *Monterey*, a vessel chartered for the purpose, steamed past McNab's Island and southward in heavy seas, rolling like a schooner with goose down for ballast.

Black clouds scudded low across the sky and the wind howled out of the southeast, thrumming in the *Monterey*'s rigging in what Jim said was the key of A. Giant waves attacked her, like rabid wolves foaming at the mouth, and she faced them boldly, climbing high to their summits before dropping into the trough on the far side, her foredeck awash and her iron hull shuddering as she laboured to climb the next one racing toward her. Heavy rain lashed her decks and super-structure so that even on the peaks, water engulfed her. The only ray of hope in this bleak picture was a faint light that gradually began to grow across the eastern horizon, signalling a break in the weather.

Below, the decks reeked with the foul odour of vomit from men heaving as badly as the seas beyond the hull. Many were in their bunks or hammocks, incapacitated, and felt that a bullet might be a better fate than what they were suffering. The latrines were planks sloped off the ship's rail, which explained the adage that an ill wind blows no good. Conditions were almost unbearable and we'd only been at sea for two days.

I wasn't bothered as much as others by the rolling of the ship. My stomach was a little queasy but I attributed that to the horrible smell that permeated almost everything. Jim also had his sea legs, so we spent as much time as possible with the horses because they were having a wretched time of it.

We put them in canvas slings so the heavy seas wouldn't toss them around in the stalls, but some still fell, their long necks swinging like pendulums with the rolling motion of the ship, chafing against the boards that held them in. It was a heart-wrenching sight, made worse because we were helpless to do more for them. Two horses died our first day out, 11 on the second, and as each day passed, we lost more. On the worst day, we fed 26 to the sharks which were trailing the ship in the dozens because of the feast we were throwing them. Of the more than 500 horses we had taken on board, 162 were cast into the sea, most having succumbed to pneumonia. Nearly 90 per cent of the animals had been infected and more might have been lost had it not been for the men's diligent attention, keeping the stalls spotlessly clean and watching for the first sign of illness.

Then, as the sea flattened and the weather grew warmer, another problem arose. Thrust suddenly into summer, the horses still had their winter coats, which made it difficult for them to cool down. Nevertheless, their condition improved remarkably, as did the disposition of the men.

The top deck was active with drills, revolver practice and lectures on scouting. Men queued for typhoid inoculations. The canteen was open for beer at lunch and at supper. Huge hoses were connected to the ship's pumps and the men stripped naked and gave each other saltwater baths, hands cupped around their private parts. This was not out of any sense of propriety, but because the stream from the hoses could double a man over, as if he'd been kicked between the legs by a horse.

After our departure from Halifax, I received a promotion to corporal and now attended, with other NCOs and officers, detailed lectures ranging from scouting to how to handle men. Steele believed that the best leaders lead by example and insisted that we treat the men as responsible adults at all times. "If they behave like children and require punishment," he said, "then it must be fair and fit the crime. The best advice that I can give you is that in the odd circumstance, if a man behaves badly, it is sometimes best to look the other way. Any officer or NCO found being cruel, or even officious, will only get one warning before he is relieved of his duties."

He explained how the Boer army was organized. The "commando" was their chief unit and consisted of two field *kornetcies* of about 200 men each. The kornetcies comprised eight corporalships, each corporal being in charge of approximately 25 men. At best, though, it was a very loose organization and reminded me of the Cree when I lived among them, since a man could serve under any leader he chose. A well-liked corporal might have twice as many men as one less popular. None of them received any pay. It seemed an undisciplined, almost laughable way to run an army but Steele warned us that they were not to be underestimated.

"They are not Indians, nor are they black. They are as white as we are and are crafty, skilled horsemen and expert marksmen. And they are utterly ruthless and you'd best not forget it. Believe me, you will have your hands full dealing with this enemy!"

We crossed the equator, with extra rations of beer for the men not on duty, and did our training during the relative cool of the early morning and late evening. Only those with unavoidable duty had to work in the fierce afternoon heat, but no man did more than his fair share. Ascension Island and St. Helena, blue smudges on the horizon, slipped by very slowly as the *Monterey* bore southeast at a steady 12 knots, unbothered by the sea. On April 10, we raised Table Mountain and crept past Robben Island into Table Bay, and docked at Cape Town's South Arm Quay.

TEN

A Slow Start

ANYONE WHO HAD ANTICIPATED a large welcoming party must have been disappointed, for if our departure from Canada was distinguished by fanfare and huge crowds, our landing in South Africa was notable for a complete lack of both. The only people to greet us at the docks in Cape Town, besides a small contingent of British officers, were black workers who were everywhere, even manning the long line of wagons waiting to take our tents and sundry other things to the bivouac area.

Over the next few hours we unloaded the horses and all our gear, marched over to Green Point Common, less than a mile from the ship, and erected our conical canvas tents. The lush grass that had given the common its name had long been trampled into oblivion and turned into loose sand by the large number of soldiers camped there. The town—a city really, for its compacted dirt streets were lined with grand, modern buildings and jammed with iron-wheeled carriages and trolleys—sat in an incredibly beautiful, natural amphitheatre formed by Devil's Peak, Table Mountain and Signal Hill. The quality of light made both town and mountain and even the sea look like a painting, in which the artist saw everything in various shades of blue. It was an exquisite setting, the portal to a land evidently worth fighting for, if the seething masses of khaki-clad soldiers were any indication.

Steele wasted no time in imposing a rigorous training schedule and replacing the horses we had lost at sea. After we had disembarked, an additional 44 animals were put down because of glanders. Through sheer force of will, Steele managed to acquire 118 British remounts and 200 Argentine.

The British animals were of superior quality, the Argentine were not. Many of the men were unhappy with them because they were so unlike our Canadian horses. They were squat and short legged, less than 15 hands high, and not very attractive. The arch in their necks reminded me of pictures I'd seen in a book of Alexander the Great and his horse, Bucephalus. But they were sturdy, with plenty of stamina, and that was important when the measure of an animal was the weight it could carry over long distances. Saddles alone were more than 30 pounds, and the gear, which ranged from grooming tools to weapons, often weighed in excess of 50. Add to that a man of Jim's size and the horses were often carrying well over 300 pounds. If they couldn't handle it, plus move along at nine miles an hour, scout among the hills all day and still have energy in reserve in the event of an attack, they weren't of much value to us.

As we waited for orders to move out to the front, many of

the men came down with dysentery, a result of the water and the local fruit. Sick parade every morning was a long line of soldiers with exploding bowels. Many had piles, but few complained, as the doctor's remedy was to put the complainer on a horse and have him ride hard till they burst. I wasn't bothered to any serious extent by either but there was one day when I couldn't stray farther than spitting distance from the latrine.

A week passed, then two, and the men became bored and irritable. Steele showed more sense than other commanders, who confined their men to camp in the evenings, by allowing us to take advantage of Cape Town's varied amenities. He reckoned that since we were older than the soldiers in most of the other regiments, we could handle the freedom. Even so, there was much drunkenness during this period and Steele ignored it when he could. When it was impossible, a fine of a day's pay was the usual punishment, which was nothing for a lot of the men, who did not need their $30 monthly salary. One of the worst fines was a loss of two weeks' pay for contracting a venereal disease, deemed a self-inflicted wound.

But a man would find out just how hard Steele could be if he lost any part of his equipment. All of it was difficult to replace and besides warranting fines, it usually meant a court-martial and time in the guardhouse.

Steele's cleverness of command was never more evident than when Jim and I and a few others were returning to camp from a saloon in town where we'd been celebrating the relief of Mafeking along with everyone else. It had been a cool, rainy day, the evening air was chill, and a few whiskies or a couple of quarts of beer became an extra blanket for bedtime. So we were in our cups and singing loudly, led by Jim, with his lovely clear voice, a melancholy song about young men gone off to war and their mothers wondering where they were. It fit the mood we were in.

> Where is my wandering boy tonight, the boy of my tenderest care,
> The boy that was once my joy and light, the child of my love and prayer?

We were building to a rousing finale when an officious British staff sergeant on patrol duty rode up behind us.

"You're making too much noise, lads," he said, the statement saturated with self-importance. "Rowdiness is not permitted. Keep it down or you'll be up on charges."

I was the senior rank in the group and since the road we were on was empty, and singing was a harmless activity for men who would soon be risking their lives in battle, I said, "Hold on, Staff. We're just enjoying ourselves and not bothering anybody. Where's the harm in that?"

The staff sergeant, already rigid as a board, on a small Argentine horse, stiffened even more at my impertinence. "You will tell your men to be quiet, Corporal, and straighten them out, or you will answer for it!"

"Aw, don't be so stiff, Staff," Jim said, and giggled at the alliteration. "Singin's good for what ails you. You oughta try it sometime. Why, it might even melt the iron rod you've got up your arse!"

The staff sergeant was enraged. "Right, then!" he thundered, addressing me. "Corporal, you and your men will come with me. The lot of you are under arrest!"

Before I could do or say anything, Jim shouldered me aside, grabbed the foreleg of the horse in his left hand and its underbelly with his right, and with his shoulder against the animal gave a mighty heave. It toppled over like a felled tree, hit the ground with a huge grunt and sent the staff sergeant tumbling onto the road, cursing. We fled into the night, laughing like maniacs.

"You bloody fool!" I said to Jim, gasping for breath between running and laughter. "We'll all be thrown in jail!"

"It'll be worth it," he wheezed in reply.

In my own perverse way, I had to agree. I doubted that the horse was hurt—horses are tough—and my only wish was that I could have stayed around long enough to see the staff sergeant after he had got up off the ground.

By the time we reached camp, I managed to quieten everyone down to an acceptable level. We went directly to our tents, like others who might have had a night on the town. "Mum's the word," I told them. "Until this thing has blown over."

Under different circumstances, I might have had to put Jim on charge but in this instance, I would have had to include myself because I became an accomplice when I ran. My take on the situation was that the Brit got what he deserved and I would defend Jim if push came to shove. But I didn't think we had much to fear; it had been too dark for the staff sergeant to get a reliable description of us. He would be able identify us only as Canadians, one of us a corporal, for we were all wearing Stetsons and we all sported moustaches, which described most of the men in the regiment. Few were as big as Jim, though, and that made me a little uneasy.

The following day I was rein-training one of the Argentine remounts, a stubby, brown gelding with black legs, mane and tail that I had claimed for my own. He had a spirited temperament but responded well to the reins and I couldn't resist naming him Bucephalus. I was about to call training him a job well done when I saw Steele approaching. He wasn't walking with his usual purposeful stride—it was more of a stroll—but I didn't think for a moment that he was paying a social call. I dismounted, came to attention and saluted.

"Good afternoon, sir."

"Not so far, Strong," he said. "The commandant of one of the British regiments paid me a visit this morning with an interesting tale about some boisterous Canadians, a corporal among them. Must I elaborate, or do you know what I'm talking about?"

"It doesn't ring a bell, sir. Maybe with more details I could help."

"He maintained that a giant, drunken Canadian attacked one of his staff sergeants and toppled him and his horse. Is that enough detail for you?"

"A drunken giant, sir?" I asked, hoping I was the picture of innocence. "We have a few big men in the troop but there are no giants, sir. Especially drunken ones."

"I see." Steele stroked his moustache with a finger and thumb. "Well, it did seem a little far-fetched to me. Carry on, Strong."

"Yes, sir!" I snapped my best salute at him.

"Oh. One more thing, Strong. If at any time you discover

who the culprit is, then you will tell him that I'll not have any horse, British or otherwise, treated in that fashion. Do I make myself clear?"

"Perfectly, sir." I saluted again and Steele left. He had done his duty by asking and wasn't going to take it any further. And I would have bet a month's pay that the image of an officious British non-com getting his comeuppance had given him a laugh or two in private.

Our orders to move came after six weeks of waiting. They were secret and we didn't know our objective until we were on board ship. We sailed north, along the east coast, into two false starts.

Our first destination was Kosi Bay, which straddles the Portuguese East Africa—South Africa border where it meets the sea. From there, the unit was to make a 200-mile trek over the mountains, demolish a bridge and defend our position against expected Boer counterattacks. The plan fell through when we learned that our secret was no secret to the Boers, who were waiting for us.

Our new orders sent us back down the coast to Durban where Steele informed us that our mission was to be resumed. He had persuaded his superiors of its feasibility simply by changing the route to avoid the Boer ambush. We would strike north by rail, 70 miles along the coastal plain to the railhead at the Tugela River, and march overland from there. We weren't more than a day beyond the Tugela when, for reasons undisclosed to the men, the mission was cancelled permanently.

Our orders now were to join General Sir Redvers Buller's Natal Field Force and put our scouting skills to use by guarding his flank as he and his troops advanced into Boer territory. We returned to Durban and the following afternoon were on another train that belched smoke and steam as it carried us far from the coast, climbing among the hills beyond the city, passing splendid mansions and villas with luxurious tropical gardens among gum trees, Norfolk pines and bamboo. Some of the men took the time to write letters, Jim among them. He never mentioned how much he missed Maggie but he wrote to her at every opportunity, which in itself spoke volumes. Before long, the men broke out in song, Jim's voice soaring above the others, as we sped toward the mountains and towns whose names we knew of only as battlefields. When we reached the first, the singing stopped.

Colenso, 115 miles up the line, sat in a loop of the Tugela River. On the 15th of the previous December, Buller's forces had advanced on the lines of defence established there by the Boers. The purpose of the offensive was to push the Boers back and relieve the town of Ladysmith which was under siege 15 miles to the north, but Buller failed spectacularly and it was not difficult to understand why. We could see where the Boers had dug in on the hillsides, sometimes in trenches, at other times behind low stone walls, so well hidden that Buller believed he was fighting an invisible enemy. His soldiers were like lame ducks crowded on a small pond as they made their way along the river; the proof of it was still there in the decaying horses and mules that lay scattered about, and the wagons blown apart.

We passed a small cemetery beside the track but there must have been others in the area, for Buller had lost 1,100 men, killed, wounded or captured, to the Boers' 38. It affected our men profoundly and some cursed Johnny Boer while others grew pensive. It reminded me of Frenchman's Butte and Loon Lake, although the enemy here was clearly different from Big Bear and his warriors, and vastly better armed. I glanced at the weathered faces around me and wondered who among us might not return. I hoped it wouldn't be Jim. He had far too much to lose.

Ladysmith, on the banks of the Klip River near where the railroad lines from the Orange Free State and the Transvaal intersected, was a key point in the struggle for the British colony of Natal. More than 13,000 soldiers had been there, and for four months, Boer forces kept them pinned down, bombarding the town daily with their Long Toms and pom-poms. When the townsfolk weren't scurrying for their lives, boredom was their worst enemy and for something to do they pitted tarantulas against scorpions and trapdoor spiders against each other, betting on the outcome.

Water- and food-supply lines were cut off and everyone was soon eating horse feed; when that ran out, they began eating the horses. The cavalry didn't like it, but once food for the horses was gone, eating them put the animals to effective use. Health plummeted and enteric fever caused more deaths than the exchange of fire between the opposing sides. The Intombi hospital camp was two miles away, behind enemy lines, although the Boers allowed unrestricted passage to it. Nevertheless, it was supposed to handle only 300 patients and was crammed with nearly 2,000. As men and women died, their corpses were removed, placed in trenches and covered with a thin layer of soil so that there was room to pile more bodies on top.

In a second attempt to relieve Ladysmith, Buller's forces moved west along the Tugela River, crossing over near Spion Kop and into another slaughter. It wasn't until the middle of February that he was able to save the town and rid the area of Boers.

The orchards edging the town as we entered were the first indication of the long battle that had taken place. They were in ruins, trees splintered as if they were mere twigs and the ground pockmarked by shells. Within the town limits, wooden buildings with corrugated tin roofs lined the broad main street and still showed severe damage, though many were under repair. The clock tower on the town hall had a huge bite out of it and most of the roof on the Royal Hotel had been smashed in. We stopped only long enough to water the horses and have breakfast. With a simple turn of the head, any fool could see that keeping the town under siege must have been child's play for the Boers: hills rose from the *veld* in almost every direction around it.

Beyond Ladysmith lay a prairie of parched grass that was like anywhere southeast of Calgary, the only difference being the boulder-ridden mesas or *kopjes* edging it and the native *kraals* and cornfields. The country remained wide open with kopjes and hills poking from the yellow-brown grasslands in no perceivable pattern. Seventy miles farther on, we reached Newcastle, another cluster of tin roofs over nondescript buildings set among low hills. The weather had turned cold and drizzly but the predominantly English inhabitants greeted us warmly.

It was the end of easy travel for us. Right up ahead, at a place called Laing's Nek, the Boers, in their retreat, had used explosives to block a tunnel.

ELEVEN

The White Flag

THE FOLLOWING MORNING WE prepared to march. The weather turned for the better and we could see how prettily Newcastle was situated, nestled among rolling, tawny prairie hills, with the Drakensberg off to the west and flat-topped hills to the north and northwest. The pass between the two most prominent of those hills was Laing's Nek, and our route would take us there.

We struck out over the veld along a much-trampled road that would have been mud the day before but was drying out nicely in the heat of the day. We climbed gradually through the dry, grass-covered slope toward the pass, which was the border between the British colony of Natal and the Boer Transvaal. A short, steep climb took us to the summit where several dry-stone breastworks, manned by British soldiers, were guarding the pass. Majuba Hill rose on our left like a truncated pyramid.

During the first South African War, the Boers had occupied the pass because of its strategic location on the main road between Durban and Pretoria. The British believed that being atop Majuba Hill would give them a distinct advantage and force the Boers into retreat. But as they had done many times before, the British underestimated their enemy and the Boers, with their superior knowledge of the landscape, swept Majuba Hill clean in short order. In the process, the Boers lost only one man while the British lost nearly a hundred. The white crosses of their graves were plainly visible as we rode by. "Remember Majuba Hill" was the battle cry as Buller's troops crossed the Tugela River on their second attempt to relieve Ladysmith but had they remembered it correctly, they would never have climbed Spion Kop.

Three miles beyond Laing's Nek was Charlestown, originally a Customs post on the border, but now a military base guarding the railway and the road to the east. A short distance farther on we reached Volksrust, a Boer town and already the site of a prisoner of war camp.

The imprisoned Boers looked bedraggled in their drab clothes of grey or brown. One or two wore rumpled black suits with tails and top hats that were half the size of most I'd seen. They were officers, we were told. They stared at us from behind a wire fence, the epitome of hopelessness. And who could blame them? Here we were, more soldiers added to a force that already vastly outnumbered their own.

The town sat on the edge of a small prairie, beyond which were more of the rolling hills of the high veld, punctuated by kopjes rising from the sun-baked land like blisters. We turned northwest along the summits of a long range of low hills paralleling the rail line, which ran another 120 miles to Johannesburg.

The days were mostly bright and warm, tunic-weather, unless a fierce, cold wind forced us into our greatcoats. The nights arrived with no twilight and were always frigid, some- times damp and misty, sometimes so frosty that at first glance in the morning, it was easy to believe it had snowed. Either way, we slept in our greatcoats; they didn't keep us warm as much as they kept us from freezing. Such was winter on the veld.

When the sun rose, it brought out the flies which got into everything. In the evening the flies were replaced by thick clouds of smaller insects that invaded your nose and mouth if you weren't careful. And then there were the ants—black, brown, red and white—all equally annoying. They'd get inside your bedroll, even in your underwear. In the end, we won the war against the Boers but it was no contest against the insects. They soundly trounced us.

We joined Buller at Zandspruit, near a flat wetland cut by a winding stream and flanked on the east by a low kopje. We arrived in the dark, around 8:30 at night, and saw a sea of lantern- and candle-lit tents. Bucephalus whickered as we approached, recognizing the presence of others of his spe- cies, all strangers. Somewhere, someone was singing an unrecognizable song, and the breeze carried whiffs of barn- yards, latrines and wood smoke from cooking fires. But it wasn't until dawn next morning that the vast size of the gen- eral's force became apparent.

The camp was not unlike a new gold-rush town, but in place of miners, there were soldiers in an assortment of uniforms, and in place of mining equipment, 12- and 15-pound field guns. Its population was about 55,000 men, who spoke with a variety of accents, mostly from the British Isles, and there were black men by the hundreds, all teamsters and labourers. If there were any women around, I didn't see them and that was a good thing: in situations such as this, men got along much better without them.

Yet despite its size, the camp could vanish completely in a few hours, as this one soon would. There was an air of urgency about the place as the force prepared to move out. Wagons were loaded and hitched to mules, as were the field guns, and the cavalry readied its mounts while the foot soldiers gathered their kit.

Strathcona's Horse formed for inspection, with the sun already warm after an extremely cold night. Buller climbed on a partially loaded wagon and welcomed us, then spoke briefly and fondly of his time with Steele during the Red River Expedition in Manitoba. "This is not a conventional war we are fighting now. There is no front line against front line; rather, the Boers use the guerrilla tactics of ambushes and sudden attacks. Anyone on picket duty or patrol has to be meticulously vigilant, but if there is a regiment anywhere on Earth capable of handling such responsibilities, it is surely Strathcona's Horse." He finished by proclaiming, "Though you have yet to fire a shot in anger I have no doubt that you are one of the finest regiments in South Africa!"

That was General Sir Redvers Buller, always using outrageous compliments to make his soldiers feel good. A big, jovial, ruddy-faced man with a moustache like frayed cable ends, he had the jowls of a St. Bernard and, some said, an IQ to match—not unlike many of the British ruling class. In addition to the Red River Expedition, he had fought in the Kaffir and Zulu wars, as well as the first war against the Boers. He'd even won the Victoria Cross. He had come to this war as commander in chief but his strategic blunders at Colenso and Spion Kop had led to reduced responsibilities, and he was now the general officer commanding the Natal Field Force. He had been replaced by the diminutive Lord Roberts, affectionately known as "Bobs," who was his complete opposite in more than just size and was now moving north toward Johannesburg and Pretoria.

Buller's job was secondary, to protect Roberts's eastern flank while driving the Boers back along the railroad line. But he was getting older and more cautious, stung perhaps by his failures or by the fact that he had too little time left in life to begin squandering it now. Whatever the reason, Buller always moved slowly, to keep pace, it was rumoured, with the supply wagons carrying his champagne and caviar. The men joked that he always appeared to be moving backwards instead of advancing and this, combined with his retreats, had earned him the nickname "Old Reverse," a play on his first name which was pronounced "Reevers." Yet despite his shortcomings as a tactician, his knack for winning the affection of those he commanded made him an effective leader.

After Buller's speech we decamped and moved out, the Horse leading the way, doing at last what we had come to do. Another warning came from Steele, specifically to be on the alert for white rocks, painted by the Boers in their retreat and used as range markers for their snipers and field guns. Any distance up to 1,000 yards was within the capabilities of their sharpshooters. The hills among which we marched could hide the man who held your life in his hands and you wouldn't ever know he was there, nor would you hear the bullet that ended it. Steele sent out advance patrols, often consisting of a non-com and two or more troopers because officers were favoured targets of the Boers. We scanned the hills relentlessly with binoculars and spyglasses but saw nothing, which was not surprising. We knew that we wouldn't see anything until it was too late.

We reached Perdekop by mid-afternoon and Standerton, a large railway centre, the following day. As we approached the town, a loud explosion brought us up short. Other than the thousands of soldiers around, it was our first indication that there was actually fighting going on. Steele sent two scouts to investigate and discovered that the Boers in their retreat had destroyed the railway bridge over the Vaal River. But they had left behind 18 locomotives and 148 railway cars, gifts for the British. Railway buildings were burning fiercely and Buller had the Boer workers who set them on fire held as prisoners of war and sent to the camp at Volksrust. In the town itself, hundreds of British citizens crowded the main street, crying "Welcome, Canadians!" Women wept openly and threw flowers at us, and men shook our hands, though one spouted pious nonsense and a promise of Armageddon. We had liberated our first town without firing a single bullet.

Instead of chasing the Boers, we stayed in Standerton for a week, which was typical of Buller and the kind of inaction that exasperated many of his troops. The engineers from the British regiments, unable to repair the steel railroad bridge damaged by the explosions, began building a wooden trestle to replace it. Meanwhile, the Horse were sent out on patrols into the surrounding area. Jim and I volunteered for them, as it was boring in camp and the town was off-limits.

On our first patrol, with a half-dozen others, under a sergeant, we happened upon an abandoned Boer farmhouse, low and squat, whitewashed, with a thatched roof. Two door-size windows flanked the door itself. We approached cautiously, acutely aware of the possibility of an ambush, and fired a pistol shot to bring out any innocents who might not be aware of our presence. Nothing stirred. We went around to a windowless side of the house and dismounted, feeling slightly foolish because if the enemy were in the house they would either have already fired at us or hightailed it out the back door. As we suspected, the place was deserted. Anything that could be loaded into an ox cart had been taken by the occupants when they fled; the larger items, mainly very rustic furniture such as tables, beds, chairs and chests of drawers, had been left behind. In one corner of the living room was an old spinet. Powerless to resist, Jim sat down and began to play. He fumbled a bit at first, trying to find the right chord structure, then began to sing.

> Goodbye Dolly I must leave you, though it breaks my heart
> to go,
> Something tells me I am needed at the front to fight the foe,
> See, the boys in blue are marching and I can no longer stay,
> Hark, I hear the bugle calling, Goodbye Dolly Gray.

The rest of us sang lustily along and as we did, we piled furniture in another corner of the room and did the same in the other rooms. Once it had been collected, we stuffed crumpled-up paper around the bottom of the piles and set them on fire. The tinder-dry wood and varnish ignited quickly and the piles became roaring infernos, the flames licking the walls and ceiling, on their way to consuming everything. Then we set fire to the kraal and a small field of corn, anything that might be useful to the Boers.

Rejoining the main force, we moved out for Greylingstad, another 30 miles closer to Johannesburg. Every mile was a mile deeper into dangerous country, for we knew we were stepping on Brother Boer's tail. Steele dispatched several smaller advance patrols to gather intelligence. I led one with Jim and another private named Bob Rollins, a cowboy from Red Deer, a damned fine marksman and almost as natural a tracker as some of the Indians I'd met in the Territories.

During the morning of our second day on patrol, we came to a small stream a mile and a half north of the Johannesburg rail line. The night had been freezing but a warm sun now blazed in a blue sky, heating the land and us too. It was dusty and we stopped to let the horses drink before continuing. Since Volksrust, the country had remained rolling, rocky prairie. A mile or so farther on we were stopped by the sight of a farmhouse, some 300 yards off. I called a halt, pulled out my spyglass and scanned the place. It was typical of many Boer farmhouses in the area, built of stone with a tin roof. Nearby were three small outbuildings, a kraal and a few scrub trees. A white rag fluttered from a pole in the front yard.

Steele had also warned us about white flags. More often than not, their purpose was simply to let approaching soldiers know that non-combatants were in the house, a Boer wife and her children perhaps, or older folks. It was possible, too, that the occupants had decided to abandon the farm and forgotten to remove the flag. But the flags could also be traps, false signs of surrender or truce designed to draw us in close enough so the concealed enemy was certain of a lethal shot. Through the glass, I could plainly see that the front door was closed, as were the window shutters, and the place looked deserted. But it could still prove dangerous; the surrounding area offered little cover for a safe approach.

The rule of thumb was that we should investigate farm-houses only with a troop of men and not a small patrol, because they might hide something sinister. Nine times out of 10 they didn't, so it was ultimately a discretionary call on the part of the leader. But I didn't think I should make such a call without first consulting Jim and Rollins.

In our present position, we were sitting ducks for snipers so I said, "Let's get behind some protection and talk about this," and jerked my head toward a knoll. I slipped the spyglass into my saddlebag and pulled out my revolver, to fire a warn-ing shot into the air and let any innocent occupants know there were soldiers approaching. But before I could squeeze the trigger, a shot rang out and I saw a hole torn in Rollins's tunic below his right collar bone. He jerked back in the saddle but caught himself before he lost his balance. A look of shock and confusion came over his face. "I'm hit," he said. Then he slouched down on his horse as if someone had let the air out of him, and fell off. More shots went whizzing by.

"Shit!" cried Jim, as we kicked at our horses to escape the enfilade. It was perhaps 20 or 25 yards to the protection of the knoll, but it might have been all of Africa. The only thing in our favour was that we were now moving targets and harder to hit at a distance. Jim, on a much faster horse than Bucephalus, reached the knoll first, and I was almost there when I heard a bullet smack flesh. Bucephalus let out a grunt, stumbled and crashed to the ground while I flew over his head in a somersault, arms and legs akimbo. I landed on my back on the hard ground, which knocked the air from my lungs and stunned me. My pistol went flying. I felt Jim's big hands grab my ankles and drag me into the protection of the knoll.

"You all right?" he asked, breathing hard. He handed me my gun, which had nearly hit him.

I hadn't acquired any broken bones or bullet holes. "I think so." I holstered my weapon. Though my mind was functioning, I felt disconnected from everything around me. I turned over onto my hands and knees and Jim helped me to my feet.

"Where's my spyglass?" I asked, then realized that I had put it away before the bullets began flying. "Damn it, it's in my saddlebag! Do you have a glass, Jim?"

"They don't issue them to privates, Jack, remember?"

I had forgotten, in the confusion. They didn't issue them to corporals either, unless they were in charge of a patrol. I half-staggered to the far end of the knoll and found a place from which I could see the farmhouse without getting my head blown off. At that distance, most of the detail was lost to me; nevertheless, I could see that the shutters on both windows were now open. Other than that, I couldn't detect any movement. The place looked as deserted as it had before.

I returned to the near edge of the knoll where Jim was crouching.

"Bob is still alive!" he said, amazed by the discovery.

I could now hear Rollins moaning, crying for help, even over Bucephalus's struggles to get up. My horse had taken a bullet in his lower left rump that had hit an artery and was bleeding profusely. I wished that I could save him, but I couldn't; nor could I leave him there to suffer. I pulled out my revolver and with a shaking hand shot him, as his eyes found mine. Just as I squeezed off the shot, he jerked his head and the bullet went straight into his eye. He screamed in pain, an almost human sound that shocked me, and I shot him again, hastily, cursing myself for hurting him even more.

Jim was pale, despite his weathered face, and I'm sure I looked no better but we needed to turn our attention to Rollins. "Somehow we've got to get him," I said. "And soon. If we leave him there until dark, he might bleed to death. We've got to get him to the hospital, fast!"

"I'll go," said Jim.

"The hell you will," I told him. "You're too much of a target."

I was grateful for Jim's offer but the job was my responsibility. It was in my favour that the ground between the knoll and the farmhouse wasn't even. Over the distance to where Rollins lay it dipped once, not deeply, but enough to hide a man from a shooter a few hundred yards away. Unless of course the shooters were on high ground but there wasn't any in the immediate vicinity and I was certain that those shutters hadn't been open when I first scanned the house. The shooter or shooters had to be in there, if they were still around at all. In the old days, we would have seen smoke from where the bullets were issuing but smokeless powder was in use now by both sides. Since the smokeless powder didn't corrode a weapon as black powder did, it meant that rifles could be more precisely machined, giving them a greater firing distance and higher accuracy. It was good for the shooter, but not for the person being shot at.

Bucephalus lay about six or seven yards from us and he would provide my first cover. The dip was about halfway between him and Rollins. That left another 10 yards or so to where he lay, 10 yards over which I'd be exposed to fire. We would have been better off had his horse been shot at the same time, because that would have given some protection closer to him, but it had followed Jim and me to the cover of the knoll and was grazing, unhurt, a hundred yards beyond.

I discussed the plan with Jim and he had nothing better to suggest. "Get your rifle," I said. "The shooters are in the house at the windows. If they start firing at me, alternate your shots between the windows as fast as you can. Keep a few clips handy, just in case."

Each clip held eight bullets and was ejected automatically when the last round was fired, after which another clip could be inserted. With any luck at all Jim should be able to keep the shooters pinned down until I got back with Rollins. I hoped the damned thing didn't jam, something the Lee-Enfield had a habit of doing every now and then.

I took a deep breath. "Here goes." I was surprised at how steady my voice was because I was quivering inside and my bowels were preparing to collapse.

I got on my belly and wriggled over to Bucephalus, inhaling dust all the way, and reached him without incident. The quivering on the inside had turned to shaking on the outside, and I knew that if I hesitated behind Bucephalus too long I would have to take Jim up on his offer. I counted to five, leapt to my feet and ran madly in a crouch, my legs feeling doughy, then dove and rolled into the dip, the rocky ground scraping my hands and face. So far, there had been no firing but if they were watching, the shooters would now be aware of what I was doing. I lay there for a moment trying to still my heart and catch my breath.

When I had gained control of myself, I sprang to my feet and ran again, keeping low and weaving a path toward the wounded trooper. I heard gunfire coming from behind me and in front, and felt a bullet tug at the arm of my tunic. I expected to stop one at any second, but it didn't happen. I reached Rollins, knelt, got an arm under his shoulders and another beneath his knees and struggled to lift him. He was a dead weight and moaned in such distress that I feared I'd torn him apart. "It hurts! Ohhhh, shit, it hurts!" he cried. It took every ounce of strength in my possession to get to my feet.

Jim was still firing and I moved as rapidly as I could toward the knoll, Rollins groaning every inch of the way. With each step, he became heavier and heavier and every thump of my feet on the hard earth loosened my grip on him until I couldn't hang on any longer. I made it as far as the dip and had to let him go. I crashed to the rocky terrain on my knees and cried out in pain, but my cry was lost among Rollins's screams of agony when he hit the ground too.

I was half on top of him, which didn't help, and I rolled off. "Jesus, I'm sorry, Bob," I panted. "I couldn't hold you anymore." But he was sobbing with pain as involuntary tears rolled from his eyes and he wasn't listening.

"Jack!" It was Jim calling. "Are you okay?"

"I'm okay," I called back. "Hang on!"

I had to collect my thoughts. The shooting had died down but I didn't think I could lift Rollins again. I had to devise a different plan. My knees hurt like hell and my mouth was as dry as the veld. Sweat was rolling off me in torrents. I was still shaking but now it was from anger—anger at myself, the bloody Boers and the bloody English for getting us into this mess in the first place. I found it hard to think.

Rollins was moaning again and I didn't know how much longer he would last. His face was pale and around the wound, his uniform was soaked in blood. I couldn't tell if it had stopped bleeding or what damage the bullet had done but as he was gasping for breath and had blood in the corners of his mouth, I assumed it had lodged in his lung.

It was now about noon and I knew that I could stay where we were until dark and make my escape but Rollins couldn't. The idea crossed my mind that if I waited long enough he would die and I wouldn't have to put myself at risk. But while the thought was there, the action wasn't. I had to get him out of there.

A solution came out of sheer desperation and I called to Jim. "Throw a lasso over here! I'll tie it around Bob and you can haul him in. But first, I need a rifle so I can give you cover. Get Bob's lasso and throw the loop to me. Get his rifle, too, and tie it to the other end so I can drag it over here. Make sure the clip is full!"

A few minutes later, I heard the lasso whistle through the

air. It landed square on me, something I would have expected from any cowboy worth his salt. I put the noose around Rollins's chest and underneath his arms so that the knot was between his shoulder blades. It was awkward, working in a prone position, and the dip was like an oven. Every time I moved Rollins, he yelped in pain. I had just got the rope secured when the other lasso sailed over.

"Haul away, Jack!"

Hand over hand, I pulled at the rope and in a few seconds, Rollins's Lee-Enfield was beside me. Jim had stuffed a hanky in the barrel to prevent dirt getting into it. I pulled it out and checked the clip to make sure it was full. Rollins was still struggling for air. It was now or never. I called to Jim again. "On the count of three, you pull and I'll start shooting. Got that?"

"Count when you're ready!"

I said to Rollins, "This is going to hurt like hell, Bob, but it's the only way to get you out of here."

"I can do it," he said, his lips barely moving, his voice weak. If he passed out from the pain, it might be the best thing for him.

"You ready, Jim?" I shouted.

"Yeah!"

"One! Two! Three!"

Rollins started sliding across the ground much faster than I expected but then Jim was a man who could fell horses. I stood and began firing at the house, while moving backward beside Rollins. Bucephalus wasn't in Rollins's path, although he brushed against his hind quarters as Jim pulled him past. I wasn't as lucky. I tripped over him and landed heavily on his stomach, then rolled over in behind him. But Rollins was safe and I was flat on the ground, out of harm's way. I pulled my rifle out of its scabbard because I didn't want to leave it for the Boers, then reached across Bucephalus's body and loosened the saddle tie strap and unbuckled the cinch. Luckily, the stirrup hadn't caught underneath him but it still took some effort to pull the saddle off. I flung it over to Jim and wriggled back to the safety of the knoll.

TWELVE

A Shroud of Fog

BOB ROLLINS DIED THE next day in the hospital. He'd lost too much blood and his wound had become badly infected. We buried him one morning on the farm where we were bivouacked, while Boer pom-poms echoed in the distance and fingers of mist touched the low-summited hills. It was a sad affair for every man in the Horse. Though we had lost men to enteric fever, Rollins was the first killed in action. He wouldn't be the last.

Once Buller was made aware of the episode at the farmhouse, he sent in a Royal Artillery battery and removed the place from the face of the Earth. By then, though, the Boers were long gone.

Steele summoned Jim and me to his tent. With him were B Squadron's commander, Major Arthur Jarvis, and his second in command, Captain George Cameron.

"A commendable job, gentlemen," Steele said, and shook our hands, as did the others. He handed me a chevron. "I shouldn't waste any time adding it to those, Strong," he said pointing to the pair already on my right sleeve. I was now a sergeant with a commensurate pay raise of $2.40 per month.

"Thank you, sir."

He then gave corporal's chevrons to Jim. "Fine work, Spencer. It's gratifying to know that you're putting your enviable strength to a variety of uses here in South Africa."

The veiled reference to the episode in Cape Town was Steele's inimitable way of telling us that few things happened in the regiment that he didn't know about.

"Yes, sir. Thank you, sir." Jim never batted an eye.

Steele spoke briefly of the responsibilities that the new ranks demanded, mainly that our conduct in front of the men must always be exemplary, then dismissed us.

I was pleased with the promotion but I couldn't help feeling a bit hypocritical. On the surface, it looked as if I had selflessly risked my life to save Rollins but I wondered if that was really true. Sure, I had wanted to help him but more, I was the NCO in charge and I couldn't have faced the regiment had I not shown responsibility for those in my command. So in one sense I had probably done it as much for myself as I had for him. But Jim said, "It don't matter who you do it for, Jack, as long as it gets done."

Jim and I were the talk of the regiment for a while. And like the true friend he was, he apologized to everyone for saving me and said the next time he would try to exercise better judgment.

That all happened at the beginning of July, a month that

dragged on like a bad cold. The Horse's activities consisted mainly of holding operations and we saw very little action. Steele was annoyed. He hadn't raised a regiment and brought it to Africa to sit on its collective hands. He complained to his superior officers that they were wasting our talents while "mere shop boys"—meaning British soldiers—were right in the thick of it. He kept pressing and by month's end got his wish. Buller and the Horse were to move east to Amersfoort, along the route we'd already taken, and then push north to join Roberts, who had already taken Pretoria and was preparing to ram the Boers eastward into the sea. We would connect with his troops somewhere near Belfast or Machadodorp, along the rail line to the coast.

We set off, the Horse providing escort duties for a ponderous, three-mile-long supply-wagon train and a convoy of several hundred mule teams. It was movement on a grand scale, which made the Boer *voortrekkers* and Canadian overlanders seem puny by comparison. Dust from the tramp of hoofs filled the sky in a brown haze for miles as native muleskinners snaked whips that cracked like pistol shots. Horses snorted, mules brayed and oxen bellowed; wagons creaked and groaned against the constant grinding noise of iron-rimmed wheels against the rocky roadbed. And while the whole thing lumbered along like some great, sinuous beast, the Horse skirmished with Boer sharpshooters who harassed us most of the way. In one sense, the scene epitomized the entire war: the ponderous British forces were laden with provisions and equipment, meant as much to reduce hardship as to be used for battle, while the highly mobile Boers travelled with few things beyond their weaponry and bedrolls, living off the land. For a bunch of farmers, they were acquitting themselves far better than anyone had expected. But then we were fighting for a symbol and $30 a month; they were fighting for their farms, their families, their livelihood and their country.

At Perdekop, we had our first pay parade since leaving the Cape and received our first batch of mail. There was nothing for me but Jim had several letters from Maggie that he went off to read by himself. He was a much improved man when he returned.

"You're almost bearable, now, Jim," I told him afterward.

"It's funny you should say that. I'm findin' that you're not so bad now either."

Five hundred remounts broke out of a temporary kraal and ran off into the veld, with a thunder of hoofs that made the earth tremble. It was a thrilling sight and you could sense the freedom that was coursing through them, like prisoners escaping from jail. It provided several members of the Horse, including me, with as much fun as a man could expect in the middle of a war. We rode after them, lassos twirling, and rounded them up, much to the delight of the Tommies who gathered to watch the spectacle as if it were Buffalo Bill Cody's Wild West Show. Our reward for rounding up the animals was having first pick of them.

I didn't name my remount; I hadn't named the one I had after losing Bucephalus. Getting attached to them wasn't wise; they were a dispensable commodity here. In fact, by the time the war ended nearly a half-million horses would be lost, many to overwork and malnutrition. Some died because altitude changes affect horses more severely than they do humans. Much of South Africa's interior is at a level of between 4,000 and 5,000 feet or more, and horses unaccustomed to it, and subsequently overworked, broke down from heart failure.

This is not to say that they weren't cared for and groomed each day; indeed, we did the best we could for them under the circumstances, knowing that one day our lives might depend on them. And often, the connection went deeper than that. I saw a trooper cradling his downed horse's head in his lap while he rubbed its forehead and ears, talking to it in soft tones, tears streaking the dust on his cheeks, explaining why he was going to have to put a bullet through its brain.

We pushed on, with B Squadron scouting in advance, fanning out from a branch road leading northwest from Perdekop to Amersfoort and the main road to Belfast. We knew the trek would be difficult, for not only would the terrain worsen, it was also dense with Boers. As proof, we hadn't gone four miles before we encountered them in a series of challenging hills called the Rooikopjes.

The column changed direction so many times through the maze of dusty uplands that we shifted from the lead to the flank and back to the lead again, in what seemed like organized confusion. Enemy field guns and pom-poms pelted us with fire all day long but we outmanned and outgunned the Boers and drove them north, mile after mile, until we owned the heights above Amersfoort.

We held our mounts at the edge of the slope and scanned the town through spyglasses. A single highway ran through it, intersected by a few short side roads. There were perhaps 15 or 20 horses hitched to posts in the streets on the near side of town; otherwise it looked devoid of life. Yet only a fool would have believed that; it was merely a matter of which of the houses down there hid the enemy. Then the officer in command shouted to us, "I do believe Brother Boer is at home, men! Let's pay him a visit!" There was a roar of approval.

With his arm, the OC motioned us forward and B Squadron swept off the brow of the ridge, line abreast, followed by members of the King's Royal Rifles, a British infantry regiment. We yelled like madmen, our guns blazing over the thunder of horse hoofs. Memories of Loon Lake and the charge down the hill with Steele to confront Wandering Spirit and his warriors flashed through my mind. Like then, I could sense the blood lust building in the voices of the men, a volatile fuel that propelled us even faster down the grassy slope. Our bullets tore into the buildings as the Boers threw open the shutters in several of the houses and sent a return hail of bullets zinging past us. The resistance lasted for only a few seconds before collapsing in the face of the onslaught. The Boers who were able turned tail and ran. We gave chase, shooting at their backs without much effect; as near as I could tell they all escaped unscathed. At the edge of town, we stopped and posted sentries in case any of them decided to return.

"The yellow bastards!" one trooper muttered, but the Boers' flight had little to do with cowardice. They lived by the adage "He who fights and runs away, lives to fight another day." It was a cardinal rule for them. If they had been British, they would have made a heroic last stand and found their place in history. But the Boers couldn't waste lives on what to them would have been an utterly foolish endeavour.

Now that the brief battle was over, civilians began pouring into the street, Boer women, children and older men. We searched every building in town and discovered that our luck had been better than the Boers'. Our indiscriminate firing had resulted in the deaths of six of them, three in one building, two in another, and one, a boy no more than 16 years old, in a shed by himself. He was dressed in homemade clothing and wore soft hide boots. A floppy-brimmed hat lay on the floor beside him. He face was peaceful and if it weren't for the bandolier of ammunition slung across his chest, he might have been having a rest before going off to school or to milk cows, instead of trying to kill us. We gathered all the bodies and turned them over to the civilians for burial.

There were also four wounded, one seriously, and the townsfolk took him into one of the houses to do what they could. The KRR claimed the others and detained them in the town jail until there was transportation to the prison camp at Volksrust. The only casualty we sustained was an infantryman wounded in the jaw.

The wagons hadn't caught up yet and the reason sat thick and high on the western horizon. A wall of smoke was lifting skyward, turning the setting sun blood red. Boers retreating from the flanks had set fire to the veld and temporarily severed our supply line. If nothing reached us until the next morning, it meant that a long night awaited us, as none of us had enough clothes to keep warm and worse, we had no food.

When the sun sank behind the hills, a thick, cold fog descended over the town, and in the course of an hour, the summery day turned into a wintry night. The men grew increasingly cold and hungry.

I can't say how long it was between the last voiced complaint and the first explosion of breaking glass but it was probably only minutes. It seemed like a signal for things to come, as more explosions followed in quick succession. Men ran through the streets, some from B Squadron, smashing shop windows and taking whatever pleased them, mainly liquor and food. They stole it from stores and from the townsfolk. They took geese and chickens, and wantonly slaughtered sheep and pigs, bayoneting them and slashing them into roasts. Some grabbed clothing, mostly items to keep from themselves from freezing but one man, a KRR private, donned a woman's dress, and several of the Horse tied silk stockings around their necks as scarves. Others started a huge bonfire in the town square, then carried and dragged merchandise and furniture from the stores and added them to the flames. They smashed pianos and organs in order to carry them to the fire, and destroyed anything else, from bicycles to baby carriages, that wasn't useful or readily burnable.

It was sheer madness. Jim and I stood at the edge of the square and watched the destruction, along with the officers who were powerless to stop it. He lit his pipe and the smoke mixed with the fog, but the sweet aroma lingered. There was a thin line separating those of us standing and watching the looting from those participating in it, and I thought I understood. None of us had come here with this in mind but the dark ride down the hill had built into a bloodthirsty rage and still held many of the men in its grip. I had felt its power too; it was what got me to the town. Otherwise, I would gladly have ridden off in the opposite direction. Jim had sensed it as well, but we'd been able to let it go while others hadn't. The looting, smashing and burning were substitutes for the blood they hadn't spilled, and it would stop only when they were empty of the savagery needed to make the charge in the first place. That they could hide in the fog made it that much easier. I figured we could count ourselves lucky if we got through the night without a lynching.

The rampage lasted well into the small hours of the morning as the men, several now dressed in women's clothing, sang and danced around the fire like some primitive tribe. That they neither molested the townsfolk nor commandeered their homes was all that could be said on their behalf. When they grew tired, they found spots in shops or other places of business, curled up with the extra clothes or blankets they had stolen and went to sleep. The rest of us used our saddle blankets to keep warm.

The fog turned from milk to thick cream and the town fell into an eerie silence, punctuated only by the occasional pop of a cinder exploding in the fire and the distant barking of the odd dog. I was thankful that the night had ended without further trouble and wondered how it would play out when the rest of the column arrived. For the first time since leaving Canada, I felt a long way from home, that I was among barbarians and was not more than a half-step removed from them myself. It was an unpleasant discovery to say the least.

The morning light came suddenly, but the fog was still thick and it was like the lifting of eyelids over cataracts. I awoke chilled to the bone, having barely slept at all. Gunfire echoed down from the north edge of town as the Boers attempted a minor assault, but poor visibility hampered their efforts and they retreated. When the column and supply wagons finally appeared around 11:00 A.M., the fog still hadn't dissipated.

The destruction of the night before was less grim in the pervasive greyness than it really was, but what had gone on was apparent to anyone with eyes. Even so, none of the senior officers asked about it. Not a single question. And since they didn't ask, no one in B Squadron or the KRR, neither officers nor non-coms, volunteered any information; nor did the townsfolk, who kept silent in fear for their lives. There was no point. How could those in command put so many men on charge without seriously jeopardizing the push north? It was best to pretend that nothing had happened and move on, that it was nothing worse than what the Boers had done in many English towns when they rolled over half of Natal.

THIRTEEN

A "Pretty Little War"

THE FOG KEPT US in Amersfoort all that day but by the next morning a hot sun had burned it off. We moved out, over rolling grasslands cut by small streams, for Ermelo, the next sizeable town, some 35 miles north, clearing small pockets of resistance in the form of snipers. Two days later, during a severe dust storm, B Squadron took Ermelo with little opposition. The Boers had entrenched themselves at the edge of town but were unprepared for the squadron assaulting their position. Most fled, and the handful that didn't were taken prisoner. They were all teenagers. Major Jarvis led the squadron this time and conducted an orderly search of the buildings. We found and seized many small arms and a fairly large cache of ammunition. He then posted guards at all buildings vulnerable to looting, while he and the other officers imposed themselves upon Boer families in the best houses in town and ate their best food. The men watched in envy but said nothing. They had got off scot-free at Amersfoort and were unwilling to stir the pot.

We continued the march north, across prairie-like country, through the choking smoke of deliberately set grass fires, clearing villages and waiting for the column to catch up before advancing again. And as the Boer retreat outpaced our advance, we met less and less resistance. It gave us a heady feeling to know that we had them on the run, that we were beating them.

There was minimal resistance at Carolina, and the Horse resumed its customary scouting duties, trying to draw fire from any Boers who might be lurking atop the kopjes, then calling in the big guns to rout them out. I was in charge of a small troop of a half-dozen men, including Jim, when we encountered some scouts from the South African Light Horse, a regiment of irregulars consisting mainly of *uitlanders,* or foreigners. These were mostly disenfranchised British gold seekers, forced out of the Transvaal when war became inevitable. They went to Cape Colony where their true hatred for the Boers led to the formation of the regiment. Like Strathcona's Horse, though, many of their officers were regular career soldiers on temporary assignment. This time, it was a conceited British lieutenant by the name of Ramsay. He had a posh, upper-crust accent, a thin face and a handlebar moustache that he must have taken the time to wax every morning. He had little patience with his men and they gave me the impression that they'd rather be anywhere than riding patrol with Lieutenant Ramsay.

As we plodded along, Ramsay told me that he could not understand why the Boers bothered resisting at all. "Oh, they might give a stiff little show every now and then," he said, "but it's nothing we can't handle. Really, they are awful idiots to fight. They are accomplishing nothing except wasting their lives and our time."

He fancied himself a bit of a poet and often emphasized his thoughts by quoting a line of poetry. "Byron, dear boy," he'd then say or "Kipling, old chap," correctly presuming I didn't know who had written it.

I found him a condescending bore and was in desperate need of a diversion when we came over a low ridge and saw a farmhouse among some trees in the shallow valley below us. Every time we encountered one my heart rose into my throat and I remembered poor Bob Rollins. We reined up. There were the usual outbuildings and a large, rectangular kraal built of dry stone, larger than most I'd seen, as was the stone house, which was quite lovely and fronted with a vine-covered veranda along its entire length. There were goats in the kraal and a white rag hung limply on the front door. The goats meant that there was someone around, perhaps a farmer's wife, but no one came out of the house. It was entirely possible that they hadn't seen us because they were preoccupied, so I was all for firing a warning shot or giving the farm a wide berth until we could determine if it was safe to move in. Then, if need be, we could bring in a machine gun or pompom for reinforcement and give the place a good raking over.

Ramsay, however, was of a different mind. In his opinion, the Boers were on the run. He gave me a disdainful look. "Don't bother yourself, old chap. We'll handle this one." He turned to his non-com and said, "Sergeant, put something white on the end of your rifle to show we mean no harm and take three men and see what we've got here. It looks safe enough but mind your step. Off you go, then."

The terrain was wide open between us and the house, so it was a questionable order at best. I said, "I'm not sure that's a good idea, sir . . ."

I was going to tell him about Rollins when he cut me off. "Need I remind you, Sergeant, that I am the ranking officer here? When I want your advice, I will ask for it. Carry on," he said to his own sergeant who gave me a look that said "God save us from empty-headed officers." But an order was an order.

"Yes, sir!" he said and selected the three men closest to him. He took a large, dirty, white handkerchief from his pants pocket and tied it to his rifle barrel, then stood the stock on his thigh. I pulled out my rifle and held it at the ready. All Jim and the rest of the Horse needed from me was a nod and they did the same. The four men set off down the slope leading to the farmhouse.

My eyes flitted between the kraal and the house, watching for any sign of movement. I saw it, but too late. The troopers had covered about half the distance when a barrage of shots knocked all four of them from their horses. Hit in the chest, one animal crashed to the ground while the others ran off in a panic, raising red clouds of dust.

"Sonofabitch!" I yelled.

The shots had come from the kraal and I began firing at it. "Shoot!" I yelled at the others and a deafening roar of gunfire arose as the Light Horse troopers joined in, all except the lieutenant who was stunned by the turn of events. I didn't wait for him to take charge.

"Jim!" I shouted, slicing our troop in half with my arm.

"Take these men and ride around to the right side of the kraal! The rest of you follow me!" Motioning to Ramsay's men, I called, "Keep firing on that kraal and for Christ's sake try not to hit us!"

Less than a minute after the shooting we were bearing down hard on the enclosure, angling in on its corners, firing at will. Our bullets and those from the ridge pinged off the stone walls, sending chips flying and ricocheting everywhere. There was no return fire. Suddenly, the gate flew open and out ran six Boers with their hands in the air.

"Don't shoot! Don't shoot!" one of them cried in English. They dropped to the ground on their knees as we reached them. Four of them were middle-aged, the other two were in their late teens and looked like brothers. The Light Horse thundered up behind us, raising more dust.

"Search the house!" I yelled and several troopers hustled onto the veranda, their boots ringing on the floorboards, their spur rowels clinking noisily. Just as they reached the door, it swung open. An older woman dashed out among them, surprising everyone.

"My boys!" she cried. "My husband!"

She ran toward the Boers but two troopers caught her by the arms. She fought to get loose, screaming, "Let me go! Let a poor woman go! These are my boys! He is my husband!" She indicated the man who had led the surrender and who had spoken English. Clearly the leader, he was of medium height, his beard streaked with grey, his dark eyes alert beneath a wide-brimmed hat.

"Be calm, woman!" he commanded and his strong voice settled her down a little.

Upon questioning, he told us that they had been waiting, positive that a British patrol would happen along sooner or later but they had expected one much smaller. They had contemplated escaping but left the decision too late and their only option was to shoot their way out. When we descended on them so fast, escape became impossible.

We tied their hands behind their backs. The youngest of the teenagers was trembling but all of them were scared and for good reason. There was an ugly mood among the men, British and Canadian alike, and the Boers could sense it. They knew who they were dealing with, that the Light Horse would not let them off easily. I could see the fear for their lives in their eyes.

Lieutenant Ramsay had by now gathered his wits together and was attempting to take charge but with little effect. I wasn't doing much better controlling my own men, even Jim, who was angrier than I'd ever seen him. Several of the Light Horse had retrieved the bodies of the slain troopers, thrown across the three surviving horses like bags of barley. Their arrival at the house was salt rubbed in the wound. Some of the Boer bullets were dum-dums, which an international agreement had banned nearly a year before. They made a small hole where they entered but left a gaping exit wound. The back of the sergeant's head looked as if someone had taken a sledgehammer to it. A Light Horse corporal, a hard case who might have been a street brawler, walked over to the Boer leader and slapped him hard across the face, rocking him onto his heels.

"You murderin' bastard!"

The Boer did not cower but stood his ground, the fear in

his eyes replaced by a fiery defiance. He spat out a mixture of saliva and blood that landed on the front of the corporal's tunic. The corporal was enraged. He doubled his fist and banged it against the Boer's chest.

"You just signed your death warrant, Boojer. Where we come from you don't shoot a man showin' white and you don't trick him in to doin' it by hangin' out a white flag yourself. And you *never spit on your superiors*. Get some rope!" he called, to no one in particular, but there was no shortage of volunteers. "Let's give these fuckers their due!"

"Hold on, Corporal!" Ramsay exclaimed. "You are forgetting who's in charge here. These men are prisoners of war and will not be harmed!"

"Sez you," said a Cockney Light Horse trooper. He raised his rifle and pointed it at Ramsay, and the corporal followed suit. As I was next in rank, the trooper shifted his weapon in my direction. "If anyone else 'as any objections he'd best keep 'em to 'imself."

"Don't be a bloody fool, man," I said. "This is murder, as much as what the Boers did!"

He gave me a look of disbelief. "Murder? Bullshit! I can murder you or you can murder me but we only *kill* the enemy and ain't that what we came 'ere to do? What the 'ell does it matter 'ow we do it?"

Jim, who was standing beside me, intervened. "It matters," he said. "We're just as bloody angry as you are but this is downright criminal!" He stepped forward and the trooper moved his aim from me to him.

"It's war, guv." The trooper was disdainful. "Stay where you are. You ain't too big for a bullet."

"Think about this, men," Ramsay said. "I'll see that you spend the rest of your lives in prison for this, if not shot." His eyes took in the others. "So will anyone else who participates."

But events had gone beyond his ability to handle them and his voice lacked conviction. The trooper swung the gun back toward Ramsay's chest.

"Ain't no one goin' to prison, guv. Because ain't no one goin' to know about this, if you catch my drift."

"What about the woman?" I interjected. "You going to kill her, too?"

"She may want to do that 'erself after this. If she don't, 'oo's gonna believe a fuckin' Boojer and a female at that?"

He spun away from me because he had finished arguing. He and the others wanted blood and were determined to get it. A couple of my men threw in with the Light Horse troopers and there was nothing I could do about it. I would have only risked a bullet for my trouble and I wasn't about to die defending Boers who abused the white flag of surrender and used dum-dum bullets.

With a ladder from an outbuilding, a trooper threaded ropes between the veranda's corrugated tin roof and its rafters, one for each man, and fashioned a noose at the end of each rope. Other troopers brought out six chairs from the house and set them beneath the nooses. The Boers were prodded at gunpoint to climb onto the chairs where their ankles were tied. None resisted. The Light Horse corporal placed the nooses over the men's heads and cinched them tight around their necks, with the small knot behind their ears. While some troopers held the men steady, others pulled the ropes taut and secured them around the veranda railing.

Watching her husband and sons about to die, the woman could not contain herself. "You cowards!" she screamed at the troopers. "Take me, too!" She tore open the buttons at the top of her dress, exposing the cleavage of her ample breasts. "Shoot me! Shoot me here! My heart is great!"

The Cockney trooper said, "And spoil yer fun of watchin', luv? Don't be daft!"

"Pull those chairs away!" roared the corporal. There was a scraping sound of wood on wood and then creaking as the rafters and railing took the load. It was a strongly built veranda, there was no denying that.

"My God!" the woman screamed and collapsed to the ground in a dead faint.

The hanged men kicked and jerked as much as they could with their ankles tied together and made awful choking, gurgling noises. Their faces turned a deep purple-red, their eyes bulged. I thought their heads would explode. This wasn't a hanging; it was slow death by strangulation. I turned around for I could no longer bear witness to it. Ramsay bent over and vomited.

"For God's sake," I cried. "Someone have mercy and shoot them!"

"Leave the fuckers swing!" snarled the corporal, brandishing his pistol.

Most of the men who didn't actively participate in the lynchings couldn't have moved even if they wanted. The sight of six human beings in an agonizing, losing battle to cling to life for a few seconds longer had them utterly transfixed.

As the house was stone and its roof tin, it was unburnable, so the men brought all of the furniture out to the front yard and set it on fire. As the flames rose into the sky like the Hell this place was, two troopers placed the unconscious woman on small tick mattress they had saved. We found some spades in one of the sheds and in the shade of an old tree dug a shallow, common grave for the dead British soldiers. After we laid them to rest and said a few words over their graves, one of the troopers placed a spade on the ground beside the woman who had regained consciousness and was now sitting up, rocking to and fro in a state of shock and mumbling incoherently.

"You'll need this, luv," he said. "When you're feelin' up to it, of course."

The woman continued rocking, oblivious to the trooper.

Several of the men smashed out the windows of the house with their rifle butts while another found some dark paint and a brush. On the wall behind the hanged men, he scrawled, "We remember Majuba, Boojer."

As we rode off, a strong wind that had been building since noon blew small red dust devils across the veld and the corpses swayed like silent wind chimes. The sun burned down from a cloudless sky and pressed like lead on my shoulders. A "pretty little war" was what Buller would later call the South African conflict in a telegram to his wife. A pretty little war.

FOURTEEN

Losses

I SWEATED BLOOD ALL the way back to the regiment over whether or not I should report the lynchings to my squadron commander. Threats from the Light Horse troopers hovered over me like those of a schoolyard bully and my own men's involvement didn't make it any easier. But I couldn't in good conscience let it slide.

Jim, though still angry, was more philosophical about it. He shrugged. "I didn't like it any more than you, Jack, but if you want my opinion, I don't think anything'll come of it. The brass have got more important things on their plate than to worry about what happened to a handful of murdering Boojers."

"They can do what they want with it," I said, "but I still have to report it."

"Then you'll want to make sure you keep your distance from the Light Horse."

As it turned out, Ramsay went straight to his commander and reported it and I barely had time to unsaddle my horse before an order came from Steele himself. He wanted to see me, immediately. I hustled to his tent on the double and told the story, exactly the way it happened. He took it all in, without saying a word. When I finished he said, "Right. I appreciate your candor, Strong. I will investigate the matter. Meanwhile, it's information that you should keep to yourself. Do I need to repeat that?"

"No, sir."

"Dismissed."

I saluted and left.

I waited for the lion's mouth to open and devour us but it never did. Several weeks later, when allegations of the lynchings filtered down from the higher echelons, Steele denied having any knowledge of them, insisting that his men were a fine, upstanding lot who would never do such a thing. He wasn't alone in the lie. The Light Horse commander denied any involvement on the part of his troops, too. That was as far as it went.

I came to terms with it. It was a dirty, nasty war with more than its fair share of ruthless men, and while that didn't make it right, it was the reality.

The Boers had gathered east of Belfast, near a place called Machadodorp, on a great ridge running north-south, intent on making a stand with their heavy guns and a concentration of men. They would need every ounce of force they could muster as they faced Roberts's massive column to the west and Buller's smaller force to the south. Together, the British numbered nearly 19,000 men against 6,000 to 7,000 Boers spread thinly along a 20-mile front. A red-earth kopje on a farm owned by a family named Bergendal became the Boers' Spion Kop.

About three acres in area and covered with a jumble of boulders, the kopje protruded from the ridge like a salient, and the men on the Boer line—mostly tough Johannesburg policemen—had orders from their commanders to hold it. But British artillery, 40 guns in all, bombarded them and adjacent parts of the line at a rate of 19 shells a minute for three hours.

The Horse did not participate in the battle but had front-row seats for one of the greatest spectacles on the planet: men hurling death and destruction at each other. Safely out of range, I watched the battle through a spyglass, as enormous rocks were blown into man-size fragments that flew threw the air like pebbles. God help anyone who might have been hiding behind them. Yet the Boers held their ground. The infantry charged up the slope in a hail of bullets from flanking enemy fortifications, their khaki-clad figures lost occasionally in explosions of dirt and dust of the same hue. They flopped prostrate on the ground behind the myriad anthills dotting the slope when they couldn't reach the preferred cover of a boulder. During lulls in the shooting, they would advance a few more feet toward their objective, firing all the while. I saw several men brought down by bullets, some killed instantly, others badly wounded.

But when an artillery shell blew a man apart, I yanked the spyglass from my eye, unable to believe what I had seen. This couldn't be real. Did I actually see a human being torn to bloody bits? Is that what my father had seen during the American Civil War, only close up and many times over?

Something my mother had said long ago echoed in my brain: "Your father saw horrific things in the war. He was no more than a child given a rifle to shoot at other children. He saw the heads of his friends blown off their shoulders and saw others fall around him with their insides hanging out, screaming for their mothers. That has to affect a man no matter how tough he thinks he is."

How much could a man see, I wondered, before he needed to numb his mind with whisky for the remainder of his life?

On the kopje, the onslaught eventually proved too much for even the toughest Boers and they fled to fight another day. The noise of the battle, even from a distance, was almost deafening. Then, as if some god of war had thrown a switch, the firing stopped.

The ensuing silence seemed almost unnatural. Smoke and dust drifted across the battlefield, carrying with it the stench of lyddite, a high explosive containing picric acid. Before leaving the kopje, one of the Boers had taken the time to write a short note for the British soldiers. Stuck in the crevice of a rock so the wind wouldn't carry it off, it read, "Dear Khaki, we are not feeling very well today; but trust we shall meet you some other time. Yours ever—."

That was the battle of Bergendal Farm, which took place on August 27 and proved to be the last great battle of the war. All that the Boers had left was a narrow strip of country barely 70 miles across, between the British forces and the Portuguese East African border, and they wouldn't retain that for long. Everyone figured the war was as good as over, that it was time to go home. But no one told the Boers.

Fifty miles north of Machadodorp was Lydenburg, a Boer recruitment and supply centre, and Buller wanted to take it. We pushed the Boers in that direction, skirmishing with them, and halted for the day near a lovely farm called Badfontein. Steele sent men to a low ridge a half mile ahead where they established an outpost until British staff officers ordered them back. They felt the outpost was too far from the camp and wanted it closer in. The decision angered Steele. The ridge was the high ground and he believed that vacating it was a serious strategic error. Events the following morning proved him right: the Boers returned in the night and, unbeknownst to us, lined the ridge with their heavy artillery.

At dawn, Steele and a brigade major were preparing to investigate the ridge themselves when a shell burst close by. The explosion nearly knocked Steele and his horse over while it blew the head of the major's horse clear off. The animal dropped, trapping its rider beneath it. As Steele was trying to control his own mount, panicked by the blast, some foot soldiers rescued the major. Several more shells exploded, killing four horses and a pair of mules. Steele bellowed, "Everyone move back! Move to the cover of the wagons!"

The order didn't need repeating. We beat a hasty retreat, secured the surviving animals in a *donga*, or shallow ravine, and dived beneath the wagons.

The Boers shelled us for much of the day. We could see the flashes of their big guns along the ridge, each flash followed by about 20 to 30 seconds of nerve-wracking silence during which we contemplated our possible demise. Then we would hear the actual report of the gun being fired and, with a little luck, the sound of the shell bursting a few seconds later, sometimes overhead and sometimes on the ground, sending columns of earth into the air. Shrapnel rained down on us, bouncing harmlessly off the wagons where we hid in frustration. We were helpless until our artillery caught up with us. At dark, the guns fell silent and a fog descended on the valley. We crawled out from beneath the wagons, thankful to be on our feet again and able to move around.

The next morning an icy mist lay over the landscape and the Boer guns were silent. Had they gone? No one knew. But the British officers now saw the strategic value of the ridge and ordered Steele to find a way to recapture it. He sent for me and when I arrived at his tent, he could not hide his anger.

"Strong," he said, his words clipped, "as much as it displeases me to give this order, I want you to take some men and check out that ridge for Boer activity. I would prefer to wait until the fog lifts but we can't let the rascals get too far ahead of us. If they're gone, set up an outpost and reconnoitre the area. See if you can find out where they are and report back to me. I don't doubt that they've slipped off in the fog and darkness and you'll find the ridge empty, but I don't need to tell you that Brother Boer can hide behind a blade of grass and shoot your eye out, so use extreme caution."

"No fear there, sir."

I chose Jim and a half-dozen other reliable men from the troop and we saddled up in the chilly morning air, the horses snorting clouds of steam.

"There's no sense in giving a sniper an easy shot, so we'll spread out," I told them. "We'll ride line abreast at a distance where the outside men can just see each other. Jim, you take the left side and Harold" (this was Harold Dexter, a Lethbridge cowboy), "you take the right. I'll take the centre along the road. You others space yourselves out at even intervals between us. Stay in line and when I stop, everyone stops. It isn't likely we'll find anything there but as we get closer to the ridge, stay low on your horse's neck so you make a smaller target. I don't want anyone taking a bullet, so keep an ear cocked and your eyes peeled for any movement or anything that doesn't seem like it's part of the landscape. If that happens, we get the hell out of there, fast!"

Visibility was 200 yards at best but the road was well trampled by the Boers and easy to follow. The slope on both sides of the road was grassy, with clusters of rocks here and there but nothing big enough to hide behind. I never took my eyes off the point where the land blended with the fog. We stopped twice on our way to the top, for a full minute each time, but heard and saw nothing. We inched up the gentle incline and reached the crest of the broad, flat ridge without incident. Visibility was improving by the minute but we saw no movement anywhere.

Steele was right: the Boers had indeed vacated the ridge. We could see where they had placed their Long Toms, saw spent shells and the tracks where they had withdrawn. They had left early in the morning, since the tracks weren't as dewy as the ground adjacent to them, and that meant they were not too far ahead. We stopped at the far side of the ridge and could see several hundred yards down its equally gentle slope but there was only the churned-up road, disappearing into the thinning fog. I motioned for the outside riders to come into the centre and, once they got close, ordered two men to stand guard on the ridge and sent a third man to Steele with our intelligence. The rest of us spread out again, at 50-yard intervals, and began working our way off the ridge.

To the sides, large clumps of boulders scattered across the landscape made me jumpy; they were plenty big enough to hide a sniper without a horse. Still, we saw nothing. We rode on for perhaps a half mile, the road rising and falling like ocean swells. The air was cold but I was perspiring and didn't feel it. The fog had all but dissipated when we came to the rim of a broad valley that stretched on for miles. Far down on the valley floor we saw what we'd come for: the Boers and their Long Toms. For some reason they were stopped. I pulled out my spyglass. They were nonchalantly eating, which didn't make sense to me. Why hadn't they left pickets on top of the rise to warn them of advance patrols?

The answer was rifle shots, Mausers, that rang out from somewhere behind us. Simultaneously, I saw Harold Decker, on my right flank, fall from his horse, a gout of blood spurting from his neck where a bullet caught him. The trooper between Decker and me was felled too, his horse shot out from under him. A bullet hissed by my nose and another tore off the top half of my horse's right ear. It screamed and bucked and rather than stick with it, I leapt to the ground and scrambled for cover behind some rocks. Out of the corner of my eye I saw Jim jump from his horse as it reared up, while Art Hume, the trooper between us, was leaning over his animal's neck and spurring it back in the direction we'd come from. That was asking for a bullet and he got one, or at least his horse did. It stumbled and fell with a sickening sound. All of this happened in moments. Bullets were flying everywhere, caroming off rocks and punching the ground with small explosions.

Then the shooting stopped as suddenly as it had started, presumably because there were no targets left. I couldn't see anything out to my left, but Jim's large Strathcona boots were moving behind some rocks to my right, which meant that he was still alive. I didn't know what had happened to Hume, if he'd been shot along with his horse or if he too had managed to reach cover. I wasn't about to stick my head up to find out. I turned and leaned against the rocks and took stock of our situation.

The snipers had been behind us, off to my right, and given the number of shots, one on top of the other, there were two or three of them. Decker had been closest to them and the easiest target; the trooper between us less so but still a sitting duck. The rest of us were lucky that the snipers hadn't been better shots but they did get our horses. From where I sat, I could see movement in the main column of Boers in the valley. My guess was that riders were coming to relieve or rescue the snipers. If so, they would be here in a few minutes and there was no place to hide from them. I hadn't had time to grab my rifle, which left me with my revolver and extra rounds of ammunition in my bandolier. I held no heroic notions about fighting to the death, but I had no white hanky to wave in surrender, either. Maybe the Boers would shoot me, regardless. Two or three minutes passed and I could see horsemen leave the valley floor and begin the long ascent to our position. I couldn't make out their number exactly but there might have been six or seven of them.

I called out, "Jim! Are you all right?"

"I'm good," he answered.

Hume's voice cried out, "I'm okay, too!"

Jim, who had a vantage point similar to mine, called. "Do you see what I see comin' up the hill?"

"Yup."

"Any ideas?"

"I'm thinking!" I said.

There was complete silence for a moment. Then I heard horses' hoofs in the distance, not from down the hill but from the road behind us, and a few seconds later, more gun-fire—Boer Mausers—followed by several rifle shots tumbling over each other. These were different weapons, Lee-Enfields rather than Mausers. I peeked over the rocks and almost cried out for joy. A troop of Strathconas was reining up on the road. Steele must have sent them out immediately after receiving our message.

I arose and scampered around the rock, yelling at the others to come forward. Jim and Art were on their feet too, and we began firing at the Boers ascending the hill. They were well out of our revolvers' range and the bullets fell short but they clearly got the message when our horsemen lined the brow of the hill. They did an about-turn and fled.

My heart was still thumping madly as we checked out Harold Decker and the trooper nearest him. Both men were dead. A dum-dum bullet had entered Harold's neck below the hairline and blown out his Adam's apple. The other man took one in the spine. Art Hume had broken two of his fingers when they shot his horse out from underneath him and he tried to break his fall, but other than that he was all right. The snipers had also managed to kill two men from our rescue troop before succumbing to bullets themselves.

We walked over to where they had been hiding. Blood was spattered everywhere, across the ground and the rocks they'd used for cover. There were three of them, bearded young men in ragged clothes, with bandoliers crisscrossing their chests. They didn't look like cold-blooded killers and were probably not expert snipers; otherwise, they might have got us all.

In a few hours, Strathcona's Horse had lost nearly half the men it would lose in battle during its entire stay in South Africa. Steele was fit to be tied. He did not like to lose men under justifiable circumstances, let alone foolish ones, and he openly blamed the brigade's staff officers for forcing him to withdraw from the ridge in the first place.

From Lydenburg the road twisted and turned eastward through the Mauchsberg Mountains, climbing to an elevation of more than a mile above sea level before descending into the jungle-covered lowland beyond. It ran through narrow gaps between green and gold mountains and around high bluffs, and crossed three great ridges split by deep ravines. Day after day, we chased the Boers across that magnificent landscape, seizing kopje after kopje, at times under so much fire from their Long Toms that the men began to call the route "Long Tom Pass." As the rugged road climbed and dipped, we once saw a long line of them far ahead in their march east. Our artillery might have reached the rearmost part of the line but they had placed their ambulance there as protection.

With their backs against the Portuguese East African border, the Boers turned north. Curiously, Buller decided not to pursue them. His critics would later say that if he had, he might have captured the renowned Boer general, Louis Botha—it was he whom we were following—and ended the war. But that was not Buller's kind of war. Chasing an enemy in retreat was simply not an honourable thing to do. Instead, we halted for almost two weeks and not a soul complained. We'd been on the march for nearly two months and were exhausted.

We camped on a grassy meadow by a very pretty little creek edging a splendid mountain, and enjoyed not being under constant threat. Farms in the surrounding area provided us with lamb, poultry and beef, bought and paid for this time, and it was a vast improvement over our rations of tinned bully beef and biscuits.

Across the creek, several tunnels had been bored into the mountainside and it didn't take long for the more knowledgeable among us to discover that they were gold mines. In fact, those who knew the history of the area said that the gold rush had begun in 1873 with the discovery of two 2-pound nuggets, ultimately kept in their natural form and named Emily and Adeliza. But men had hardly needed that incentive. In no time at all, a small rush was under way as they put metal plates and biscuit tins into service panning for gold. Some even found colour, but as in all gold rushes, most went home with nothing. However, a more lucrative opportunity presented itself to B Squadron.

About three miles north of our camp there was a deserted but working mine, along with the requisite stores, and our commander sent us there to protect it. It was like sending hyenas to guard a downed antelope.

The heart of the mine was a 10-stamp mill, an ominous-looking device used to free gold from the rock containing it. A hydraulic engine turned a belt and rotated cams that raised two heavy stamps, attached to each of five vertical rods which, when dropped by gravity, crushed the rock beneath it. An elevated wood bin with a sloping bottom fed the ore to the stamps which pulverized it at the rate of 90 beats a minute.

We soon had the mill running, emitting an ear-splitting racket that was audible for miles. At first, we worked a large heap of ore left unprocessed when the site was abandoned, and that yielded enough gold to send us into the mine for more. While most of the squadron sat and watched, a dozen or more of us worked the shaft as if we owned it. In two days, we had pocketed several ounces of gold each but we kept the information to ourselves. Unfortunately, the noisy work attracted a great deal of attention. By the third day, the brigade's provost martial had got wind of our activities and ordered the mill shut down. Then, much to everyone's surprise, he had the lot of us arrested for looting.

We were extremely lucky that it was Buller we had to face. From the outset, he seemed to have more important things on his mind and showed little interest in our deeds. He pretty much said, "Boys will be boys," gave us a mild reprimand and ordered us to turn the gold over to him. He would ensure its return to the mine's rightful owners, whoever they might be. I surrendered all that I had, which amounted to several ounces, but I can't say for sure if the others did, because no one searched us. What happened to the gold that we handed over is hard to know but when Buller dismissed us, I had the uneasy feeling that I'd been looted myself.

So much looting was going on, in fact, that a special parade was held and Lord Dundonald, one of the brigade's senior officers, lectured us sternly about molesting the locals. "It is not war to loot poor people," he said. He singled out the Horse specifically but Steele objected.

"Certain young colonials have turned down the brims of their felt hats and put dents in the crowns to make them look like Canadians," he insisted. "But they have not fooled me because their saddles tell the true story."

By that he meant the horns, and there was little doubt that he was referring to the South African Light Horse who typically wore one side of their hat brims pinned to the crowns.

Rumours of peace flew along the column and dreams of going home generated much excitement in the regiment, which was now only a ghost of its former self. About 200 men, a third of the regiment, had lost their horses to the ravages of war and disease and were now on foot, and a few wiser ones had chosen to stay behind in Lydenburg to await remounts. Not that it mattered much. The reality was that the war was winding down for us; the Boers were constantly in retreat, and we had all signed one-year contracts that would end in about four months. That meant Steele would have to return us to Canada before the expiry date and since that could take six to eight weeks, it didn't leave much time for fighting. We sat around campfires at night singing melancholy songs such as "Red River Valley" and "My Old Canadian Home," our version of "My Old Kentucky Home." But it was as much the wishful thinking of ragged and dirty men, tired of the fight, than anything else. And most of us weren't so naive as to think that the brass wouldn't try to get as much mileage from us as possible.

Buller's commitment had ended, though, and he was ready to go home. He wanted to get the column to the rail line at Machadodorp but he had orders to loop north first and clear the country of Boers. Few were happy with the decision and those of us in the Horse had to be satisfied that it was a route home, however roundabout.

FIFTEEN

Exeter Farm

WE REACHED LYDENBURG AND after a four-day lay-up in rainy, cold weather, we turned south and left the Boers to their own devices. They were now merely fleas on an elephant. We retraced our steps south to Machadodorp, where the train would take us to Pretoria and on to Johannesburg and Cape Town.

The dead horses we'd left during our passage through the valley a few weeks earlier lay here and there along the road. They were bloated and grotesque, and vultures were growing fat from the unexpected but welcome feast. Some were still perched on the carcasses, tearing off bloody strips of meat. Those who had finished were so heavy they could not take flight and simply lumbered off at our approach. Dozens more sat on the ground, awaiting their turn and fighting each other to be next in line, while a hundred or more circled above, their huge wings silver against the sky. It was a ghastly sight, worsened by the fact that many of the animals were still recognizable as old companions, with names and once-distinctive personalities.

At Machadodorp, we formed up in the town square where Buller bade us farewell. The war was over for him. He was the last of a dying breed, men who believed that wars ought to be fought honourably and on gentlemen's terms. This war hadn't been and it would only get worse after he was gone. When he climbed on the wagon his eyes were dark and baggy and he looked as dead tired as the rest of us felt.

"I have never served with a nobler, braver or more serviceable body of men," he said. There he was again, making us feel great about ourselves, so we gave him three cheers and a tiger, even knowing he said that to all the boys.

We had to turn our horses over to the Dragoon Guards, who would continue pursuing the Boers. For many men it was a heart-wrenching task. I had not wanted to become attached to my horse but found it impossible not to. She had been a reliable companion since Perdekop and I was not happy handing her over to a complete stranger, despite not having given her a name. She didn't care much for the change either and bucked her new owner off.

Sam Steele and B Squadron were the first to leave for Pretoria, in open cattle trucks that were cold and uncomfortable but were taking us far from the war. Or so we thought.

In the Boer capital, the British flag now flew above the colonnaded government buildings. The jacaranda trees lining the roadsides were laden with purple, trumpet-shaped blossoms and the town was flooded with people, horses and wagons. The air of optimism about the place could have fooled one into believing the war had ended. The place was so overcrowded with soldiers that we spread our bedrolls on the hard station platform for the night. We would have spread them on shards of glass as long as we were on our way home. But we awoke to find that Steele had been busy while we slept.

Buller was gone, Bobs was going and Lord Kitchener was now in charge of operations. He told Steele there was one more job that he wanted the Horse to perform. The Boer general, Christiaan De Wet, who was still causing no end of problems for the British with his hit-and-run tactics, was laying siege to Fredrikstad, a rail station about 50 miles south-west of Johannesburg. Our assignment was to relieve the town and capture De Wet. Steele didn't like it one iota. He knew we were exhausted and he argued on our behalf, but Kitchener was not a man to be denied. We remounted and re-kitted and were following the railroad tracks out of Pretoria the following morning, across a desolate landscape of scrub bushes and thorn trees, our heads spinning at how swiftly events had shifted. And more than a few of us were describing Kitchener's ancestry with what we believed was pinpoint accuracy.

The Boers became even less visible and more elusive. It galled Kitchener and made him determined to leave them with nothing that would even possibly offer support. He sent us out to burn farms wholesale, crops and buildings included, and anything else that might be useful. We were to tell the people it was for their own security, to protect them from the "Kaffirs," or black South Africans, now that their menfolk weren't around. It was far from pleasant work. What do you say to a woman who answers your knock at the door by inviting you in for tea or milk? "Thank you anyway, Madam, but

I'm here to reduce your home to ashes. But don't let it bother you; it's for your own good."

Granted, some of them were spies and some had arms and ammunition cached beneath the floorboards of their house, sewn into the tick of their mattresses or stashed inside a spinet, but the majority were innocent people whose only crime was getting in the way of the war. Undoubtedly, they were all patriotic to the Boer cause but why on Earth wouldn't they be? Most stood by helplessly, weeping as we set fire to their homes. Some refused to leave and had to be carried forcibly outside. In one instance, I lugged out an eight- or nine-year-old girl wearing a gingham dress and bonnet, with tears streaking her dirty face, kicking and screaming, so that her equally distraught mother would follow.

In another, an old man spat at me. "We were told it was the Kaffirs we had to fear, not you!" he said. It shamed me so much I could not look into his eyes; indeed, I can scarcely admit to it. I left him, tears staining his stubbled cheeks, watching the fire consume the centrepiece of his life. As we rode off, I could see pillars of smoke rising into the sky along the horizon where similar scenes were being played out and other farms burned to the ground. Other women and children crying; other old men spitting and cursing. I was not proud of myself. None of us were.

That wasn't the end of it; we burned many more. The farms were fairly evenly spaced across the veld, 16 miles apart. Some houses were built of stone, others of mud and wattle, but all were indicative of the hard life of subsistence farming, of eking out an existence in a land that demanded every ounce of one's energy and gave very little in return. Most of the dwellings were sorry excuses for homes, but they *were* homes and provided shelter to those who dwelled in them. Some were British farms, and it was always a relief to encounter those and not have to carry out our despicable task.

Toward the end of November word came that De Wet was headed for Cape Colony; he planned to foment more dissent among the Boer farmers who had opted to remain under British rule and were now close to revolting. We boarded a train to Springfontein, a railway junction in the Orange Free State, then marched southwest to the swollen Orange River where we were told that De Wet had turned northwest instead of crossing over into the Colony. To find out, Steele sent out a few intelligence-gathering patrols to some of the farms across the river, both British and Boer.

Jim and I rode together on what we deemed to be an easy assignment. We clanged over a guarded iron bridge and rode northwest through the Orange River Valley on a muddy, orange-red track paralleling the river and lined here and there with willows. Flat-topped hills sloped down to the wide valley bottom, and sagebrush and thorny acacia trees grew in abundance. The rainy weather had given the land more green vegetation than it had for most of the year, and the air had been freshened by the unsettled weather, which was a combination of bursts of rain and intense sun that raised steam on the horses and heated my bones.

We rode, lost in reverie, for I don't know how long. It might have been a few seconds or a few minutes. Either way, it was a foolish thing to be doing even though we were now in British territory. The river formed the boundary and was guarded at the main fords but there was still a possibility of

Boers sneaking across and if we were going to survive this war and get home, we'd do well to keep our eyes open for any sign of movement. But the only movement we saw was a solitary kestrel soaring overhead, hunting for a meal.

We checked an English farm but the owners, an elderly couple, had seen nothing. But it wouldn't hurt to check Exeter Farm, they said, a few miles along the road. We found it nestled in the opening of a wide cleft between two kopjes. A neatly hand-painted sign proclaimed its name—"Exeter"— and it was from all indications an English farm, as it was well kept and in a better state of repair than many of the Boer farms we'd seen. A wagon with two horses still in harness stood nearby, as if someone had recently arrived or was about to leave. As we approached, two women came out of the house, off the porch and stood in the front yard, waiting to greet us. One of them smiled and waved as we rode through the open gate. I could hear the sound of chickens clucking.

"Afternoon, ladies," I said, pulling up.

The women nodded and said hello with lovely English accents. The one who had smiled and waved was rather plain, while the other was especially pretty. At closer quarters the smile on the plain woman's face looked as if it had been pasted on. Both women were fidgety. Had I been more alert I would have noticed that they were talking to us with their eyes. But I was tired, distracted by the pretty one and thirsty, and so was Jim. I was about to ask for a drink of water when the front door of the house was flung open and out came two Boers with Mausers levelled at us.

"Don't move!" one shouted. "Get your hands above your head, and don't move!"

There was no choice; we raised our hands high. Damn it! We were almost done with this godforsaken war, but we'd stupidly let our guard down and now were going to pay for it. My mind was racing, searching for a way out of the mess.

We had received new uniforms at Springfontein, and the Boers wore rags, so I didn't think we would be shot before they got our clothes without any blood on them. The Boers had a nasty reputation for stealing enemy uniforms—like white flags, they were a cunning way to draw a patrol within firing range—and I felt certain these guys wanted ours. It was not an uncommon occurrence and once the prisoners had been interrogated and any pertinent information extracted from them, they were usually allowed to return to their camp on foot, stark naked and humiliated, either sunburned or frozen depending on the weather. On the other hand, some never returned. The Boers employed a wide range of interrogation techniques, a few of them sadistic.

"Get off those horses!" the Boer ordered and it was in that split-second that I decided I was going to be neither humiliated nor shot in cold blood. As I swung to the ground I left-reined my horse, which made her a partial shield between the Boers and me. At the same time, I drew my pistol from its holster, fell to the ground and began snapping off shots beneath the horse's belly. The Boers split apart and began firing too. I hit the one on the left in the leg and he yelped in pain, staggered a bit and fell on the porch, losing his rifle. A slug thudded into my horse and she stomped on my leg as she bolted off a few yards before collapsing. The women screamed and ran to the wagon, out of the line of fire.

Jim's horse had also bolted as he was dismounting and sent him tumbling to the ground. I felt a hot, searing pain in my chest that for some crazy reason made me think of branding calves rather than a bullet wound. My right arm seemed to lose strength and the gun felt twice as heavy but I had plenty of adrenalin to keep me squeezing the trigger and my last bullet found its mark dead centre in the chest of the second Boer. He reeled back against the wall with a thud and slid to the floor. All of this happened in the length of time it took to squeeze off six bullets.

I was able to get to my feet, although my right shin was painful where the horse had stepped on it. But that was the least of my worries. When I put my hand to my chest it came away sticky with blood, and the sudden realization that I had indeed been shot, and might be dying, nearly made me swoon. I limped to the porch, trying to ignore the pain. The second Boer was slumped against the wall, dead. The other was busy trying to staunch the flow of blood from his leg, more concerned with saving himself than being a threat to us. I scooped up his rifle and gave it to Jim who had recovered from his fall and now thumped onto the porch with jingling spurs and his gun drawn, his eyes wide and alert.

"Holy Christ, Jack!" he exclaimed. "You crazy bugger! What the hell were you thinkin' of!"

"I'm fine," I gasped. "Kind of you to ask. I just need to sit down for a bit."

My legs were weak and I felt out of breath. I sat down heavily on the porch steps as chunks of black began floating across my vision. I vaguely recall the women hovering over me as the chunks fused together and engulfed me.

SIXTEEN

Ree

I AWOKE FROM A wild dream of fantastic characters, some of whom were trying to kill me, and animals that were only partly recognizable as beasts I'd seen before. I was on a cloud with an angel standing above me. Then I realized that the cloud was a soft feather bed and the angel was the pretty woman from outside. A lamp was burning on a bedside table, another on a chest of drawers across the room. There was someone else with us, standing off to the side.

"How do you feel?" the woman asked, her voice tender and low.

"Not dead, but I can't be sure," I croaked. Someone must have stuffed my mouth full of veld dust.

She smiled. "Well, you're not dead, I can assure you of that, and according to the doctor you won't soon be. Can I get you anything?"

"Water, please."

There was a pitcher of water behind the lamp on the bed-side table, and a glass. She poured a small quantity into the glass and held it to my lips, tipping it slowly. The cool liquid was a Rocky Mountain stream sliding down my throat. A shape loomed up beside her. It was Steele.

"Trying to get out of the war are we, Strong?" he said, a half-grin on his face. "If you'd only been patient, you might have done it with a lot less pain and bleeding."

"Yes, sir." I was pleased he had come.

A web of red veins streaked his eyes, as if he'd been on a bender the night before. I expect that the war was taking its toll on him, the way it was on everyone else. Moreover, he took every casualty in his regiment personally, even the men he didn't know, and he'd known me for a long time. He explained what had happened after I had passed out on the porch, which was not mere moments before, as I had assumed, but several hours.

While one of the women tended to the wounded Boer and locked him in an outbuilding until he was formally taken prisoner, Jim had carried me into the house and put me on the bed. He had removed my tunic and undershirt so that the angelic woman could clean my wound, then had ridden pell-mell to the regiment for help. He returned with Steele himself, a handful of troopers and the regiment's doctor. After a thorough examination, the doctor determined that the bullet which, to my extreme good fortune, was not a dum-dum, had gone clear through my right chest wall, missing my lung but cracking a rib in the process. My horse had badly bruised my right leg when it stepped on me, but nothing was broken. I had momentarily regained consciousness while the woman was assisting the doctor in bandaging my chest and he administered some laudanum, although I had only a vague recollection of it.

"Where's Spencer?" I asked.

"He escorted the doctor back to the regiment. As for you, you'll rest up until we can get an ambulance out here. It may take a day or so until one is available but it'll get you onto a train to the Cape and a proper hospital. You did some exceptional work here, Strong, and I'm going to recommend a citation. Our Boer friend that you spared had lots of interesting information that he was more than willing to share."

Steele patted my shoulder lightly, an uncharacteristic display of affection, and said, "I'm leaving you in Mrs. Lawrence's capable hands." He nodded toward the woman. "Do try to be a co-operative patient, although I expect it's contrary to your nature. I've posted two men outside to guard the farm, so rest easy. With any luck at all the regiment will be stood down and we'll meet you at the Cape."

With that, he gave thanks to our hostess, bade us goodbye and returned to the war.

The woman offered more water, which I eagerly accepted. I took the glass myself and sipped at it, dribbling a little water onto my chin when I raised the glass too high. The arm movement gave me a jolt of pain, so I switched the glass to my left hand and felt better, though less adept. But as long as I didn't move my right side too much there was very little discomfort. I felt pretty good, in fact: I was glad to be alive and thought the wound was a small price to pay to be in the company of this charming woman.

"Thank you." I handed the glass to her. "I'm sorry. I know Colonel Steele said your name but I didn't quite catch it."

"Lawrence," she replied. "But I do hope you'll call me Ree."

"Ree?" I repeated. It wasn't a name I had heard before.

"Yes. It's short for Rianne, which is an Irish name. My mother is Irish," she explained. "I'm named after my maternal grandmother. My father is English. But you need rest, Sergeant. We can talk more in the morning."

"Yes, but please call me Jack."

"Jack, it is, then."

She gave me another dose of laudanum. I slept deeply at first but fitfully for the rest of the night, as it was difficult to get comfortable. Nevertheless, I felt much improved in the morning and wished I could get out of bed and move around. Ree had one of the guards come in and help me into a semi-sitting position. She brought a basin of warm soapy water and bathed my face and hands, which did wonders for my disposition. I can't say I liked having to depend on a stranger for such intimate care, but I found the softness of her touch thrilling, despite my condition.

Afterward I could hear her busy in the kitchen, heard the sizzle of bacon frying and eggs cracking open. The smell was mouthwatering. The guards came in one at a time to eat and when she brought food for me, I tried my best not to wolf it down. When I had finished she took the tray of dishes away, washed them and returned to the room. In the far corner stood an ornately carved rocker that she pulled close to the bed. She sat down, apparently content to chat for a while.

In answer to my question, she explained that Lawrence was her married name; her maiden name was Carrington. She had been born in Exeter, in southwest England. Her father was a solicitor and it was through his business acquaintances that she had met Oliver, her husband. He was an enterprising man with itchy feet and an adventurer's heart, and it was his idea to come to South Africa to carve out a new life: buy a farm, breed sheep and raise children. She and Oliver had done all right until the war came along. The British army had requisitioned much of their stock, leaving only a few sheep and a milk cow, and they'd yet to see any money for it. Local blacks sometimes stole the animals for food. Without help or a dog, it was almost impossible to keep an eye on them. She had spent much of her time alone, except when her neighbour, Daphne, whose husband had also gone off to join the fight, and Daphne's daughter, Elspeth, came to visit. They had been on the way to Exeter Farm when the Boer soldiers had commandeered their wagon, and they hadn't been in the house more than a few minutes when we rode in. The Boers sent the women out as bait, keeping Ellie as hostage. They said that all they wanted was our uniforms and they'd be on their way.

"I've never faced such a dilemma in my life." Her eyes glistened with tears. "I didn't know whether to believe them or not. They seemed so utterly desperate. I offered them all of Oliver's clothing and all the food they wanted but they were determined to have your uniforms. I don't know what I would have done if they had shot you in cold blood but they threatened to kill us if we didn't co-operate. They said they would have their guns trained on us all the time. I was petrified." She smiled ruefully. A slight overbite lent an alluring fullness to her mouth. "That was either a very brave thing you did out there or very foolish. I haven't quite decided yet."

"I wish I could say that I coolly worked the whole thing out before I acted but it was really pure instinct. I suppose I'd heard too many horror stories about what Boers do to their prisoners, but I could have gotten all of us killed and I'm sorry. I'm thankful it worked out for the best."

"Oh, dear," she said, alarmed. "It wasn't my intention to make you regret your actions and I do apologize if I've done so. I'm very grateful that you acted—period. So are Daphne and Ellie, by the way. They had to get back to their farm but they asked me to thank you before they left. A lot of men might not have done anything."

She left to do some chores and returned with a lunch of lamb stew and bread. I didn't want her to leave again, so I asked her more about herself. "Do you have children? I haven't seen any about."

She sighed. "No. And I can't say that I'm too disappointed, given this awful war. This country is no place for children these days. Indeed, it doesn't seem to be much of a place for anybody except soldiers. It has changed so much since the war began. Irrevocably, I sometimes think."

The war was not only making enemies of some of their neighbours, it had taken her husband, who was involved in the hunt for Louis Botha, the Boer general. It had also drained what little black hired help they had and then, as if that weren't enough, her dog had died and left her feeling even more vulnerable.

"I know it sounds disloyal, but sometimes I think we British want everything, that there is no end to our greed."

"It seems to me that it was the Boers who started the war."

"If they hadn't started it Britain would have. There was too much at stake not to. I won't deny that the Boers are an intransigent people but the only thing our neighbours ever wanted was peace and to be left alone. It's all Oliver and I ever wanted, too."

"And yet Oliver went off to fight."

"General Buller is also from Exeter, so how could he not? Besides, he really had no say in the matter. You're on either one side or the other here—there's no in-between. I don't blame the Boers in the Free State and the Transvaal for being so protective of what they've got. They went north hoping to be rid of us British and our liberal ways but we keep returning like their worst nightmare. Then men like you come here without really knowing what the war is all about beyond some vague notion that the Empire is threatened or that it's a not-to-be-missed opportunity for personal glory." She paused. "I'm sorry. That sounds very accusatory. I didn't mean you personally, but sometimes the whole mess makes me very angry."

"That's all right," I said. She had spoken with such a complete lack of malice that I did not feel offended.

She went on to explain that after the Boers had trekked north and defined their territories, an extraordinary stroke of good luck turned into their greatest misfortune. The upside was that the Transvaal was rich with gold and diamonds, richer than any place in the world; the downside was that the British wanted it. To go after it they used the disenfranchised uitlanders as an excuse for war.

Naturally, I hadn't heard many positive things about the Boers, but the worst was that they were slavers and had left the

Cape only because the British abolished slavery, which meant the Boers would lose their cheap labour. I mentioned this to Ree. "It seems to me they're a little slow in catching up with the rest of the world. Even the United States has been without slavery for nearly 40 years and they were considered slow. I'm amazed you have any sympathy for them at all."

She shrugged. "We all have to find our way in the world, Jack, and the Boers use the bible as a guide. It says that the fate of the descendants of Ham's black children is to remain hewers of wood and drawers of water forevermore. Slavery to them is not a business; it's part of the natural order of things, a right granted by God to whites. Did you know that they call giraffes camels because giraffes aren't mentioned anywhere in the bible? And when Mr. Joshua Slocum and the *Spray* sailed into Cape Town not long ago, claiming that he was circumnavigating the globe, the Boers scoffed at him. The Earth wasn't a globe, it was flat. I mention these things not to justify their behaviour but to explain it. They have their faults as we all do but they're a decent people—hardworking, reliable and loyal. One could do worse than to have a Boer as a neighbour. Heaven knows they've helped us when we needed it."

We talked for most of the afternoon, between small absences for chores Ree had to do. She was baking bread, too, if the smell filling the bedroom was any indication. Dinner was more lamb stew and more bread, for which she apologized. "Lamb stew is a bit of a staple these days. And the rains have played havoc with my garden, so I have to rely on the root cellar for vegetables that aren't very fresh."

The bread was not long out of the oven and she had slathered it with home-churned butter. The stew was hot, meaty and delicious, far superior to army food, and I told her so.

"How very kind of you." The compliment clearly pleased her.

"This proves beyond a doubt that the ingredients are only half as important as the person who puts them together." I held up the bread. "Especially this. It's a slice of heaven."

She remained quiet while I ate but after I had finished, she said, "Perhaps I should leave so that you can rest."

I was tired but I did not want her to go. There are some people in whose presence you feel instantly at ease, as if you'd been friends for a long time. That's how I felt with Ree and I could tell that she felt the same way with me. She appeared relaxed and happy to have male company, even if I was an invalid, and I was more than happy to be with her. "Please stay," I said. "You've no idea what a pleasure it is to be in the company of a woman again, not to mention being in a real bed, without the smell of wet canvas and everything being damp."

"As you wish. Just give me a few moments to wash the dishes and make sure the guards don't need anything."

She was a vivacious woman, in her late 20s or early 30s, with a long, fine nose and a sweet, full mouth. And while the gingham dress she wore did not accentuate her figure, it did not hide its loveliness. Her chestnut hair gleamed in the light. She had it piled on top of her head and held it there by barrettes and hairpins. There were the beginnings of crow's feet at the corners of her hazel eyes, from many hours squinting in the hot African sun which, at the same time, had lent her skin a glow. She was tired from running a farm on her own, never mind having a deadly shootout on her front porch. Still, it was quite amazing how some women can manage to look lovely despite a heavy burden of responsibility. I could hear her in the kitchen, washing the dishes, and was impatient for her return. I doubt that she was gone more than a half-hour but it was still too long for my liking. She poked her head into the room, her smile all the medicine I really needed.

"Would you like tea?"

"I would love a cup. Thank you."

I heard her ask the guards if they would like tea, and fix it for them, then she brought in a small pot on a tray with two cups and filled them with the dark, steaming liquid. Even pouring tea she was graceful. She sat in the rocker and asked how I was feeling, and we made small talk for a while, sharing snippets of our lives. She was curious about Canada and wondered what it was like, for she and her husband had contemplated emigrating there. I described its beauty and vastness as best I could, then slowly, as often happens when strange or dangerous circumstances bring people together in dim lighting, the conversation grew more intimate.

"Tell me, Jack, if you don't mind my asking. What brings you halfway around the world from your home to fight someone else's battles?"

"Many things. Mostly a debt I felt I owed to someone. A sense of duty, too, I suppose. Answering the Empire's call, that sort of thing." I hesitated because I didn't really want to say what was forming in my mind. I thought it would be an admission of weakness and didn't want it held against me. Yet I believed I could trust her. "Sometimes, though, I think that deep inside I felt I had nothing left to lose."

She raised her eyebrows. "Except perhaps your life."

"That wasn't a consideration."

She digested my words. "I'm curious. Is this the sort of life you imagined for yourself as a child?"

"Not especially. I dreamed of being a cowboy and owning a ranch. I got to be a cowboy but I never got around to buying a ranch. Life keeps interfering. One day, though."

I was reluctant to ask her the same question, because it felt too personal for a married woman, but a wish to know outweighed my sense of propriety. "What about you, Ree? Are you living the life you imagined for yourself?"

She smiled wryly. "This is too hard a life for anyone to imagine and I doubt I would have chosen it if it had been solely my decision. Now it's not only hard, it's lonely. I find myself talking to the chickens. I've even given them names, which I don't think is a good idea if you plan on eating them one day!" She paused and gave a small, half-embarrassed laugh. "During my toughest moments I sometimes imagine a knight on a white charger coming to rescue me from all this. But in the end, there are no knights on chargers. It's up to us to save ourselves."

It was such an intimate detail to divulge that I wondered if she was happy in her marriage to Oliver. Perhaps I was reading too much into it and it was simply the thinking of a woman who had spent too much time alone. Whatever the case, I was pleased that she felt she could trust me as I had trusted her. We sat in silence for a while, listening to the house let go of the warmth of the day. Then she spoke again.

"You said, Jack, that you may have joined this war because you had nothing left to lose. That must mean you have lost everything already. I don't wish to pry but is it something you want to talk about?"

No, it wasn't something I wanted to talk about. In fact, I had never mentioned it to anybody, not even Jim. And yet, I found myself thinking that maybe I could to Ree. I pondered it for a long moment. The silence dragged. Then I surprised myself by saying, "Yes. I do." And I told her about Charity and Becky and that horrible day on the bridge. It tumbled out of me and I did not stop until I had told her everything.

AFTER THE funeral I could not stay in my house any longer. It seemed such a desolate place that I moved in with Joe Fortes. I offered to sign the deed over to Alex McRae who would not hear of it.

"Nonsense, Jack," he said. "It's your house to do with what you will. By all means, sell it if it will bring you solace."

I still didn't think it was mine to sell but had not the heart to argue. The only thing that would bring me solace was not possible. I was burdened with guilt; I was lethargic and unable to motivate myself to do anything. I returned to work but it was meaningless. Every morning I awoke in a dismal space in my mind, and every night when I went to bed, I prayed that the morning would be different. It never was.

I spent far too much of my free time at the cemetery, sitting between the two monuments, asking why the lives of such beautiful creatures had been snuffed out in such an ugly fashion. Why they were snuffed out at all. I did not put the question to any god. No god that I could imagine would have done such a thing. Yet I envied those people whose faith was so strong that they could find a reason for everything that happened, who could say with utter conviction, "It was God's will." To me it was life at its most insane, and the ostensible randomness of the accident plagued me daily.

Nightmares haunted my sleep. I would be back in that cold, dark water and invariably Charity and Becky would be within my grasp. But there were so many pairs of hands reaching out that I did not know which ones to grab. In my confusion and indecision, they began drifting out of reach, their eyes begging me to save them. I would try to swim after them, but my arms and legs would turn as heavy as bridge timbers, impossible to move. As my loved ones floated off into the darkness, I cried. I could feel tears rolling down my cheeks, distinct from the sea water. The frustration of it and the subsequent sorrow and profound guilt that coursed through me when I awakened tore at me like a hungry beast. My life became an endless litany of "if onlys": If only I hadn't taken my family to Victoria; if only I hadn't persuaded them to come to the parade; if only I had stayed on the prairies; if only, if only, if only.

Joe told me, "It's better that you pull yourself together, Jack, and not tear yourself apart. There's always someone willin' do that without you helpin' them."

Yet I scarcely felt capable.

What I needed most was a change of scenery—to escape from the mill, from the cemetery and from Vancouver. I considered taking a long vacation to a warmer climate, or a sea journey, for I could well afford it, but feared there would be too much inactivity, too much time to think. I could also carry on with the plan of buying a small ranch in the foothills but the idea was less attractive without Charity and Becky.

I had to tell McRae that I was quitting the mill and leaving town. At work I said, "Alex, I need to talk to you and Eleanor. Would you mind if I stopped by the house tonight?"

It was clear that my father-in-law wanted to ask what it was about, but he replied only, "By all means, Jack. Why don't you come for supper? I'll let Eleanor know."

During a dinner of roast pork and sweet potatoes, we chatted about everything except the reason for my visit. McRae, who usually moved directly to the point, did not seem anxious to reach it, and Eleanor apparently did not feel it was her place to broach the subject. We did not speak about Charity or Becky; their absence from the table said enough. After we finished eating, McRae and I retired to the parlour with brandies while Eleanor tidied up and Charity's brothers went off to their rooms.

"What's on your mind, Jack?" McRae asked, as we sat down.

I came straight out with it. "I'm leaving, Alex. I can't live here without Charity and Becky. I feel like I'm digging myself into a hole that gets deeper and deeper and if I don't leave now I won't ever be able to climb out. I hope you and Eleanor understand."

McRae gave a slight nod of his head. "We suspected as much. Can I ask where it is you are going?"

"Alberta. The foothills, I think. Maybe find a job on a ranch and learn a bit about the business. Maybe I'll have a ranch of my own some day."

"Yes. I believe you've mentioned that a time or two. I confess I didn't lend it much credence."

I almost mentioned that Charity and I had all but finalized our plan to buy a ranch out there but held my tongue: the revelation might only be hurtful. Instead, I said, "It might not do me wonders but it's not likely to do me any harm, either."

"Do you know what you're giving up, Jack? I shouldn't need to tell you that there's a great future for you here and that you've already invested a lot of time and effort working toward it. It would be a shame to have it go for naught."

"I know what I've lost, Alex, and at this point in my life that's what's moving me. Maybe a change of scenery will help me get around it. I don't know. What I do know is that I've got to go before the ghosts around here drive me crazier than I already feel."

"I see. Well, as long as I am the manager, there will always be a job at the mill for you, if you're ever in need of one."

"Thank you, Alex. I truly appreciate your helpfulness. Not only now but over the years." I managed a weak smile. "We got off to a rough start that was entirely my fault but you turned out to be more of a father to me than my own father ever was. Thank you for that, too."

McRae remained silent for a moment. "Eleanor is going to be disappointed. I know I am. It won't be easy losing another family member." He sighed and stroked his beard. "We'll adapt, I suppose. We always seem to. Well, I'll have your pay ready first thing tomorrow morning."

"Thank you. There's not a second goes by that I don't wish things had turned out differently. Every time I think of it, I try to force my way back in time, to before the accident, where I can make the decision to *not* get on that streetcar." I paused, unsure that I should continue. "Charity didn't want to go that day, you know, because Becky wasn't feeling well. She wanted to stay at the hotel but I talked them into the streetcar ride."

McRae took a sip of brandy and crossed his legs. "You shouldn't blame yourself for any part of that, Jack. After all, if you are to blame for them getting on that trolley, then Eleanor and I have to accept blame for allowing you and Charity to marry. Then where does it stop? Shall we blame our ancestors for bringing us into the world to experience this suffering? I think not. If you want to blame somebody, blame the City of Victoria and their decision to send an over-crowded streetcar across a rotten bridge."

There was a tone of scolding parent in his voice, which may very well have been appropriate. I understood the point, though, and said so. What I didn't say was how hard it was to believe, and that I wondered if I ever would.

When Eleanor joined us and was informed of my intentions, she nodded almost imperceptibly. "Oh, my," she said quietly, resigned to the further unravelling of everything she held dear.

The air was heavy with sorrow and McRae changed the subject.

"Have you sold the house yet?"

I was hoping that question wouldn't arise, for I hadn't and wasn't about to. I had already been to a notary and had the deed signed over to the McRaes, with the promise that it would be sent to them once I was gone.

"Not yet," I lied. "But things are progressing nicely."

"Ah. Well, if I can be of any help, let me know."

"I will." To my relief, McRae didn't pursue the matter.

The McRaes walked out onto the front porch with me to say goodbye. In the stillness of a warm August night, the muffled noise of machinery came from the direction of the mill and the smell of sawdust permeated the air. It was so different from where I was going I ached to be there as soon as possible. With emotion she had never shown before, Eleanor hugged me, tightly, as if a part of Charity had somehow rubbed off on me. For a while, I didn't think she would let me go. "I do hope you will write, Jack. We'll always want to know how and what you are doing."

All I could say was yes, because that's what she wanted to hear. But I wasn't entirely convinced that I would follow through on it. Writing letters had never been my strong suit.

Instead of shaking my hand, Alex took it between both of his and squeezed hard. "If the opportunity doesn't arise at the mill, I'll say this now. Go well, son."

Son. The word caused a huge lump to form in my throat. No one had ever called me that, not even my own father, and I wondered why I was leaving a world that had demanded all of my resources to enter. Its power pulled at me as I stepped off the porch, but I did not turn back.

In Calgary, the change in physical landscape did little for my mental landscape. While one held broad vistas and a limitless horizon, the other was hemmed in by mountains that were images of Charity and Becky, my mother and even my father. The mere thought of making the first step to put my life in order was overwhelming and I mistakenly believed that whisky might be the catalyst I needed. I soon found myself in a hole that was deeper than the one I'd dug in Vancouver.

REE LISTENED intently. When I finished, I could see, even in the lantern light, that she had turned pale. I had not realized that she had leaned forward and taken my hand in hers and I don't think she had either. We became conscious of it at the same time and she quickly let go.

"I'm so sorry, Jack," she almost whispered. "You must really have loved her."

"I did. I do. I guess I always will. She was a wonderful woman, and Becky . . ." I stopped. "I'm sorry. I shouldn't have burdened you with all that."

"No, no. It's quite all right."

Yet I knew that I had touched her in ways she hadn't imagined. She rose from the chair and said tenderly, "I'd best let you rest, Jack. The ambulance will be here in the morning. Can I get you some laudanum to help you sleep?"

"Yes. I think so."

Not only would it help me sleep, I hoped it would end the thoughts I shouldn't be having about a married woman. I didn't know what to make of my feelings but I knew they were more than just proof of the old saw about male patients always falling in love with their nurses. I had an overwhelming desire to take Ree in my arms and feel her close to me. And it wasn't entirely sexual; it was something much deeper than that. I cared for her, as I hadn't cared for a woman since Charity. She stirred something inside me that I assumed had died in the water off Victoria.

Wild dreams plagued my sleep, Ree woven in and out of them, and I awoke in the morning feeling unsettled. The opportunity for another chat never came; indeed, little passed between us beyond pleasantries, which may have been for the best. The ambulance arrived soon after breakfast.

The attendants came in with a canvas stretcher and gave me more laudanum for the move to the train. The road was rough, they said, and all the bouncing around was bound to aggravate my wound. Despite the precaution, I couldn't ignore the pain completely and grunted even as they lifted me onto the stretcher and carried me outside to the ambulance, a mere wagon with a canvas cover stretched tautly over a rectangular frame and a red cross emblazoned on each side. Two very patient mules stood in front it. I heard Ree say to the attendants, "May I say goodbye to Sergeant Strong before you leave?"

"Yes, ma'am," one of them replied. "But you'll need to hurry. We have a train to meet."

They helped her onto the step-up and into the wagon. She knelt by my side, a soft look on her face. Rain began to pelt the canvas roof. Taking my hands in hers she said, "I'm sure they'll give you the best of care at the Cape, Jack. You've been a most congenial guest. Till I see you, then."

I gave her hand a squeeze. It was warm and moist. "I can't wait," I smiled. "Thank you for your kindness, Ree. I won't forget it. Or you, for that matter."

I could see in her eyes that there were words that could not pass her lips, just as there were words that could not pass mine. We were too late. She climbed down from the wagon and stood there in the rain, unmoving, arms folded in front of her. The ambulance driver snapped the reins and urged the mules into motion. We started with a jerk and swayed out the gate and I watched her until we rounded a bend and I could no longer see her.

SEVENTEEN

Turnaround

FOR MUCH OF THE train ride to the Cape my thoughts fluctuated between Ree and the Boer I had killed on her front porch. I had shot at other people before, faceless people from a distance, at Loon Lake as well as in South Africa, but had never really known if I'd hit anybody and had never seen the results if I had. But I'd seen my bullets hit the Boer, snatching his life from him, and I found no gratification in it whatsoever, even though he was the enemy and would have shot me in a trice if he'd had the chance. I sensed a crack in my humanity and was glad that my part in the war was over.

The hospital in Cape Town was a horrific place and almost made me wish I were in the field again. The true carnage of war was on display: men with holes ripped through their bodies, men with limbs blown off, men turned blind or deaf and were struck dumb and men in an appalling state of shock. The only thing that made it tolerable was the nurses in their starched uniforms who cared for their charges with loving efficiency.

I was one of the lucky ones. I was healthy compared to most of the others, which left me lots of time to think, and Ree dominated practically all of my waking hours. I had concluded, rightly or wrongly, that she was unhappy in her marriage, and I saw myself returning to Exeter Farm, the white knight come to save her from an unfulfilled life. What kept me from actually doing it was the knowledge that if something like that had happened with Charity, I would have been devastated, and I couldn't see how it would be any different for Oliver. According to Ree, he was a decent, caring sort who treated her with respect. Had their situation been different I might have felt justified in requesting my discharge in Cape Town and taking the first train north.

I suppose I could have gone to speak with her but it seemed such a presumptuous notion. What if the feelings I perceived in her were nothing more than those of a lonely, frightened woman in need of a man's company? I might create an awfully awkward situation for both of us. Still, it did not prevent the fleeting, selfish image of an 11th-hour telegram arriving from Ree, informing me that Oliver had managed to get himself killed.

I stayed in the hospital less than three weeks and was released right before Christmas to make room for more wounded and maimed. I was temporarily bivouacked at Green Point with other Canadian soldiers awaiting repatriation. Christmas packages came from home for the lucky ones, although some gifts, such as woollen mittens and knitted scarves, were obviously from senders who either forgot or didn't know that South Africa was in the midst of summer and the weather was sweltering.

It was a lonely time for me, surrounded by people I had no desire to be with and who no doubt had less desire to be with me, for I was not agreeable company. I was never very sociable at the best of times and these were far from that.

I ventured downtown only for reading material at a bookshop in Adderley Street and to watch the New Year festivities. Native troupes, all men, paraded down the streets, dressed in gaudy uniforms, playing banjos, guitars, violins and tambourines. Drum majors led them, the men sometimes marching like soldiers, sometimes dancing and singing. Banners attached to staffs advertised each troupe's name, such as "Cherry Pickers" or "Diamond Eyes," but a few honoured the freed slaves in America and called themselves "Mississippi Darkies" or "Alabama Coons." The celebrations went on for days until the participants grew weary of the fun and simply stopped showing up.

Meanwhile, there was much talk around the camp about the formation of a South African police force. Indeed, Steele himself would eventually accept an appointment as a full colonel in the force once his duties as the Horse's commander were behind him. Lord Baden-Powell would be the commanding officer and its official name would be the South African Constabulary. It was to act as a permanent British garrison whose long-term function was to police the Boer and native populations, in case they failed to recognize the end of the war when it finally came. The force wanted volunteers and the word was that any man from the Horse would be given special consideration and a promotion to boot. The idea of staying in Africa and possibly seeing Ree again was tantalizing and I was almost ready to volunteer. But it would have been for the wrong reasons. In the end, I decided that going home, far from temptation, was the wisest thing to do. I was also tired of being a soldier, always at someone else's beck and call, and tired of war.

In January, the Horse returned to Cape Town. The war was over for them now, too. They had chased De Wet in circles and would have caught him but for the incompetence of some of Steele's British superior officers. In fact, they never caught the Boer general and he ultimately attended the signing of the peace treaty a year and half later, when hostilities ended.

Steele fully expected that the men would get drunk and end up in trouble. It was what most of the regiments preceding them had done and was quite understandable: after months of deprivation in the field, most believed they had earned a drunk-up. Nevertheless, Steele wanted to avoid any possibility of an ignominious ending so instead he marched the Horse in the broiling heat directly from the train to the ship and sequestered them there for a day and a half prior to sailing. The rabble-rousers of the regiment groused loudly but the rest of the men were content to be taking one more step toward home.

I was already on the ship, having boarded first with the other wounded. I had heard that the regiment had suffered no more casualties, which meant that Jim was all right. I was keen for his company again and I stood at the rail until I caught sight of him in the crowd of soldiers ascending the gangway.

"Jack!" he shouted when he saw me, and waved. Despite the smile, he looked quite worn out.

The ship was purposely free of alcohol—for the men, that is, not the officers—but Jim had managed to purchase a bottle of whisky from a bootlegger in one of the train stations where they had stopped to stretch their legs during the trip south. He claimed that he had our reunion in mind when he bought it, hoping that I'd not already gone home. While we waited for the ship to leave we found a dim corner in the men's quarters in the forward hold and passed the bottle back and forth, sweating profusely in the stifling heat. The liquor went down like fire and brought on more sweat but it drained the tension lodged in my gut. We didn't have to worry about officers: non-coms ruled here. Besides, we weren't the only ones with a secret stash and as long as no one caused any fuss, the officers were content to ignore it.

Jim spoke of the futility of chasing De Wet with the British cavalry, a couple of hundred miles back north again, through heavy rain, along muddy roads and across swollen rivers, all of it a colossal waste of time and human lives.

"We ran out of everythin'. Didn't have a pot to piss in. On our second-to-last day in the field, the Brits lost 17 men to Boer snipers. That was in less than an hour. Seventeen fuckin' men, Jack, who were thinkin' of goin' home! The best thing I can say is that it was none of the Horse. We had no choice but to retreat, but the bastards followed us for three days, snipin' at us every step of the way. They had us on the run and must have thought they were winnin' the war.

The Horse rode rearguard, so we were knee deep in it 'til the end. How we never lost anybody, I don't know. In fact, it's a bloody miracle. Jesus, I can't tell you how good it felt when Steele told us we were goin' home! I could have kissed the ugly bugger."

He admitted to being exhausted and grateful that the ordeal was over, to have survived it and to be going home to Maggie with all of his body parts intact. Especially the one they would need most to raise a family. The first thing he was going to do on his return to Ottawa was ask for her hand in marriage.

"How're you doin', Jack? Shit, I should've asked before I got so caught up in myself."

"Don't fret about it. I'm all healed. And while you were out there trying to get yourself killed, I was enjoying myself here in Cape Town." Since he didn't ask, I didn't tell him about Ree. He might have offered advice that I didn't need to hear.

"You deserved it, Jack, after what you did. Man, that was somethin'! You're getting a medal for it, you know."

"Yeah. That's what Steele said. But I don't care. I'm only glad I didn't get us killed."

Jim swatted me on the shoulder to show his appreciation, the painful impact of the blow lessened substantially by the whisky. We talked more about the war, getting drunker with each drink. Inevitably, we talked about going home because now it was about to happen.

"We're gonna get that ranch, partner. You and me and Maggie. Hey, you'll be my bess man, eh?" The whisky was taking its toll on his speech.

"You're damned straight I will." The reply demanded my full concentration in order to say it right. But I meant it, drunk or sober.

He turned maudlin. "I might not be seein' Maggie again if it weren't for you, Jack. I owe you."

"You owe me? Weren't you the guy that pulled me out of that bog in the Yukon and saved my skin at the farmhouse? But then you're bigger 'n me and needed more saving than I did. Oh, sing a song or two and we'll call it square."

He broke out into Stephen Foster's "Beautiful Dreamer," which nearly reduced me to tears. I know that music is often used to incite men to war but when Jim sang, it was war's antithesis, full of beauty and grace. He finished off with "The Maple Leaf Forever" and barely got through it. But the quality of his voice still astonished me. Had he wanted, he truly could have made a living on the stage.

After the songs, our stamina, like the bottle, was down to its dregs. We drained both and staggered to our hammocks. Neither of us moved until we fell out at reveille the following morning. I was so hung over I was virtually numb which, in a way, was a blessing because I was barely able to think about what I was leaving behind and in no shape to jump ship if I had been.

As January drew to a close, we sailed from South Africa, leaving Kitchener and his army to deal with the Boers. We were done with the place and few would miss it. Clouds curled down threateningly from the top of Table Mountain but the sky to the northwest was an electric blue and our bow pointed in that direction. The wind was beginning to gain muscle and on the far side of Robben Island, the ship lumbered to starboard in a low ocean swell and set a course for England, rather than Canada.

The destination wasn't everyone's cup of tea. Many wanted to go directly home but Steele was determined to show us off to Queen Victoria and to Lord Strathcona himself. During the 24-day passage, we were issued new uniforms and ordered to cut our hair and shave our beards, so as not to offend Her Majesty's sensibilities.

As it turned out, the queen died while we were at sea. She had been on the throne for nearly two-thirds of the 19th century, had seen her country become an industrial giant and a world power. A world mourned, a country wept and I bribed a steward in the officer's mess for enough rum to get Jim and me drunk again.

Upon our arrival, English newspapers praised the Horse and our commander, renaming us "Fighting Sam and his Headhunters." In London, we lined The Mall, opposite the Coldstream Guards, resplendent in their impressive uniforms and spotless white gloves, while the new king, Edward VII, rode past in his carriage on his way to open Parliament. When ordered to present arms we had been in the field too long and had forgotten the proper way to do it. Some of us merely came to attention, others sloped arms and some did nothing at all. The Coldstream Guards were like a well-oiled machine but they hadn't seen action and we had. It was the Horse that the crowd cheered.

The following day we formed up at Buckingham Palace where we were inspected by the king and more lords than was decent to have in a single place, among them Strathcona and, of course, the diminutive Bobs. Old Reverse, Buller, was there, too, as jowly as ever. All had been grandly paid by their government for their hand in the war, despite their ineptitude and inability to win it. None had the savagery of Kitchener. As for us, the king handed out awards. The entire regiment received the Queen's South Africa Medal, as we had served under Victoria, not Edward. We also received the King's Colours, while Steele accepted the Royal Victorian Order, 4th class. The rest of us would have to wait for our return to Ottawa to receive any other medals. After several verbal pats on the back, they let us loose on the town.

Steele warned us to behave ourselves, to do nothing that would tarnish our stellar reputation, but it was an order almost everyone ignored. We were heroes in London and there wasn't much we could do, short of murder, to diminish that status. Everywhere we went there were free drinks and we took full advantage of it, some much more than others, and the town turned a blind eye toward our childish misdeeds. Ironically, Steele himself proved to be the worst violator of his own orders, getting blind drunk at a banquet for the officers sponsored by Lord Strathcona. When he went searching for a bathroom, he staggered into the kitchen by mistake, urinated against the stove, then reeled into the banquet room and vomited all over the floor. Strathcona was fuming. He punished Steele by withdrawing a $10,000 bonus for services rendered.

After the open veld, London was a dreary place—its trees naked, its air bad enough to make my eyes itch and its streets jammed with cacophonous, iron-tired vehicles and solemn people. I was glad to leave it. Word of Steele's punishment filtered down to the men and we gave him a thunderous ovation when he showed up at the Liverpool docks prior to our departure. It wasn't money but I believe it meant nearly as much to him. We sailed from Liverpool near the end of February and thousands of appreciative citizens came to bid us farewell, waving white handkerchiefs and hats while a band played "Auld Lang Syne."

The Atlantic Ocean, when we reached it, was wild and storm-tossed, and we spent most of the two-week journey confined to the hold, the seas being far too rough to allow any of us on deck. Just as when we left Canadian shores a long year before, the stench of vomit and diarrhea below decks was appalling. A rogue wave tore off half of the ship's propeller and swept two of her crew overboard. There was much consternation on Steele's part as well as many of the men that we'd never see home again, that the sea would do to us what the war hadn't. We had given many a cheer over the past year but none as hearty as the one we gave after sighting the lights of Halifax, six days overdue.

Steele officially disbanded the regiment in Halifax, rather than Ottawa, for two reasons. First, because the ship was late the expiry date of our contracts was rapidly approaching, and second, the Exhibition Buildings in Ottawa, the site of our planned medal ceremony, were now a recruitment and training centre for the South African Constabulary. So they held a hurriedly arranged celebration in the Halifax drill hall. Medals were distributed and Jim and I each received the Distinguished Conduct Medal for trying to save Rollins's life. Added to mine was a silver bar with laurel, for my crazy actions at Exeter Farm. Even better, in addition to his pay, each man received a $194 bonus and a train ticket to anywhere in Canada, with a two-month stopover privilege. Steele's parting advice was, "Boys, never forget that you are Canadians and that Canada, as a country, has no superior in the wide world. Be proud of being Canadian!"

Jim and I caught the first train for Ottawa and I stayed to be best man at his and Maggie's wedding and to see them off to Niagara Falls on their honeymoon. Newspapers often describe brides as being "radiant" and Maggie was a perfect example. She radiated happiness and beauty, and all those things that I had seen combined in a woman only once before. Jim was as proud as I'd ever seen him.

He cornered me before their departure. "Jack," he said earnestly. "Let's meet in Calgary. You may get there before us, so if you do, have a look around. See if you can find somethin'. What's good enough for you is good enough for me, you know that." He stuck out his hand and I took it. "Thick or thin, partner."

"Thick or thin," I agreed.

But the truth was I didn't know what to do. After the train left, I wandered around town for a while, at loose ends. Nothing out west stirred my blood; it was Ree I wanted to see. I figured that I had performed one of the dumbest stunts on the planet by falling in love with a woman who not only lived nearly 8,000 miles away, but was married as well. *Put her out of your mind*, I thought. *You've got a free ride west. Go there without further delay and find that ranch that you and Jim always wanted.* Yet I found myself walking along the banks of the Rideau Canal, drawn toward the Exhibition Buildings, the octagonal roof of the pavilion standing high above the rest, acting as a beacon. I stood outside the entrance to the grounds for the longest time, watching people come and go, some in uniform, others not. Then, because Jim was not around to call me a crazy bloody fool and forcibly pin me to the ground, I went in and offered a year of my life to the South African Constabulary.

EIGHTEEN

The Search

IF I ASKED MYSELF once, I asked a dozen times—why, when I could have well afforded steerage on a liner to Cape Town and gone there as a civilian, I submitted myself to a year of misery with the constabulary. I rationalized that it was because the recruiters were handing out the cash for the voyage and that I might as well take advantage of it; British law did not allow men to enlist outside the country where they were to serve, so suitable men were simply handed passage money to South Africa and trusted to enlist when they got there. The heart of the matter, though, was that it delayed something that, deep inside, I was afraid to do. It was a bit of a coward's way of doing things but there you have it.

My unit's field of operation was in the Free State, about 120 miles from Exeter Farm. By the time I reached Bloemfontein, the operational headquarters, the entire countryside within a 50-mile radius was held by the British and free of recalcitrant Boers. But Kitchener wanted to expand the area so our initial objective was to push west, scorch the land and gain control by establishing posts and clearing out several troublesome roving commandos, some of which numbered more than 300 men. Once we were in control, the endless patrols began: stumbling out of bed long before dawn, in the freezing cold, and riding into the searing heat of the afternoon or a deluge of rain, and sometimes both. The days were long, wearing and mostly boring, the monotony relieved only by brief but fierce encounters with the enemy. I gritted my teeth, did my duty and waited impatiently for the year to move full circle.

In the end, it was a numbers game and our numbers were greater than the Boers. They sued for peace in April of 1902, just as my contract ended, and surrendered in May. It had been a prodigal war, as wars often are, and cost the British more than £200,000,000, not including the millions spent to repair all the damage done to the farms. There were more than 100,000 casualties and the South African veld was the final resting place for many of them. The Boers lost thousands, too, not to mention the additional thousands of innocent civilians who died in British concentration camps, and the losses among the black volunteers on both sides. Then there were the half-million horses, mules and donkeys sacrificed for the cause.

I took my discharge in the capital of the Free State rather than Cape Town, my port of entry into South Africa, an arrangement that suited everyone fine. I had 60 days to take advantage of my free return passage to Canada, but that was of little concern to me.

Bloemfontein's wide streets, fine sandstone buildings, lovely parks and trees made it an easy place in which to drag my heels, which is precisely what I did. Now that I was free to go see Ree, I could not seem to act on it, even though I'd had more than a year to think of what I would say once I got there. I believed I was being selfish and, if Oliver had returned safely from the war, I would only be creating an awkward situation for her, particularly if I was right about her feelings toward me, that she wasn't only satisfying a woman's nurturing instinct. I hung around for several days before I found the courage to board the southbound train, and even then, it wasn't with an overabundance of conviction.

I disembarked at the first stop inside Cape Colony and the nearest to Exeter Farm. Norvals Pont was a busy place, filled with soldiers and concentration camp prisoners, mostly women and children, being dispersed to their homes or what was left of them. (The camps were the brainchild of Kitchener, a man who would weep over the death of an animal, yet cast a cold eye on the death of a soldier, and starving women and children.) At the local stable, I paid a premium price for a horse too old for military duty and too ornery for the average rider, then set out on the rutted wagon road that I was told would eventually join the track Jim and I had followed more than a year before. The horse, a big brown gelding that stood 16 hands, was skittish despite lacking some nether parts and took time to settle into the journey. But all animals have an innate need to know who is in charge and once he understood that it was the rider, his rebelliousness diminished. He definitely deserved his name, though, which was Skelm, a Boer word for "rascal."

Winter was approaching on the veld and the grass was dry, brittle and yellow; only along the river that sliced through the broad valley was there any greenery. The flat-topped hills angling off to the south looked as if an obsessively neat giant had come along with a scythe and sliced off their tops at precisely the same height above ground. When I neared the third one, I knew I was approaching Exeter Farm and was nervous enough to contemplate turning back. One part of me believed that I was a fool but the other drove me forward.

My first view of the farm evoked a jumble of memories that vanished with the first indication that things were not as they should be. The sign at the entrance was gone. It was about 150 yards to the house but even from that distance there was a sense of abandonment to it. There were no animals about, no sound of chickens clucking. I didn't know what to make of it. I had imagined all kinds of scenarios except this one and it took me completely by surprise.

I tied Skelm to a hitching post and walked around the house, peering in through the uncurtained windows. Most of the furniture remained but the beds in the main bedroom and the room where I had stayed had been stripped. I wracked my brain trying to remember the name of the woman who had been with Ree when Jim and I rode up. If she was still in the area, she would most likely have the information I needed. The name Daphne emerged and the more I tossed that around in my mind, the more convinced I became that it was right. And since I hadn't passed their farm on the way here, they must be farther along the river. I climbed on Skelm and coaxed him into reluctant motion, and a half-hour later struck pay dirt.

In the yard in front of the first farmhouse I came to was a young girl who might be Daphne's daughter, for she reminded me of her mother. I smiled and waved at her and she responded with a tentative wave. Then her mouth dropped open and she turned and hurried into the house. Had she recognized me? I reined Skelm to a halt and dismounted when a man came out, short and compact with a full black beard. He had a similarly broad face and walked with a limp. Behind him were Daphne and the girl.

"My heavens!" Daphne cried. "It's Sergeant Strong!" To her husband she said, "Reggie, this is the man who saved our lives at the Lawrence farm and got shot for his troubles!"

The man smiled and stuck out his hand. "A pleasure to meet you, sir! Daphne has spoken of you many times. I'm Reg Davis."

His grip was strong, his hand calloused. "Glad to meet you," I said. "Please, call me Jack."

"Indeed, it would be our pleasure," Reg said. "Let's get your horse tended to and then you must come in and rest a while."

While I led Skelm to a water trough, Reg fetched some oats. Then I was ushered into the house, to a cosy living room. A spinet sat in one corner and I thought of burning houses. They bade me sit down and Reg and I made small talk until Daphne brought tea from the kitchen while her daughter, Elspeth, followed with a plate of bread and jam. Once they had taken seats, I resorted to my white lie as my reason for being there, that since I was in the area with the constabulary I decided I should stop by and thank Ree for tending my wounds.

"Ree sold the farm," Daphne told me. "Poor thing. The ambulance had barely whisked you off when she received word that Oliver had died in the Transvaal. What a pity!"

"Yes," I said. "I'm so sorry to hear that. She must have been devastated."

The news of Oliver's death unsettled me. I had all but wished for it and the only thing that saved me from crushing guilt was the fact that he was already dead when I had done so.

"She had a horrid time. He dodged bullets for so long only to die from the fever just weeks before his release. He's buried in a churchyard in a small village north of Pretoria. Ree could not obtain permission to visit him, of course, because it was too dangerous. She wasn't at all happy about that. They were doing so well with the farm, too. She tried her best to stay on but her heart wasn't in it."

Reg interjected. "The damned Kaffirs weren't much help, either."

"She lasted about two months," Daphne continued. "She said that some friends of the family in England were interested in buying her out but not until they were certain the war was over. In the meantime, she was going to find work in Cape Town to tide her over until the sale was finalized. We bought what little livestock she had left."

"Was she planning on returning to England?"

"She didn't say so if she was, which I found odd. I couldn't see any reason why she would want to stay in Cape Town and I never asked. I didn't feel it was my business."

But I could see a light come on behind Daphne's eyes, as if she had connected the dots, though she was diplomatic enough not to say anything. Meanwhile, my heart was doing funny things in my chest. Ree must have arrived in Cape Town around the time I was leaving and she was probably there when I returned with the constabulary. "Has she kept in touch at all?"

"Only one letter. She said that the prospects for work in Cape Town were favourable and she hoped to secure something soon. I responded but I've yet to hear from her again. It's entirely possible that she didn't receive my reply. Perhaps something even worse, I fear."

"What's that?" Her tone alarmed me.

"The bubonic plague swept through Cape Town last year."

I'd heard about that in the Bloemfontein area but never gave it much thought. Knowing that Ree was there put an entirely new slant on it and made me anxious. I asked, "Do you still have her letter?"

"I believe so." Daphne turned to her daughter. "Ellie, be a good girl and run and check the box in the bottom drawer of my bureau and see if you can find Ree's letter."

The girl went off, returning a few moments later with an opened envelope that she handed to her mother. Daphne removed the letter, a single sheet of paper, and unfolded it.

"You are welcome to read it, if you like." She offered it to me.

"Thank you."

The sentences ran straight across the unlined page in neat and precise handwriting, which seemed to reflect Ree's uncluttered mind. It did not contain anything more than what Daphne had already told me. I reread it and found nothing between the lines but at the top of the page was her return address. I burned it into my memory before handing the letter back.

I wanted to leave but felt it would be bad form to rush off. We chatted about the war for a while, Reg and I avoiding our personal roles in it. He might have joined the constabulary had it not been for his leg, he said, but then again, Daphne and Elspeth needed him more than the country did. He offered a snifter of brandy, which I gratefully accepted. I wanted something to steady my thoughts, which were racing a mile a minute. Daphne invited me to stay for dinner and overnight but I wanted to be alone to digest the information whirling around in my mind. I declined, thanking her for the kind offer and the hospitality. She and Reg were clearly disappointed.

I tried not to hurry as I took my leave. Outside, Reg thanked me again for what I had done at Exeter Farm and insisted that I was welcome in their home at any time. Daphne echoed his sentiments.

"It's generous of you," I said. "Thank you." I pretended to be nonchalant but I really wanted to get to Cape Town. I had a sinking feeling that I was already too late.

We shook hands goodbye, Daphne grasping my hand with both of hers.

"Goodbye!" Elspeth said. "Thank you!"

I mounted Skelm and despite his protests spurred him out the gate toward Norvals Pont. Once on the road he set a good pace without any further prompting. He might not have been able to smell the stable from that distance but he knew we were heading in the right direction.

The stable owner seemed crestfallen that I had returned so soon and surprised, if not disappointed, that I hadn't any bruises or broken bones. I was lucky to get a room at a seedy hotel that offered little more than a roof over my head, and I was at the station the next morning, pacing impatiently while awaiting the train.

We steamed across the parched vastness of the Great Karoo, speeding like the wind among its flat-topped kopjes and down its ancient river valleys, stopping here and there in nondescript towns of dusty buildings with sun-tarnished, corrugated tin roofs and pepper trees that all looked the same after a while. We descended through the twisting mountain passes of the escarpment, where the train doubled back on itself, then emerged in a lowland of peach orchards and grape vines, and soon I could smell the sea. Finally, late in the evening, we rolled into Cape Town itself. I had forgotten how breathtaking its setting was, even at night, nestled at the foot of Table Mountain and stretching around Signal Hill, both black shadows against the starlit night.

I found a modest hotel in St. George's Street, with views of the two landmarks, and stretched out luxuriously on the bed, enjoying not having to sit up in coach class anymore, relishing the peace and quiet of a city nodding off to sleep instead of the constant clickity-clack of steel wheels on steel rails.

I awoke early on the Sunday and after breakfast set out for the address I had memorized from Ree's letter. The desk clerk gave me directions and said it was within walking distance but I was anxious enough to hail a cab.

White cloud covered the top of Table Mountain, spilling over its folded granite sides as a strong wind blew from the south. It was a recurring wind that Cape Towners called the "Cape Doctor," because it carried off all the garbage in the streets; it had done so for years until it occurred to the townsfolk that it might be better for their health if they dealt with the mess themselves. Otherwise, the Cape was enjoying blue skies and much warmer weather than the veld, which was some 5,000 feet higher.

I had only known the town when it was overrun with soldiers and it looked odd with fewer of them about. Buildings of European architecture now provided a background for distinctly African faces, ranging from pitch black through varying shades of brown. And native garb was much more colourful than the khaki that once painted the streets. People were happy that the war was over and it wasn't difficult to find a smile. That too was different.

The sun shone warmly as the hansom cab clattered through town to a residential area and stopped in front of a whitewashed, weather-beaten block of flats. I asked the driver to wait for me, climbed an ornate but worn stoop to the entrance and tried the door. It was locked. I pushed a button on the wall and could hear a faint buzz. A cranky-faced crone answered the door and I asked if she knew Ree. She hesitated for so long that I assumed she was either deaf or so offended by the impertinence of a stranger asking questions that she couldn't speak. But she had only been thinking.

"The young lady who lost her husband," she recalled, wheezing slightly as she breathed.

"Yes. I'm a cousin from Canada," I lied. "I've been up north with the constabulary for the past year and would very much like to contact her."

Mentioning the police force impressed her. "I see. I'm afraid I can't help you. She left six months ago and gave me a forwarding address but I no longer have it. I saw her once at the town market but that was some time ago."

"When? Do you remember?"

"Oh, two, perhaps three months ago."

"Do you have a telephone?"

"I do but it isn't for public use."

"I understand. But could I trouble you to check your telephone book to see if it lists a Rianne Lawrence? I can't tell you how much I would appreciate it."

She nodded brusquely and closed the door in my face. The request was a long shot because Ree had probably not been in her new home long enough to be in the book but it was worth a try. Anything was worth a try. A few moments later, the door swung open.

"There is no such listing, I'm afraid. I took the liberty of calling the exchange but they have no number listed for her either."

That meant Ree didn't have a telephone. Now what? I thanked the old woman for her trouble and left.

The only thing I could think of was to check the records at Government House in the event the plague had claimed her. If her name wasn't there it would eliminate that possibility. And perhaps an ad in the daily paper would bear fruit. But such things would have to wait until the following day when everything reopened. Since there wasn't much else to do, I thought I might as well wander around the town and its environs, and hope that by some miracle I might spot Ree. In order for that to happen, though, she had still to be in Cape Town.

I dismissed the cab and wandered up the hill toward Table Mountain, taking a circuitous route along different side streets, past thatched-roof houses and neat apartments fronted by grand stoops. I wondered if Ree might occupy one of them and harboured silly fantasies of her spotting me from a window. A brand-new Benz automobile passed noisily, its driver wearing a peaked hat and goggles. His bonneted wife sat staidly beside him and two small boys bounced in the rear seat. One of the town's wealthier families out for a Sunday drive, I supposed, showing off their new vehicle. They looked as if they hadn't a care in the world and I envied them.

I found myself in Adderley Street again, unaware of the passage of time until the noon cannon boomed its daily message. The street was much busier now that church was out. Families and couples in their Sunday best climbed into carriages or cabs, or strolled home along the sidewalk. Others boarded trolley cars. Greek fruit purveyors, diminutive Hottentots, colourfully garbed Bantu, and hustling Malaysian fish hawkers with two baskets suspended from a bamboo yoke slung across their shoulders, selling their goods from door to door, added to the general bustle along the street. Twice I saw a woman from behind who could have been Ree and my heart bucked like a wild horse. But both instances were false alarms. That I would find her in this manner in a city of more than 40,000 people was a pipe dream at best, but stranger things had happened.

I covered most of Cape Town on foot and by cab, my search resulting only in sore feet and a lighter wallet, but it was better than sitting around doing nothing. That night I strolled down to the bay and watched the fish boats come in with their day's catch. The air was electric with excitement and expectation. It elevated my spirits to be there amid the optimistic cacophony of bleating fish horns, made from dried kelp, jostled by brightly dressed wives of the Malay fishermen, small boys in fezzes and turbaned priests.

First thing next morning, I went to Government House to check the death records, even though I did not want to believe that someone as vibrant and healthy as Ree could have fallen victim to something as ugly and deadly as the bubonic plague. It was mid-morning before I got the information I wanted and it made me happy enough to forgive the obstinate bureaucrat who obtained it. Ree's name was not among the deceased. He also told me that every city kept a directory of its citizens and their addresses, and Cape Town was no exception. This publication was available at the library. It was a straw worth grasping, so I hurried over there.

The librarian, a bespectacled, grey-haired, scholarly man as thin as a willow branch, was keener to help and obtained the city directory for me. I turned to the *L*'s but found no Lawrence. I even tried her maiden name, Carrington, and while the book contained several listings of that name, none were preceded by *R* or *Rianne*. The librarian informed me that the directory was only as current as the telephone book, as both were published at the same time of year. But the exchange accumulated and updated the information for both publications and perhaps someone there could help.

"Where's the exchange?" I asked.

"Over at the General Post Office."

I did an about turn and made my way to the GPO, which was less than a block from the library. A clerk with roseate cheeks, who peered at me over the top of spectacles that sat on the tip of his nose, guarded the closed door to the exchange room where the operators worked. He said that, yes, they did keep such information but as it was constantly changing, copies were not made available to the public until publication. Moreover, the exchange did not customarily give out addresses over the phone, particularly if the resident did not have a telephone.

"Not customarily" meant I should at least try.

On the far side of the lobby, near the main entrance, were several public phone kiosks, all busy. While I waited in the queue, I asked the woman in front of me what sort of coins I needed to use the phone and dug through my pockets until I found them. When a kiosk came free, I went in and the door closed behind me. I would use the coins to get out, the woman had explained, and that would pay for the call. I cranked a single, long ring and a female voice answered.

"May I have the number you are calling?"

"Yes, well, I'm actually looking for an address and was hoping you could help me."

"I'm sorry, sir. The exchange does not give out addresses."

"I'm trying to find a Mrs. Lawrence," I blurted in desperation. "Rianne Lawrence."

There was a brief pause, then, "May I ask who's calling?"

The question baffled me. I could see no reason why the operator would need to know my name unless she was going to report me for improper use of the telephone, which did not make any sense. I almost hung up but the request was mysterious enough that I complied.

"Jack Strong."

"One moment please."

There was a click at the other end followed by complete silence. Now I was even more mystified. I thought perhaps we'd been disconnected; nonetheless, I waited, feeling silly standing there with a dead instrument held to my ear. Then there was a crackle and I heard a voice I immediately recognized.

"Jack? Dear God, is that you?"

"Ree?" I was stunned. "Where are you?"

"I'm at the telephone exchange. I'm an operator. They told me that someone was trying to find a phone number for me yesterday but they said it was a woman!"

"It was someone trying to help me."

She could tell by her board where I was calling from and asked if we could meet in front of the GPO when she got off work at 6:00 P.M. She couldn't stay on the line because her supervisor was glaring at her.

"I'll be there," I said, and we rang off. She sounded as anxious and excited to see me as I was to see her.

Finding Ree so suddenly and unexpectedly left me trembling with excitement, and I could barely get the coin in the slot in order to leave the kiosk. Outside, the sun seemed brighter, the city friendlier and my step a bit lighter, but all of the long, weary hours and days I had spent patrolling in the capricious weather of the high veld did not compare to that interminable afternoon waiting to see her.

NINETEEN

Plans and Dreams

REE CAME OUT OF the big doors shortly after six P.M., her lovely face bright with a smile. "Jack!" she exclaimed moving swiftly toward me, her hands outstretched. "My goodness! It's so wonderful to see you! I never thought . . ." Her voice trailed off. She was breathless, her eyes moist, perhaps not quite sure of herself and of the moment.

I grasped her hands and held them tightly. It was as intimate as we could get there on the bustling street, with passersby staring even at that small impropriety. It had been more than a year and a half since we'd seen each other and I had wondered if my memory of her had painted a portrait that exaggerated her beauty, but it had not. Indeed, if anything, it had failed to do her justice. The classic lines of her face, the slight overbite that made her mouth sensuous, her lively hazel eyes and chestnut hair, her trim waist and full breasts accented by the fashion of the day sent a thrill through me. The hardships of the past year were all worthwhile and I felt truly blessed by the stroke of luck that had brought me to her.

"It's a miracle that I found you," I said. "I don't know what I would have done if you hadn't worked at the exchange. Although I don't think giving up was an option."

"How fortunate for me! You've made me so happy."

Those encouraging words heartened me. "I thought we could have dinner. Are you free?"

"Yes. Yes, of course. I'll just need to make a phone call."

She lived in a lodging house for women on the south side of Cape Town and as a courtesy wanted to let the proprietor know not to set a place for her.

She excused herself and went into the GPO to use one of the public phones while I fidgeted outside like a racehorse at the gate. When she came out, she took the arm I offered and we walked the short distance down Adderley Street to Dix's Café, one of the more stylish restaurants in town. The maître d' led us through a curved archway into the Moorish Room, a colourful, ornately bedecked space with hanging lamps, carpets on the walls and a small tiled fountain at one end. The floor was a chequerboard of white and black tiles and the table was star-shaped, painted like a kaleidoscope. The chairs that the waiter pulled out for us were studded leather with T-shaped backs.

"My," she said as we sat down, her eyes taking in our exotic surroundings. "It's quite lovely."

What made it even lovelier was the fact that only one other couple shared the room with us, but they were on the opposite

side and it was as if we had the place to ourselves. Over grilled
snoek, the local fish, and a delicate Cape white wine, we began
where we had left off on the edge of the Great Karoo.

"I dreamed I would see you again but I'm not sure I quite
believed it," Ree said, flushed by the wine and, she admitted
later, a bit emboldened by it. "When you left, and news came
that Oliver had died, I was beside myself. I couldn't go to
him because of the war and I wanted so much to rush here to
find you before you went home. But I felt I was being a perfect fool."

"No more of a fool than I felt on the sea voyage back here
and a lifetime on the veld," I said, ruefully. "The odd thing is
that if I weren't such a coward, we might have been together
long before now."

I explained that I could well have afforded my own passage
to South Africa as a civilian and gone to the farm straight off,
under the guise of paying thanks for her nursing skills. But I
had chosen to join the constabulary instead, as a way of pre-
tending that I wasn't returning to destroy a marriage. "I could
have kicked myself when your neighbours told me what had
happened. I felt awful for you and for Oliver but annoyed
with myself for wasting an entire year. Then, to find you
here . . . to find you, period . . ."

I didn't know what else to say. Every time I looked at her,
I could not help but marvel at her presence, could not quite
believe how fortunate I was. For her part, she told me, she
had to pinch herself to make sure she was not dreaming, for
she had all but decided that she would never see me again.

When, shortly after my departure from Exeter Farm, word
came of Oliver's death, she felt as if the Earth had spun off

its axis. How could she lose so much in a single hour? She could not deny that her marriage had been spiralling downward, but she had held out hopes that the war, which had provided a legitimate excuse for them to be apart for a while, would somehow infuse their relationship with new life. Then I entered the scene. She was convinced that my feelings for her were as strong as hers were for me but hurrying to Cape Town to find me would have been indelicate. She waited over two months, growing wearier by the day of the demands of the farm, and by that time, her friends and neighbours understood her need to leave.

She was stunned to discover that my ship had sailed for England the day before she reached Cape Town. She wanted to weep. *Maybe he'll come back*, she thought, but told herself it was a childish notion, something that happened only in romantic novels. At one point, she had even wondered about writing Sam Steele, hoping that he could reconnect us, but decided that idea was as foolish as the other was childish. So she found work to sustain herself until the war ended and the money for the sale of the farm came from England. Her parents had offered to wire the fare for her passage home but she was determined to be self-reliant. The newspapers gave front-page coverage to the arrival of the Canadian volunteers for the constabulary but she never imagined for a moment that I was among them. She had recently received the money for the farm and had given notice to the telephone exchange, her employer, and was in the midst of preparations for her return to England when I called. She had already booked passage on a ship leaving in just over two weeks.

Two weeks? We had almost missed each other again. "Exeter was the next stop on my itinerary. I wasn't going to let you off that easily!"

She laughed. "I'm so glad! The idea of searching the wilds of Canada for you was a bit daunting."

We stayed longer at Dix's than we ought to have, sipping wine and talking, smoothly slipping back into each other's lives. She was curious to know what had happened to Jim. She remembered his size and strength, and how effortlessly he had lifted my unconscious form and carried it inside her house.

"Jim survived the war, but not bachelorhood. He married a wonderful girl named Maggie. He met her in Ottawa while we were there training. After their honeymoon, they were off to western Canada to buy a ranch and raise kids and cattle. I was supposed to join them and I hope they're not too angry that I didn't show up, but I'm afraid you were my first priority. Besides, I figured I'd only be in their way. I would have written to let them know, but I have no idea where they are. I feel bad but knowing Jim, I expect he'll be doing okay. Even so, it isn't a good thing to do to a friend. If I had told him about you, he would have known what happened but I kept it to myself. As I said, I thought I was being foolish. Anyway, I hope he'll understand. If he gets a chance to meet you, I know he will."

"It was obvious," Ree said, "that he cared a great deal for you. He wasn't at all happy when your commander ordered him back to the regiment and he had to leave you in my care. I'm honoured that you forewent a ranch to come look for me because if I remember correctly, owning one was a boyhood dream of yours but life kept getting in the way. It looks as if it still is."

"Mmmm." I smiled. "And the proof of it is that I'm sitting with you in a restaurant in South Africa. But believe me, it's no stumbling block and the long way around still leads to the same place."

It was fully dark when I took her home in a cab. The street on which she lived was, I think, one of the few I had not trod the day before in my search for her. We arranged to meet for dinner the next day. She had already given her employer two weeks' notice and even though she could now afford to quit immediately, she did not want to renege on her commitment. I helped her down from the cab and she thanked me for the lovely evening.

"I so look forward to tomorrow," she said.

I took her hands. "I hope as much as I do."

She brushed her lips against my cheek. "Till I see you, then."

At the door to the rooming house, she turned and waved, and I could see her beautiful smile in the lamplight. "Till I see you, then" was the very last thing she had said to me as the ambulance took me from Exeter Farm. In South Africa, it was as casual an expression as "How are you?" in Canada and was often spoken with as much sincerity. But when she had uttered those words on the day we parted, I wanted to believe she truly meant them.

Ree cancelled her booking to England and fulfilled her obligation to the exchange, and after that we spent as much time together as possible, getting to know each other.

Until she came to South Africa, she had led a privileged and sheltered life. Raised by doting parents, she had lacked for nothing. After Oliver had swept her off her feet, they talked of starting a new life in a far-off country, and it fulfilled a longing she had, not only for adventure but for leaving Exeter, where nothing exciting ever happened and everybody was privy to everyone else's business. They had considered Canada but decided on South Africa and put their hearts and souls into making it happen. But the hard life took its toll on their relationship. That no children were forthcoming also had a negative effect but, as things turned out, it was a blessing in disguise. Then the war came along and took Oliver away forever and brought me into her life.

Infrequent in our relationship during that period was physical intimacy, for Ree had little privacy at her lodgings and her sense of propriety would not allow her to come to my hotel room. Even so, I think we knew from the moment we clasped hands in Adderley Street that we would marry and everything else was merely the preliminaries. We did, however, manage a few discreet trips out of town and it was on the first of these that I proposed to her. We had taken the train through the farming country of the Cape Flats to Muizenberg, a resort village on False Bay, where I had booked a room at an inn under the name of "Mr. and Mrs. Strong." A single-storey, sprawling building with a thatched roof, the inn offered few amenities and the room furnishings were rough and plain. But none of that mattered to us. The anonymity it provided was first class.

At dinner, we purposely dallied over our *bobotee*, a dish of meat with curry and rice, and wine, enjoying the exquisite agony of waiting for what was to come. Later, in our room, a breeze off the water wafted through the curtains as we undressed in the amber light of an oil lamp. Ree was not tentative and disrobed like a woman confident of the beauty of what she was about to reveal. That confidence was not misplaced. I pulled her to me, cupped her face in my hands and kissed her deeply. Then I buried my face in the side of her neck to breathe the scent of her skin and hair. It smelled vaguely of lavender and the sea. We sank onto the bed and kissed and caressed each other for as long as we could stand not being truly joined together.

Afterwards, we lay face to face, arms draped loosely over each other, spent, content and silent but for our breathing. After a few minutes, I brushed back the hair covering her ear, laid my cheek against hers and whispered, "I love you, Ree. Will you marry me?"

I felt her arm tighten around me, heard the intake of her breath, her whisper, "Yes, Jack. From the deepest part of my heart, yes!"

But her commitment was not without anxiety. "I do so want children, but I worry that it might not be possible for me."

"You shouldn't think that the problem is yours. It might have been Oliver's."

"Yes, of course. Yet it still bothers me."

Though she never said as much, I knew it troubled her that if she were barren I would hold it against her, as Oliver had. But part of me was apprehensive about having children. What would I do if I lost another one?

We talked too of what to do with our lives. We had enough money to make a fresh start pretty well anywhere we wanted. "Where would you like to go, Ree?"

"Anywhere, as long as you're there too."

"Would you be happier returning to England? That was where you were going when I entered your life again."

"But I was going only because it felt like the thing to do at the time. I promised myself that it would only be a visit, to see my parents, and that I would eventually move on, perhaps to the Continent for a change. France might have been nice although I had no idea what I was going to do there. Whatever the case, I'm done with England."

We talked about remaining in South Africa, but Ree had misgivings. "The end of the war doesn't necessarily mean the end of strife here. In fact, I wonder if it will ever end. The Boers and British may have found a lasting peace but the wars with the Zulus were just an inkling of what this country will have to face in the years to come. I'm not sure I want to be around when the blacks decide that this land is really theirs. But why not Canada, Jack? Then you can find Jim and see if he's still open to a partnership. I think it would be lovely if the two of you were reunited, and I would happily settle there."

It was as if Ree knew what I was thinking. "You'd love the Canadian west and I do miss Jim, although I sometimes wonder if he feels I've deserted him. It's been a year and half since we parted, so I'd be surprised if he and Maggie didn't have a ranch of their own. Even so, it would be great to see him again and there's no denying that I owe him an apology."

A plan crystallized in my mind, something that had been brewing behind everything else for the last little while. The notion of working with cattle no longer appealed to me. I had always been more partial to horses and I knew that there was still a high demand for broken and harness-trained animals in the cities, even those with trolley cars. And other than the property—and you didn't need much—the capital investment was modest. Horses had fewer needs than cattle, especially in winter, and you had to own only a few at any one time. It was called "rawhide ranching" because most of the equipment was made from leather, and it would work in western Canada as well as anywhere. The more I thought about the idea the more I liked it. "Do you like horses?" I asked.

Ree adored them. Her father had kept a pair of jumpers and she had learned to ride as a child. She had even done some minor show jumping as a teenager. "Just in the Exeter area, of course, and I never won anything, but it was always great fun and *very* exciting!"

I outlined my plan and we discussed it until the only thing left was to do it.

We were married on a Sunday morning in late August, before the heat of the afternoon grew fierce, when the town was quiet and most people were in church. The warm sea air drifted in and blended with the sweet smell of roses and cannas, and doves cooed in the surrounding trees. Ree wore a long, dark-green skirt, a white, colourfully embroidered blouse with puffy sleeves and a hat decorated with an ostrich feather. I had a tan suit tailor-made for the occasion. A justice of the peace performed the ceremony while Ree's colleagues from the telephone exchange stood up for us. As I had been a long-term customer at the St. George's Street hotel, the management gave us one of their best suites, at no extra charge, and had complimentary wine, flowers and a bowl of fruit awaiting us.

Two days later, we were aboard a ship bound for England. Ree wanted to visit her parents in Exeter before going to Canada, because she believed it was important that they meet me and did not know when another opportunity might arise. She had written them shortly after we decided to marry but there had not been enough time to receive a response. I had no idea what to expect.

TWENTY

Thick or Thin

THE CARRINGTONS LIVED IN a lovely, red-brick Georgian house with a slate roof puncutated by four gabled dormers and as many chimneys. A dozen, symmetrical, mullioned windows faced a gated stone path running arrow-straight through a well-kept garden with splashes of fall colours. A small outbuilding and stable in matching red brick stood behind. The property comprised several acres, surrounded by a stone fence, and sat on the north edge of Exeter, among patchwork downs, with a view of the River Exe off to the east.

Ronald Carrington, a successful solicitor, was tall and thin but did not seem gaunt as some of his stature do. He reminded me of pictures I'd seen of Abraham Lincoln, only with fairer hair and fuller features. Mairead Carrington was an older, fleshier version of Ree, who smiled a lot and whose Irish accent was still noticeable. They were, as Ree had predicted, reserved at first, but only mildly so. There was a natural warmth about them that was not long rising to the surface when they saw the love between their daughter and the Canadian stranger she'd brought home from Africa.

Neither Ree nor I thought her parents needed to know that their daughter's marriage to Oliver had possibly been on the verge of disintegration when he died. It was news that might only upset them, so we kept it to ourselves.

At a party given to introduce me to all their friends, I faltered only momentarily when I was introduced to Oliver's parents. But if they were resentful that I had taken their son's place, that I had survived the war and he hadn't, they did not show it. They were gracious in the extreme.

We docked in Halifax during a November blizzard and took a train to the west, via Ottawa. From there our plan was to stop in Calgary to try to find Jim and Maggie and then head out to the coast. I wanted Ree to experience the mountains of British Columbia, and also Vancouver and Victoria, before we settled down and worked.

Ree knew, from the maps we had pored over in Cape Town, the vastness of Canada but the reality of it astonished her, in particular the seemingly endless stretch of boreal forest across the Canadian Shield. And though she had seen plenty of snow in England as a youngster, she had never seen snow that went on for thousands of miles.

"It is such a white country!" she exclaimed.

"In more ways than one. Quite the opposite of South Africa. But there are always exceptions."

It was the perfect opportunity to tell her that in Vancouver we would be stopping to see my old friend Joe Fortes, who was black, and why he was a good friend. It meant telling her about the most humiliating moment in my life: chained to a stump in the middle of the street for drunkenness. "It was punishment for a dumb mistake," I admitted, "and Joe offered to help me when most of the whites in town believed I was no better than a pariah dog. He was like the brother I never had."

I wondered if it might be a delicate subject, considering Ree had lived the last several years of her life with blacks in subservient roles, but she simply said, "It's a new life, a new country and new things to get used to. And I will. Besides, I've already met one of your friends and it would be extremely unkind of me to question your ability to make good ones."

She was referring to Jim, of course, but I realized that I did not make friends easily when it came to men. In over 30 years I had managed to accumulate only two—Jim and Joe. If I had to explain it, I would say that if a boy cannot find trust for his father, as an adult he will likely experience difficulty finding trust for other men.

A blizzard was blowing the snow pellets horizontal when we stopped in Calgary. We took a room at the Alberta Hotel and the following morning I went to the Land Registry office to see if I could locate Jim and Maggie. There were no records showing that they had purchased property anywhere in Alberta. The clerk said that there hadn't been much good land for sale for some time and what was available was extremely expensive.

That could mean only one thing: the Spencers had probably waited for me and when I didn't appear, moved on to British Columbia to look for land.

The weather did not clear until we were through the Rockies but turned murky again during the long, slow passage through the Fraser Canyon. In Vancouver, it was raining and despite the saturated clouds squatting over the city, hiding its beautiful setting, Ree found it a relief after all the snow and treacherous terrain.

We took rooms at the rebuilt Sunnyside Hotel and since Joe Fortes had once worked there, I asked the desk clerk if he knew where I could find him.

"English Bay Joe? Yes, sir. Everyone knows where he lives."

My old friend had become quite a legend during my absence, having taught many of the city's children how to swim. The following morning we went to his house, above the beach in English Bay.

"Jack!" he exclaimed when he opened the door to my knock. "You do have a way of surprisin' a man!"

He was wearing a robe over a black swimsuit and seemed mildly embarrassed by his attire in front of a woman he didn't know. Nevertheless, he unhesitatingly ushered us into his small home and cleared some papers from an old settee so that Ree and I could sit down. He was immensely pleased, not only because I had found so lovely a wife but also because I was clearly in a better frame of mind than when he had last seen me. And being the thoughtful man that he was, he didn't mention Charity, even though they had been good friends.

It was only been a few years since Joe and I had been together, but his passion for swimming had added even more muscle to his upper chest and shoulders. What hadn't changed was that he was still as gregarious and accommodating as ever. He said that he had sold his house on the inlet to the Canadian Pacific Railway for a tidy profit, as he predicted he would, and had thrown up this shack on the beach so that he would always be close to his first love, the water. It left him plenty of money for food, so he had quit his job at the Bodega Saloon, where he'd gone after the old Sunnyside had burned to the ground during the Great Fire, and gave swimming lessons to supplement his bank account.

Joe agreed to have lunch with us after his swim, so we accompanied him in the frigid air to the water's edge. I didn't need to dip my hand in to know it was cold, but it was his opinion that winter was the worst possible excuse not to go swimming. He carried a tin cup that he sat on the sandy gravel before plunging in. He swam out several yards, dove beneath the waves, surfaced like a seal, then swam into shore. He retrieved his cup, waded in back to his knees, dipped it full and drank it empty. Joe had always maintained that sea-water was much better for a body than alcohol.

Over lunch, I asked him if he had any information about my former in-laws, the McRaes, and he said that McRae still ran the mill but had become active in civic politics and was now an alderman. He had heard that Mrs. McRae was in ill health but didn't know more than that. We said our goodbyes and Joe declined my offer of a cab ride home, insisting that the walk would do him good. After a promise from us not to be strangers, he strolled off with a wave, an imposing figure even in the wide street.

The following morning I hired a rig to go out to the cemetery. Ree and I had discussed a visit to Charity's and Becky's graves and she had asked if I would rather go alone.

"I would prefer that you were with me, but only if it won't disturb you."

Her response was firm. "If you would rather I came along then I most certainly will."

The monuments were as pristine as the day they were erected and the area around them was well maintained, no doubt the handiwork of the McRaes. Ree clutched my arm tighter but said nothing, letting me deal with my own thoughts. How many times had I stood by these stones and felt that the world had ended and that I was responsible for it? More times than was healthy and that was a fact. Thanks to Ree, and time, I could now stand here unassailed by such destructive sentiments. And I knew that if it were somehow possible for Charity to be a witness to my life she would be happy, knowing that having lost one exceptional woman I was lucky enough to have found another.

Eleanor did not look at all well when Ree and I stopped by the McRae residence later for a visit. She had lost a lot of weight and her attractive face was aged, angular and pale. McRae looked tired, with dark patches beneath his eyes from overwork and anxiety, but otherwise appeared to be in good health. Both were pleased to meet Ree, perhaps because the strength and openness of her personality reminded them of Charity. I asked about their sons and they were doing well. The older one was attending law school in Toronto, while the other was following the route at the mill that I had once embarked upon. McRae had a million questions about the war and South Africa, and much of the evening passed with talk on that subject, though he mentioned briefly some of the frustrations he experienced as a member of city council, which, he complained, was "presently rife with shortsighted members." At one point, when Ree and Eleanor had gone into the kitchen, I asked, "Is Eleanor not well, Alex? She looks so gaunt."

He let out a long breath. "I'm sad to say she has a cancer. The doctors have removed her uterus and she's been treated with x-rays but I'm afraid the prognosis is not favourable." McRae was not an overtly emotional man but his eyes reflected a deep sorrow, much more than I would have expected from him.

"I'm so sorry," was all I could say. Eleanor and I had not been particularly close during the years I was married to her daughter—she was much too reserved for that—but she was, nonetheless, a fine woman and a good mother, and she and Charity had been devoted to each other. I held her in high regard and the news troubled me deeply.

Ree and I spent another day in Vancouver, exploring in dreary weather, then sailed to Victoria in plenty of time to celebrate Christmas. We found long-term lodgings in a large rooming house in James Bay, not far from where I was raised, and spent the winter enjoying the comparatively mild climate and the city's amenities. At the Land Registry office, a search of the records showed that Jim Spencer was the owner of 960 acres south of Kamloops. It was a substantial parcel of land and I wondered if he had made the purchase with a view to sharing it with a partner.

In May, we left Victoria for the Interior. We debated sending a cable to warn Jim and Maggie that we were coming but decided to surprise them instead. Kamloops, sandwiched between high hills and the confluence of the North and

South Thompson rivers, was long and narrow. A large stock-holding pen at the edge of town and the many horses tied to various hitching posts marked the place for what it was: a cow town. The sagebrush valley was already warm and dry.

According to the map, Jim and Maggie's spread was south of town. We rented a small democrat from the livery and asked for directions. The proprietor led us outside and pointed to the steep hill behind the town and the road that rose along its flank. "Follow that road over the ridge and keep right at the fork. It's about 20 miles or so."

A sturdy Canadian mare pulled us up the sagebrush-covered hillside to the ridge dotted with ponderosa pine. Beyond the fork, the road ran like a snake among aspen and pine trees, past a pothole lake and across meadows. We drove in silence, my mind on the pending reunion with Jim and Maggie. I hoped they were both well and not too annoyed by my lack of communication. We came to a driveway that branched off to our right, spanned by a peeled log supported by two uprights. A carved sign, JM, or Bar JM, dangled from chains, and that had to be short for Jim and Maggie. We could see a barn, some smaller outbuildings and a rambling log house with a covered porch across its front.

Maggie must have heard the democrat in the driveway for she came out to greet us, holding a baby in her arms. She wore a light brown dress and had her dark hair piled in coils on top of her head, held by pins. Her skin was lightly tanned and for a moment, she seemed confused. Then her face broke wide open in a smile of recognition. "Jack! You've come at last! What a wonderful surprise! Where on Earth have you been? Jim has been waiting patiently for you. He will be *so* pleased. I can't wait to see his face!" The words poured out of her. "Forgive me for yammering on but I am so thrilled!" She gave Ree an appraising glance. "And this must be the lovely reason you've taken so long to get here!"

After introducing Ree and discovering that Jim had gone to Kamloops for supplies and we had somehow missed him, I left the women to chat while I unhitched the horse, led her to a water trough and let her drink her fill. She could graze once she'd finished, so I rejoined Ree and Maggie.

"Come in! Come in!" and Maggie ushered us exuberantly onto the porch and inside.

The house was warm and inviting. To our left, a long kitchen counter and white sink sat below a window near a new, wood-burning cookstove; within easy reach, cast-iron pots and pans hung on hooks attached to a metal bar suspended from the ceiling. Off to the right, in the living area, was a fieldstone fireplace. Upholstered, wooden-arm chairs and a sofa edged a wool carpet that covered part of the fir-plank floor. The skin of the wolf that Jim had shot in the Chilkat Pass adorned one wall.

The baby's name was Peter, after Maggie's father. He was a large child—Jim in miniature with the same calm disposition—and I would wager that his delivery had probably not been easy.

Ree held Peter while Maggie put the kettle on for tea and told us how she and Jim had looked for land in Alberta but had found the costs extortionate. They had waited for me in Calgary for as long as they could, then Jim had decided that the Cariboo region of British Columbia was where they should go next. But they had stopped in Kamloops on speculation and heard about this ranch, with a house and outbuildings already on it. The parcel had everything they needed, particularly plenty of land in the event I happened along.

"Jim always reckoned that you would show up sooner or later," Maggie said, "although recently he was beginning to have his doubts."

"Well, I come with cap in hand and sincere apologies." I motioned toward Ree. "And the best excuse possible."

We heard Jim's rig rattle into the yard and I went to the window to watch as he alit. He was curious enough about our wagon that he ignored unloading his and came straight to the house. He had to stoop slightly coming through the doorway so as not to bang his head on the lintel. He looked at me, then at Ree, then at me again. Though no one could ever accuse him of being long-winded, Jim had never lacked for something to say; we had rendered him momentarily speechless. Then at last he grinned, with the look on his face of a man to whom the answer to the world's most perplexing riddle had just been revealed. "Well, I'll be . . ."

I thrust out my hand and he grabbed it in his.

Thick or thin.

Author's Note and Further Reading

THOUGH *The Luck of the Horseman* is first and foremost a work of fiction, I have tried to be as true to the historical aspect of it as the story would allow. Several books helped in that regard. For the conflict in South Africa, Thomas Pakenham's *The Boer War* (Abacus, London, UK, 1979), Carman Miller's *Painting the Map Red: Canada and the South African War 1899–1902* (McGill-Queen's University Press, Montreal, 1993) and the daily log of *Strathcona's Horse South Africa 1900–1901* (Bunker to Bunker Publishing, Edmonton, 2000) were all invaluable. Lawrence Green's *Tavern of the Seas* (Howard Timmins, Cape Town, South Africa, 1975) provided useful information on early Cape Town while Robert Stewart's *Sam Steele, Lion of the Frontier* (Doubleday Canada, Toronto, 1979) offered much about the famous Mountie. The hunt for Black Feather was based on an actual hunt in Hugh Dempsey's *Charcoal's World* (Western Producer Prairie Books, Saskatoon, 1978) and the information on cowboys and cattle came from Grant McEwan's *John Ware's Cow Country* (Western Producer Prairie Books, Saskatoon, 1973) as well as Edward Brado's *The Cattle*

Kingdom: Early Ranching in Alberta (Heritage House, Surrey, BC, 2004). What travel was like over the Chilkat Pass during the Klondike gold rush was derived from Arthur R. Thompson's *Gold-seeking on the Dalton Trail* (Wolf Creek Books, Whitehorse, YT, originally published by University Press—John Wilson and Son, Canada, 1900).

And then there is the Internet.

Acknowledgments

MANY thanks to Dave Sutcliffe of Amajuba Experience, Newcastle, KwaZulu-Natal, South Africa, for all the photographs of the route of Strathcona's Horse through his part of the country. Thanks also to Jaye, who is always there, and to Dale Lovall, who will know the reason why. Finally, thanks to Marlyn Horsdal, my editor, who manages to make my scribblings publishable, as well as to all of the talented people at TouchWood Editions, who do such a wonderful job of presenting them to the public.

THE FIRST EPISODE OF
THE WILD JACK STRONG TRILOGY

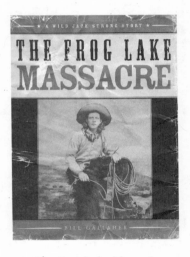

The Frog Lake Massacre
978-1-894898-75-1 $18.95

". . . very well researched and actual historical figures pop up to add to the already heightened authenticity . . . Gallaher obviously spent a good deal of time on the subject before he picked up his pen on this one."—*St. Albert Gazette*

The Frog Lake Massacre is the first book in a trilogy about a young man who is trying to forge an independent life for himself in the huge and newly-established country of Canada. Along the way, he discovers that bravery and loyalty bring their own rewards.

OTHER WORKS BY BILL GALLAHER

The Journey	*The Promise*	*Deadly Innocent*	*A Man Called Moses*
978-1-894898-99-7	978-1-894898-83-6	978-1-894898-11-9	978-1-894898-04-1
$18.95	$18.95	$18.95	$18.95

"To experience Bill Gallaher is to participate in past tales that have, in their telling, moved into the present. He is able to open our senses to the essence of Canada and the lives of those whose sojourns have made this land."
—M. Stevens, *Smith Hill Productions*

". . . rich in detail . . . [Gallaher's] writing brings to life . . . experiences that can scarcely be images in the 21st century . . . a highly readable account of one of the most interesting, and mort important, chapters in BC's history"
—*The Times Colonist*

"I decided to read just a couple of pages before sleeping. At 2:00 AM I was still sitting bolt upright, biting my fingernails as the book drew me toward its shocking, twist ending."
—*BC History Magazine*